TIDE OF WAVES AND SECRETS

C. L. MECCA

B
Boldwood

First published in Great Britain in 2025 by Boldwood Books Ltd.

Copyright © C. L. Mecca, 2025

Cover Design by JD Smith Design Ltd

Cover Images: Shutterstock

The moral right of C. L. Mecca to be identified as the author of this work has been asserted in accordance with the Copyright, Designs and Patents Act 1988.

All rights reserved. No part of this book may be reproduced in any form or by any electronic or mechanical means, including information storage and retrieval systems, without written permission from the author, except for the use of brief quotations in a book review. This book is a work of fiction and, except in the case of historical fact, any resemblance to actual persons, living or dead, is purely coincidental.

Every effort has been made to obtain the necessary permissions with reference to copyright material, both illustrative and quoted. We apologise for any omissions in this respect and will be pleased to make the appropriate acknowledgements in any future edition.

A CIP catalogue record for this book is available from the British Library.

Paperback ISBN 978-1-83656-297-9

Large Print ISBN 978-1-83656-296-2

Hardback ISBN 978-1-83656-295-5

Ebook ISBN 978-1-83656-298-6

Kindle ISBN 978-1-83656-299-3

Audio CD ISBN 978-1-83656-290-0

MP3 CD ISBN 978-1-83656-291-7

Digital audio download ISBN 978-1-83656-294-8

This book is printed on certified sustainable paper. Boldwood Books is dedicated to putting sustainability at the heart of our business. For more information please visit https://www.boldwoodbooks.com/about-us/sustainability/

Boldwood Books Ltd, 23 Bowerdean Street, London, SW6 3TN

www.boldwoodbooks.com

For every woman who has been told she couldn't, may you prove them wrong.

1

ROWAN

Estmere, Elydor

I stood with my hand on the door, unable to open it.

When I'd left, my grandfather had been reasonably well. But the second I returned home, it was apparent something was amiss. The hall of our manor house wasn't bustling with activity. Instead, I'd been greeted by our steward as if someone had died.

I pushed the door open.

Knowing my grandfather would not live forever and being confronted with the evidence of that fact were two very different things. Propped up by pillows, he sat alone.

"You look like shite," I said, striding toward him and leaning down to kiss the wrinkled, white-haired man on his forehead. Sitting on the side of the canopied bed, I wasn't surprised when he reached for my hand.

"Talk to me when you're dying," he said with a weak smile. "It is a messy business, death. With luck, you will find a way to delay your own, but I fear my time has come."

I wanted to argue with him. Tell Sir Thomas Durnell, my grandfather and mentor, he simply could not die. I'd thought he was invincible.

"The Fade?"

His frail fingers squeezed my own. "I'd always imagined it to happen much more slowly," he said.

"Would you rather it this way?"

"Now that you're home, aye. I would."

I suspected as much. "I wish I could stay."

My grandfather sighed heavily. "I already know that you cannot."

All humans in Elydor, but especially my family, had some sort of intuitive abilities. But as The Keeper, my grandfather had more than most. Only those with Durnell blood—or Harrow blood, to be precise, though that name hadn't been used in centuries—knew of it.

"What did you see?"

"The lost princess has, indeed, returned. You intercepted her and spent some time in Aethralis. You are on a mission, heading to Thalassaria, are you not?"

As always, my grandfather was entirely accurate.

"This mission of yours will not go as planned. I see nothing else yet, but worry for your safety, Rowan."

That was not information to take lightly. My grandfather had mentored me since I could wield a sword. He knew I was capable and very rarely worried for me. Or at least enough to admit as much.

"That isn't like you."

"No," he said. "It is not."

I waited, but he didn't seem inclined to elaborate. If he were anyone else, anyone but The Keeper, I could use my own intuitive skills to sense his emotion. To learn more. But he had long ago learned how to shield out others from gaining information from him: an essential skill for someone who held all of the secrets of our family's history.

He blinked, as if attempting to focus on me. All Keepers, every person with the same blood running through them, had been trained for this. For my grandfather's death. Some with more trepidation than others, but all knew the signs.

"Your eyesight?" I asked.

He nodded. "I can see you, but not as well as when you left. Tell me everything."

I started from the beginning.

"I met Princess Mevlida, Mev, on the road fleeing north. As you foretold, she'd been taken by Prince Kael of Gyoria, but in an interesting twist of fate, the two had already formed a bond. And later, a formal union," I said. "Kael has sworn his allegiance to King Galfrid."

"Mmm." Grandfather sighed. "So that is why I could see a rift between the Gyorian king and one of his sons. If either of them were to fall in love with an Aetherian woman, I'd have expected it to be Kael, and not Terran."

"I'd not have expected any Gyorian, least of all one of King Balthor's sons, to fall in love with the daughter of their enemy. But I suppose that's why you're The Keeper and I'm just a spy."

His grandfather made a sound of disbelief. "You are not 'just' anything, Rowan and know it well. If I'd ever met a more kind, loyal, resourceful—"

"Dying," I teased, knowing my grandfather did not like mincing words or being anything other than forthright, "has not diminished your overhyping capabilities."

"Overhyping? A new word for me," he said. "The meaning of

which I can easily discern. The princess must have quite a vocabulary, among other attributes from the modern world. Tell me of her."

And so, I did. Anything not to think about the fact that my grandfather's eyesight was leaving him, one of the final stages of The Fading. I recalled my adventures with Mev, Kael and Lyra, telling him what I'd learned of the modern world in the human realm from Mev. I recounted how difficult it had been to gain Kael's trust, and how, after confronting his own brother to protect Mev, Kael had eventually pledged his loyalty to her and King Galfrid. I also told my grandfather what the king had revealed to the others about reopening the Gate: that the most powerful artifacts in each clan needed to be recovered and used in a spell known only to two men—the Aetherian king who opened it, and the Gyorian one who closed it.

"This is as close as we've been since it was closed to seeing the Gate reopened once again."

"I agree." With my grandfather's frail hand still holding my own, I acknowledged the pang inside my chest at such a sight. No man in Estmere was more fierce, or determined, than him. His family had long-argued the merits of how the new Keeper was chosen. Some said that when the current Keeper died, their magic was transferred to the most loyal of those living with Harrow blood coursing through their veins. Others believed it to be someone who excelled at keeping secrets: an essential quality for The Keeper.

But I knew the truth of it.

Having observed and trained with my grandfather since an early age, I was convinced the new Keeper was the man, or woman, who possessed all of it. Loyalty. Strength. Integrity. Wisdom. Resilience. My grandfather possessed all of these things.

There was not a better man alive.

"Do not look so sad, grandson. I've lived a full life and will be glad to reunite with your grandmother. It's been an honor to serve our family, and our people. But it's a duty I gladly pass along to another."

He had served their family well, but I also knew how much my grandfather wished to reopen the Gate. He'd been alive when it closed, when so many who had come through, never intending to remain in Elydor, were cut off from their families. King Balthor had not just punished his enemy, the Aetherians, but the humans and, in Rowan's mind, all of Elydor. It had been stronger, according to his grandfather, when the free pass of information and knowledge had been allowed between Elydor and the human realm.

"We will reopen it." It was not a vow I made lightly. Many resourceful people, including my grandfather, had attempted it for many years. And failed. "Somehow," I said, "Mev was able to pass through the Gate, despite it being closed. I believe it is a sign. Her Aetherian powers are strong, and her union with Prince Kael, fortuitous. Together, we will see it done. I make that vow to you, Grandfather."

The man that had trained me... loved me... smiled.

"I have no doubt that you will."

Sighing, as if our conversation had weakened him, he added, "Tread carefully in Thalassaria. You've not spent as much time there as in the other clans. They are neither as welcoming to humans as Aetherians nor as hostile to us as Gyorians, but their neutrality toward us has been just as detrimental. Thalassarians care about their freedom above all. Remember that. There is power in unity, and hope, and a peaceful future between all of Elydor's clans is possible. But only if the Gate is reopened."

"I will retrieve the Tidal Pearl from Thalassari's queen. We *will* reopen it," Rowan vowed once again. "I will make you proud, Grandfather."

Smiling, he let go of my hand, patted it, and closed his eyes, obviously tired. "You already have, Rowan. You already have."

2

NERYS

Maristhera, Capital of Thalassaria

"*I* should return to the palace."

The woman who'd been like a mother to me, already old when my parents died and that had been many years ago, waved a hand as if unconcerned. "Look around you. The square is just coming to life."

It was true. We sat on the edge of a stone fountain, one of many in the capital. Though not far from the sea, as with most towns in Thalassaria, water could be found everywhere in Maristhera. Fountains, canals... it was our life force.

"Perhaps. But I have a new ward coming. A human."

Aneri waved to a man that I was pretty certain she was with, romantically speaking. For some reason, Aneri denied it. Neither were partnered, so her secrecy made little sense.

"A human?" Aneri's expression didn't change. Some might wrinkle their nose or frown with distaste, but not Aneri. And Nerys had been taught better than that. Still, it was unusual.

"He's passed through the border?"

I nodded. Thalassaria was the only kingdom, or clan as we called them, which did not have open borders. Even Gyorians, who despised humans, allowed them to pass freely onto their land. Of course, the humans weren't guaranteed to survive long. But they could enter freely.

"And will be arriving shortly," I confirmed, watching as two of the few Thalassari children played in the fountain, attempting to redirect the water. Their efforts made me laugh when one accidentally accomplished the feat, directly into his friend's face. "Hopefully, he won't be staying long."

"This way," Aneri said to the girl. Her legendary patience on display, she showed the girl how to control the stream of water. It brought me back to when I was her age, more than a hundred years ago, being taught the very same lesson by my mother's dear friend.

It took a few tries, but the girl managed to control the stream a bit better.

"Why is he here?" Aneri asked me.

"Unsure."

"Will he stay for the festival?"

"Also unsure. I only know word arrived this morning he was coming and that he was assigned to me."

From the moment he stepped foot onto palace grounds, the human would either be locked inside his bedchamber or escorted by me. It was an usual custom, but a Thalassari king was once murdered in his very palace and the queen took no chances when it came to her safety.

"Hmm. First, the lost princess returned. Now a human coming to the palace. Those two cannot be coincidental."

I agreed. "Either way, I'm glad for it."

Despite that my other duties as a Stormcaller would be suspended, and I had no wish to escort a man to and fro for an extended period, any opportunity to strengthen relations with the human clan was a welcome one.

At least to me.

Unfortunately, there were some in Thalassaria, including the queen, who did not agree.

Without warning, the sound of water being lifted had me up and spinning around toward the children. One of them had manipulated a large portion of the fountain's water into the air. Enough that, were it to land back where it came from, all four of us would become soaked.

I lifted my hand and, with a flick, created a bowl of water to capture its companion. Gently lowering it, I placed both back into the fountain.

The children stared at me.

"How did you do that?" the boy asked.

"I've never seen that before! Can you teach us to do it?" the girl pleaded.

I did not wish to tell them it would be many years before either could master such a skill.

"There are very few in Thalassaria who can contain water within itself," Aneri said gently.

The girl's eyes widened. "You are a Stormcaller?"

"I am."

"She is not just any Stormcaller," Aneri began.

I shook my head.

And so it went, as usual. Aneri would tell anyone who might listen how powerful I'd become. Not for the first time, I reconsidered my decision to filter some of the queen's jealousy toward me, not wanting to upset Aneri.

"With practice," I interrupted. "You might become Stormcallers too. Keep at it," I said with a smile. "And treat this water with special care. You know what it is?" I asked.

"I do," the girl said. "My mama says they are the Sacred Waters of Maristhera."

"You are correct," I said. "Many years ago, we'd not have been allowed to manipulate them for play. But that thinking has changed, and you may do so, if you remember they are special."

The girl seemed to understand. It was the same speech my father had once given me, and then later, learning of the Sacred Waters myself, I understood how special.

"I must go," I said to Aneri. "And will be more often at the palace until the human is gone."

"You best be getting rid of him before the festival then," she said. "I look forward to spending those days with you, even if you refused to challenge—"

"I look forward to it as well," I said, stopping what would be a futile new line of conversation. I kissed Aneri on the head. "I will see you soon. Enjoy yourself," I said with a conspiratorial wink.

"I have no notion what you're talking about."

Since Aneri's male friend had not stopped looking our way this entire time, I was pretty sure that was a blatant lie. But I had to get back, so I let it go.

"Keep practicing," I called to the young ones, walking across the square toward the white marble palace which could be seen easily from here. Most of Thalassaria was flat until you approached the borders. But the palace was built on a hill, for fortification.

Wondering who the human was, and what he wanted from the palace, I hurried my steps, growing more and more curious with each one. It wasn't every day a human visited us.

It was promising to be an interesting day ahead.

3

ROWAN

I'd been to Thalassaria before, but never the palace. This time, when I crossed the border, immediately being stopped by the Stormcaller guards, instead of registering myself and passing through, I was forced to wait. Though I'd seen marisol before—the teal and silver shimmering fish with teeth that could be fatal to humans—it was the first time I'd witnessed one being used. Watching as the guard leaned into the canal to place a delicate, waterproof scroll in a marisol's teeth, a bioluminescent line along its spine began to gently pulse as it swam away. The first time I'd come to Thalassari, standing along a canal with my father watching those fish messengers swim, I told him I wanted to live here. I understood, however, by the end of that mission, that a human may be welcomed to Thalassaria as a visitor, but to its fiercely independent people, I was an outsider. My place was in Estmere, in the human kingdom.

"You are welcome to pass," the guard said, interrupting my thoughts. In a remarkably short time, the message had been sent and received by palace. Queen Lirael would see me. "You know the way?"

Mounting Ember, the warhorse that had been bred over hundreds of years from Elydor's native horse stock, I made my way through the dense coastal fog that clung to the Thalassarian shores. The steady rhythm of Ember's hooves was a constant companion as we navigated the rocky path that wound along the cliffs. Below, the waves crashed against jagged rocks, their spray catching the early-morning light. The air smelled of salt and seaweed, the distant call of seabirds reminding me I was a long way from Estmere.

As I arrived in Maristhera, passing through the bustling Serenium Square and heading toward the palace, I focused on my mission in favor of my surroundings. Having long ago shed my cloak, the perpetual warm climate of Elydor's southernmost clan the reason they favored nearly sheer fabrics had me also stopping to remove the heavy tunic that I should have left in Estmere. It had been many years since I traveled this far south, and I'd not been thinking of its weather when I set off from home.

I had been thinking of my grandfather.

But now, I needed to concentrate on what I would say to the queen when granted an audience and rehearsed my speech again.

King Galfrid's daughter has returned, though we are not certain how she slipped through the closed Aetherian Gate. With her return, the king is determined, more than ever, to reopen it. As you know, we need the Tidal Pearl in order to do so.

She would refuse.

I was as certain of that fact as my own name. It was Thalassaria's most precious relic. That she'd allowed King Galfrid to use it once, when he opened the Gate more than five hundred years ago, was a surprise to all who knew of that fact, of which there were precious few.

She would refuse, but it was my job to convince her that it

would benefit her people to do otherwise. Queen Lirael may not despise humans, but neither would she lend the Tidal Pearl to Galfrid for their benefit. But for her own people? She would do anything.

If I wasn't trained as a spy, I may not have noticed the Thalassarian guards hidden behind the trees. Because it was my duty to see what typically went undetected, I easily spotted the camouflaged warriors. By the time I arrived at the palace gates, I'd passed at least ten of them on both sides of me.

No other Elydorian leader was as well-protected as the Queen of Thalassaria, whose reputation for paranoia was well known.

"Hold."

Finally, one who made himself seen. Or themselves, to be more precise. Well ahead of the gatehouse, four of the queen's guards stepped directly into the sand and shell-ridden path on which I'd been traveling.

"Identify yourself."

The guard knew well my name already. Tempted to tell him as much, I reminded myself that glibness was not my friend in this situation.

"Sir Rowan of Estmere," I said.

"Your guide has not yet arrived. Dismount."

Again, I held my tongue. Reminding the guard that a polite command was just as easily given as a rude one would serve little.

By the time my belongings and I were searched, I'd expected my guide to have arrived. Since none of the guards deemed it necessary to update me at any point, I waited without communication of any kind until a rider finally appeared in the distance.

I could see it was a woman, but little else. By the time she fully came into view, I was well and truly enamored. Wearing a teal tunic which hung off one shoulder, black, glistening, form-fitting breeches and a wide belt which appeared from her like scales of a beautiful, multi-colored fish, the woman epitomized a Thalassarian.

With one exception.

None could match her beauty. My guide's hair, a shade between brown and blonde, was tied back loosely with strands escaping everywhere. With full lips and sun-kissed cheeks, her pale-green eyes shone with curiosity as she reached me.

If I hadn't met the queen before, I would have assumed this woman was the queen, except for the obvious fact that the queen would not be unescorted. But otherwise... her bearing, the way she assessed me? Clearly, she was of noble birth.

Stopping first to speak with one of the guards, the woman clearly knew my identity yet seemed to lack disdain toward me. I would know for certain in a moment if that observation held true.

As all humans in Elydor, I possessed some measure of intuitive abilities which, in me, manifested as an ability to sense emotion. Unlike Mev, however, I could not determine intention or use my ability unless the person was close to me.

"Sir Rowan?" she asked, dismounting.

As the guards watched, she approached. With every step, any doubt I had about her capabilities were eradicated. Though she'd said only two words to me, those were enough. It was not the first time I'd been in the presence of royalty, or of those close to it in some way, to know she fit that particular mold. Yet hers was not of the haughty or entitled variety, but one of quiet confidence.

"Aye," I said, bowing to her. It was the Thalassari greeting appropriate for her station. If we were familiar, I would have embraced her. If she were a human, I'd have shaken her hand.

"I am pleased to make your acquaintance," she said.

"And I yours."

She took that final step toward me that I needed to read her.

Whether I willed it or not, a certainty filled every pore of my body. As it had been since I'd learned to control it, the sense of calm was accompanied by another feeling, this one as unpredictable as the person standing before me.

Sincerity.

If we were not being watched so closely by the guards—both those who had made themselves known, and those behind us who had not—I might have been able to sense secondary emotions as well. But when my attention was divided, as it was now, I could sense just one emotion at a time.

Shockingly, she was being sincere. A Thalassari genuinely pleased to meet me. A human.

Interesting.

"My name is Nerys," she said, her voice lilting and melodic. If sirens like the ones in my human tales existed, she would be one of them. Not because she wished to do me ill, but because I'd just lost all sense of my training, of the detachment necessary to make good judgments. I stared at her the same way I had the day my father had said, "Sit down, son. You have come of age, and we must discuss our family origins."

Nerys.

Her name suited her. Her clothing suited her. Her voice and assurance all suited her.

"Have you been to the palace before?"

"I have not," I said. "Though I'm aware of its procedures."

Most would not have noticed the slight widening of her eyes or twitch of her mouth that accompanied it, giving away her surprise. I not only noticed but felt the shift that confirmed my suspicions. It was a mistake my grandfather would have chastised me for. One the Keepers did not make.

If you speak a word, consider carefully whether or not it might reveal more than you intended. We've not kept a centuries-old secret by being careless.

It was the reason Keepers befriended few, married other humans and kept to themselves. At least, most operated in such a way. My desire for connections outside of other Keepers was a weakness, no doubt.

"So you are aware," she continued, thankfully not commenting on my retort, "that you will be provided an escort from this moment until the one you leave palace grounds?"

"I am."

"And that once inside, you will remain by my side, or within your chambers, at all times?"

I could not resist a smile. "You are my escort, then?"

Nerys's lack of reaction made me wonder at her own training. One did not become a Thalassarian guard without a great measure of skill.

What was this woman's story?

"I am," she said. "As such, I am required to ask of your purpose here before we continue."

That was not information I could divulge. "To speak with the queen."

"Unfortunately, I require more information than that."

Unfortunately, I am unable to give it to you.

I didn't say as much, however. "I've been sent to speak to your queen on behalf of King Galfrid concerning the return of his daughter."

It was information she would have already. By now, word of the return of the lost princess had spread throughout Elydor.

"Would King Galfrid not send an Aetherian for such a purpose?"

"He would," I offered diplomatically. "Normally."

She waited.

I had nothing more to offer beyond what I'd told her.

"I am afraid—"

"Princess Mevlida is a friend," I said, my words the only truth I could give her. "I have a unique perspective on her return, one your queen will wish to learn of, especially as it may impact all Elydor."

That got her attention.

"We were told the princess was taken by Kael of Gyoria and returned to her father."

"She was," I confirmed. "I will be glad to share more of that tale with you, but I've been traveling for many days, with some urgency, at the behest of the Aetherian king. If we might make our way to the palace..."

I stopped at that, my implication clear. If Nerys wished to know more about a topic every person in Elydor was curious about—why and how Mev came through the Gate—she would take me to the palace.

"Very well," she said finally. "You will be reunited with your belongings once inside, with the exception of your weapons. Those will be returned to you when you are no longer on palace grounds."

As expected.

I smiled, hoping to put her at ease since Nerys, though undoubtedly powerful, could not read my own sincerity and had little cause to trust me.

Thankfully, she turned away just as the emotion she was now feeling settled into my consciousness. It was not mistrust, as I'd expected on meeting her. Or wariness, given how little I was able to share about my intentions in meeting the queen.

It was the one thing I couldn't guard against.

Desire.

4

NERYS

He rode as effortlessly as he smiled, this human with hazel eyes that spoke of riddles. Skin nearly as tanned as a Thalassarian and brown hair, neither long nor short, marked him as a human who, unlike the other clans, had no one universally defining feature. His warrior's clothing could pass for Gyorian. Most humans were more readily identifiable, but this one blended in well as an Elydorian.

He was also exceedingly handsome.

Even more so than the one I nearly partnered with so many years ago. Like my parents, he too had met an untimely death. I'd long ago released the notion I was somehow cursed, yet I knew no others who had lost so many dear to them. Immortality was the gift Elydor had bequeathed to all those who inhabited this realm from its celestial beginnings. Even so, our death was possible and, if some were to be believed, more likely around me.

"The silver fish." Rowan, my human charge pointed to the stream we rode beside. "What are they? I don't recall them."

"You've been to Thalassaria before?"

"I have," he said, offering no further explanation. Most

humans who visited the palace were noblemen, but this one's title did not identify him as such. I was surprised the queen granted him an audience with so little information about the nature of his visit.

"They are called nera and can only be found on palace grounds. It's a sacred species tied to the history of the first king of Thalassaria."

"Which explains why I've never seen them before."

Sir Rowan said it almost absently as he peered alternately up toward coral-white posts, their lanterns casting a soft glow and down into the streams and pools of water we navigated.

"This spot," I explained, "was chosen for the palace grounds for its unique flora and fauna. There is no other like it in our kingdom."

"The first time I came here, with my father, I was in awe of everything about Thalassaria."

He finally looked at me. I almost wished he hadn't. It was easier to pretend he didn't affect me then. Because I most certainly could not be affected... in that way... by a human.

"No less in awe, I am certain, than seeing Aetheria for the first time?"

"Perhaps," he said. "But there is nothing quite like walking through soft sands." He gestured to his left. "And these shallow, turquoise lagoons." He slowed, so I did too. "Bioluminescent corals?" he asked, pointing.

Now that the sun had begun to set, the colors were even more striking. I'd made this trek so many times since I'd begun to work at the palace that I sometimes didn't notice them.

"Yes." Nodding to the many bridges woven from shells and sea glass ahead of us as we began riding once again. "Also bioluminescent. The shells absorb sunlight during the day. That bluish glow now, at dusk, is called The Tide's Gift. It lights the path for travelers but is also a revered symbol of our clan's deep connection with nature. The harmony between Thalassaria and the ocean is life-giving to us, as I'm sure you are aware. We leave our mounts here."

Smiling as we dismounted and walked into the stables, I watched the human's expression, one I'd seen many times before. Anticipating his questions, I said, "Each "stall" is an open alcove, as you see, formed from natural rock and coral. The seashell mosaics and flowing seaweed curtains have existed for hundreds of years."

"I never expected the palace to have so many unique features," he said as the stablemaster took both of our mounts. Patting Seaborn's flank, I thanked the young man and led Sir Rowan back outside. We walked toward yet another bridge, past cascading waterfalls that misted the air around us.

"It is the best of Thalassaria, according to the queen."

I should not have added that last bit. Unfortunately, he noticed. Sir Rowan stopped in the middle of the bridge and stepped toward me. Though he likely did it to hear me more clearly, with the sound of waterfalls drowning out our words, my heart still skipped a little beat.

"According to the queen?"

I rarely slipped up so easily. But something about this man made my tongue wag more freely than it should. His easy manner and smiles, maybe.

Trying to deflect the question, I asked one of him. "What is your role in Estmere, Sir Rowan? I find myself most curious about your purpose here."

"Simply Rowan," he said. "I am the son of a nobleman who wishes for a place for humans in Elydor."

"Simply?" I cocked my head to the side. "Is there anything simple about you, Rowan?"

His brief lip bite was so quick, if I blinked, I would have missed it.

"I could say the same of you. Tell me... why are you not wary of me?"

"Why should I be wary of you?" I asked, pretending not to understand his question.

But I did.

"I've never met a Thalassarian quite as welcoming to a human."

"Your answer is an honest one." *And accurate, too.* "Those who raised me have a more measured view of humans than some of my clan. But," she was quick to add, "they are not alone. More think as we do than you might believe." I could have said more but thought better of it.

"The palace is the best of Thalassaria, according to the queen." He returned to my earlier words. "You do not agree with Queen Lirael on its merits, and if I were to be bold in saying so, other matters as well."

This human was dangerous, in a different way than most.

"You have the Sight?"

He shook his head. "I do not."

Crossing my arms, I gave Rowan a look that told him I didn't believe him. Because I didn't. "You could not know as much otherwise."

His slow smile was meant to disarm me. And it worked.

"I did not know, but merely guessed. At least, not until you confirmed my suspicions."

A nobleman's son. That might be true, but he was more than that too. I was certain of it.

"What is your gift, then?" I asked, not expecting him to answer. A human's gift was their greatest power. Asking of it was considered borderline rude. And few humans would offer a free response to such a question, especially to a stranger.

"If I tell you, will you share with me what you believe is the best of Thalassaria, if not for its palace?"

"Its people," I said, the answer an easy one. "They may be wary of outsiders and often too suspicious by nature, but that is only because Thalassarians value their independence. The palace is magnificent but pales in comparison to the people who live within its borders."

He was no less surprised by my response than I was to have so freely given it.

"I can sense emotion," he said.

Had he really just told me his gift? Sensing emotion? That was not as common among humans but... I froze. That meant...

No. No, no, no.

The tug on Rowan's lips told me he knew exactly what I'd been thinking. What emotion I would have liked to conceal from him, but couldn't. Even now that I knew of his gift.

"Not to worry," he said, Rowan's voice as smooth as the tide gliding over polished stone. "If you could read emotion too, you'd have sensed the same in me since being in your presence. Shall we continue?"

Trying not to react, I stepped forward, putting one foot in front of the other as the implications of his words tumbled around in my brain.

So. He was attracted to me, too.

5

ROWAN

I sat on the same sort of bed, its insides as fluid as I remembered from my previous visit, though this one was much bigger. Waiting for the knock that would signal Nerys's return, I took in my surroundings. Sheer, translucent curtains cascaded from the bed canopy, mimicking the gentle flow of water. A large, arched window opposite me offered a view of the sea, according to Nerys, though now it opened only to darkness. Sconces fashioned from shells cast a warm glow throughout the chamber, but the most striking feature was the adjoining antechamber that I had just left. Warm water cascaded continually from the high ceiling above, an entire room dedicated to cleansing, one like I'd never seen before.

Water magic, I assumed, made such a thing possible. Even now, I could hear its echo, a soothing sound that seemed unsurprisingly to be found everywhere at the palace.

And then there was Nerys.

I stood and made my way to the window. Lights of every color, but especially greens and blues, were sprinkled across the grounds. Bioluminescent algae could be found throughout

Elydor, but this was something entirely different. Seemingly everything was imbued with the gleaming lights that could not be seen during the day but lit up spectacularly in the darkness. I could stare out this window all evening.

I could stare at Nerys my whole life.

Her beauty was as striking as the mysteries of the sea. Nerys's sun-kissed skin and aquamarine eyes lent her an innocence at odds with the rest of her. No mention of parents, but those who raised her. Her strength and resilience were evident in the way she walked. Rode. Held her head.

Smiling as I remembered her expression when I told Nerys of my gift—a revelation that had come easily from my lips, though I did not regret it—I turned toward the door, as if anticipating her knock, which came a moment later.

Though Nerys had attempted to put me at ease about the fact that my bedchamber would be locked at all times, I still found it disconcerting. Not that I was alone with such unease. Every human visitor to the Thalassarian palace complained of the same.

Opening my door, I sensed anticipation before I could block her emotion.

Nothing could have prepared me for the sight of her.

Waves of hair fell down her shoulders and back, the smallest of iridescent seashells dispersed throughout. Her dinner gown was strapless, the turquoise bodice and broken up with swaths of cream. Shells adorned the front, distinguishable up close. From far away, they would look like small gemstones.

The best part of Thalassaria might be its people, according to Nerys. And the palace, according to the queen. But from my viewpoint, it was the woman standing before me.

"You are magnificent." The words spilled out before I could

stop them, my thoughts more addled than they had been in a long time. "Apologies," I began, but Nerys interrupted me.

"None are necessary. Thank you," she said, accepting the compliment with grace. "We've likely missed the first course."

"How many are typically served?" I asked as we made our way through open corridors.

"Too many."

At her tone, and before I could reconsider it, a consideration flew from my lips. "In Estmere, it is not seen as untoward for a guest to be served privately by their host. As a way to ease them into their environment."

Nerys stopped. For a moment, I thought she might chastise my forwardness, so I rushed to add, "I mean nothing untoward by such a suggestion."

"Come," she said in response. "This way."

We walked silently through corridors of polished stone in shades of pearl and sea-green, ornate archways decorated with carvings of mythical sea creatures all along the way. Tall windows graced one side of the corridor, allowing moonlight to fill the space.

"It feels as if we are beneath the surface of the sea."

A couple, both dressed as formally as Nerys, moved past us. My guide inclined her head in greeting as both the man and woman looked at me as if I did not belong here. Which, of course, I didn't.

"Even when you do not see water, it's there. There are hidden fountains and trickling aqueducts behind each wall. Take a deep breath," Nerys said, her gown shimmering with each step.

"It smells like minerals and fresh water."

"The very palace itself is alive and breathing in rhythm with the sea. If you feel as if you are inside it, that is intentional. Just as if you feel you are among the clouds in Aethralis."

She stopped in front of a door. Opening it, Nerys stepped inside. It was a near replica of my own chamber, though larger, with a table in the corner, just beside a window that was nearly as large as the wall.

"We have a similar custom," she said, gesturing to one of the seats at the pearl stone table. "Though I thought perhaps you wished to dine in the same hall as the queen."

"I look forward to my audiences with her," I said, sitting. "But would much prefer this."

Nerys had made her way toward a wall. With a wave of her hand, what appeared to be a mirror suddenly rippled. I looked more closely. How was such a thing possible? The mirror had turned into water.

"My lady?" a faint, male voice asked.

"May I have wine and a meal for two, please?"

"Of course."

As quickly as it appeared, the water was gone. I had to see for myself. Joining her, I studied the mirror that reflected back both of us. "What was that?"

"You've not seen mirror scrying before, then?"

Mirror scrying. I'd heard of it, of course. "I thought that skill was merely a legend?"

"I can assure you, it is very real."

"And you are a Stormcaller as well?" I guessed.

"I am."

Only the most powerful Thalassarians could become Stormcallers, many of whom worked at and for the palace. Of those, I guessed very few had the skill which was so difficult, not even the Keepers had seen it performed.

I'd have asked another question, but a knock on her door was followed by two servants who hardly looked my way. Putting trays of food and wine on the table, they left without so much as a cursory glance.

"They are trained to be discreet," Nerys said, answering my silent question. "You must be hungry."

I was more curious than hungry, but when we sat, my stomach disagreed. From salad to fresh fish, both platters were filled to the brim, reminding me that I hadn't had a proper meal in days. Nerys poured us each the sapphire-colored wine Thalassaria was known for, though its sweetness, followed by a smoky aftertaste, took getting accustomed to.

"You are extremely powerful," I said between bites.

"One of the women who trained me is descended from a line of highly skilled water-wielders."

"Will you tell me of her?"

Nerys lowered her wine, the pewter's intricate carvings a reminder of the sea, as if one were needed here.

"The Great Seaquake. Have you heard of it?"

"Of course," I said. "Though I was not alive myself."

"My parents were nobles, both a part of the palace's diplomatic circles, and were on a ship headed to Aethralis when the quake struck. They were both lost to the sea."

I lowered my fork, sad to learn my suspicions were right. "I am very sorry, Nerys. That must have been incredibly difficult. You are young haranya, I assume?"

Immortals did not track years as humans did. Haranya appeared, much as Nerys, my own age, for many years. An Uninitiated human, like Mev, who was unaccustomed to being around immortals, might believe Nerys was between twenty-five and thirty-five years of age, when in truth, haranya had celebrated their one hundredth year. Most stopped counting until the telltale signs of slow aging appeared once again, at approximately five hundred years, when they were then marked as thaloran. For five hundred more years, they would appear as a middle-aged human until reaching one thousand years old, or vaelith. Those elders were, in all clans, revered.

"Very young: one hundred and twenty, I believe. And thank you. It was difficult, as Lirael had just become queen and the after-effects of the quake took precedence over finding a role for an orphan who could not seem to control her abilities. A healer by the name of Aneri, a friend of my mother's, took me under her wing. Years later, I passed the Stormcaller's Rite and began to work at the palace, as my parents had before me."

"You were brought to the palace for your skill?"

Nerys sighed. "That, and one of Lirael's men, an old friend of my father's, had been petitioning for me to come here for some time. But it was only after the Rite that I received the summons."

"Aneri," I said carefully, "must be quite skilled."

Nerys visibly relaxed. "She is, though some may consider her views unconventional."

"Unconventional? In what way?"

As Nerys finished chewing, I tried not to notice her tongue darting out to catch a bit of sauce on her lips.

"Like the Aetherian king, she has been fascinated with humans her whole life. I grew up hearing tales of them. How they first came through the Gate King Galfrid opened. The skills they brought with them that Elydor's magical properties intensified. To see glimpses of the future... or even feel others' emotions, as you do... it is fascinating."

So that was the reason Nerys had dropped her guard more easily with me than I'd have expected from a Thalassarian.

It felt like an appropriate time to tell her, to ease Nerys's mind, "I have the ability *not* to sense emotion, too."

"Are you sensing my emotions now?"

"No."

"But you did, when we met?"

"I did. I've found it useful, when first meeting people, to better understand their intentions toward me."

"To ascertain if they are a threat?"

"Precisely."

"I am not a threat to you, Rowan. It is my belief the humans should be recognized as a legitimate clan in Elydor. Your people have been here for hundreds of years."

I held her gaze, wishing there was a way for Nerys to know I was not a threat to her either. "Your beliefs are not in line with your queen's." I spoke the obvious.

She said nothing. Instead, Nerys raised a hand. With a gentle swipe in the direction of a fountain in the corner of her chamber, she lifted her hand and swirled her hand through the air. Expecting the water to move, I saw nothing, at first. Slowly, a fog began to appear, filling the space with a gentle mist that became thicker with each movement.

Though accustomed to the gentle sweep of an Elydorian's hand and the wonders they produced, there was something about hers that was more... elegant than most. I ignored the erratic beating of my heart at such a sight.

"We may speak more freely now," she said.

"A silencing mist?"

Nerys nodded. "Likely unnecessary, but I would not say these words in the absence of one. Not here, in the palace."

Waiting, I pushed away my platter, picked up the wine glass, and took a sip.

"There are many who believe as I do. That the isolationism which has come to characterize our people makes us weaker, not stronger. Those who do not mistrust humans but believe their gifts can complement Elydor, just as the other clans' gifts do. There are many of us, in fact, but the queen is highly mistrustful of outsiders, even more so than her predecessor."

I would not have expected to find an ally in my palace escort, but it seemed that was precisely what Nerys was to me. I just had to find a way to earn her trust. And quickly.

There was one way.

Though I disliked doing it after implying I would not, the stakes were too high. The secrets I kept, too valuable. Opening my mind, I allowed her energy to comingle with my own.

Hope.

She was feeling hopeful, which could mean many things. Hope that I would believe her? Hopeful for Thalassaria?

But there was another emotion too, not as obvious. Beneath that hope, a steady undercurrent of sincerity resonated. It wasn't forced, but genuine. Nerys believed the words she spoke, even understanding the risk she took in sharing them.

I made my decision, and would not look back.

"I am here to speak with the queen on King Galfrid's behalf," I said, never intending to speak these words to anyone but the queen herself. "The lost princess has returned and wishes, as the king does, to reopen the Aetherian Gate and reunite her parents along with all other families who were separated when it was closed. I am here to gain your queen's support, and aid, for such a purpose."

I closed my mind to her emotion but could easily read Nerys's surprise on her face.

"The queen's support," she murmured. "To open the Gate?"

I waited for the full import of my declaration to hit her, which it seemed to do just then.

Nerys sat back in her chair as if defeated. Shaking her head slightly, she took a deep breath and said, "Your quest is a futile one. She will never give it."

6

NERYS

I'd said too much.

How often had speaking first and thinking second gotten me into difficult situations? After all of these years, I should have known better.

When I made to stand, a hand suddenly appeared atop mine on the table.

His touch was unlike any other.

Rowan's hand was meant only to calm me. To reassure me, perhaps, that I had not spoken out of turn even though I most certainly had. Either way, my shortcomings suddenly mattered very little against the shock of his hand on mine. Rowan hadn't moved it. Nor did I want him to. I'd been touched many times over the years, but this was different.

It wasn't his hand, I realized, that made the difference. It was the way Rowan looked at me while he held it there, as if I were something more than ordinary. The temperature was as moderate here as all of Thalassaria, and yet a flush began to creep from my chest upward. I breathed deeply, in and out, willing it away.

He removed his hand.

"I do not easily trust others," he said. "And can understand your hesitancy. But I assure you, Nerys, we are on the same side in this."

I relaxed a bit. He was a human, after all, and not some Thalassarian politician who would run straight to the queen with whispers of my disloyalty. Not that it was disloyal to have a different opinion about how our clan would best thrive into the future. But I was fairly certain Queen Lirael would disagree.

"Why do you believe she will not give it?"

Instead of dropping the mist and ending our conversation, I reached for the glass of wine and, seeing it empty, refilled it.

"I do not know precisely. Since the Gate's closing, her views have changed. She has become more guarded than ever. The queen has always valued Thalassarian independence, as we all have, but there was a shift that saw her policies become more inward-facing than ever. She is not King Balthor, openly despising humans and advocating for their downfall, but neither do her beliefs align with the Aetherian king either."

His expression revealed nothing.

"Perhaps the return of Princess Mevlida will convince her. I've not found your queen's policies to be openly hostile to Estmere, as you've said."

Rowan refilled his wine as well. Sitting back, he appeared more relaxed than before. He was a knight, as the humans called it, but there was something more to him as well.

"You know more of me than I do of you," I pointed out to him. "Tell me of your upbringing in Estmere."

He hesitated. "Both of my parents were born in Elydor, as were their parents before them. We are a noble family, from the northern reaches of Estmere in a region called Calamoor."

"I've not heard of it before."

"My people keep to themselves, the dense forests and fortified towns in Calamoor lending to an independent nature your Thalassarians would be proud of. Or at least, some of them," he qualified, a twinkle in his eyes.

He smiled often, this human. There was a hint of mischief about him that I could not place. The warmth threatened to return if I did not control my body's response to his every movement.

"I do value independence," I said, realizing the silencing mist still lingered. With a wave of my hand, I moved the moisture in the air back to the fountain in the corner of my chamber. "But not at the expense of alliances and free trade."

Rowan's eyes narrowed. "That is an advanced skill, is it not?"

"You know more than most humans of our ways?" I said, not meaning for the question to sound like an accusation. It was a fact, though, that the majority of humans knew little about the inner workings of my clan.

"Not as much as I would like."

I waited, but he offered no further explanation.

"It is an advanced skill," I said finally. "Though not among Stormcallers. During the Rite, it is one of the first we are expected to perform."

"The Stormcaller's Rite," he said, taking a sip of wine. "Now that is a tradition shrouded in mystery. I know only that it is held twice each year, but not much else."

"I've never understood the desire for such secrecy around many of our customs. All of Elydor knows of the Gyorian Rite of Stone and Soil and The Trial of the Tempest in Aetheria. Why we should conceal our own makes little sense to me."

"Is it true outsiders do not attend your Festival of the Tides?"

"Not precisely. Just last summer, King Galfrid attended our festival, as Lirael attended his the year before."

"Another is imminent, is it not?"

"Indeed, it is," I said.

"Will there be a challenger?"

For a moment, I thought he could see through me. With luck, Rowan was not reading my emotions now. "No. There has not been one for many years."

Each clan's festival began the same way: as an opportunity for the current leader to be challenged to a feat of ability – wielding air, land or water—in order to determine if there should be a new king or queen. When Elydor was united, before the separate clans emerged, the leader was chosen based on unmatched power. They ruled until their death or until someone more powerful was revealed to take their place. All three clans continued that tradition.

"These days," I said, "the Festival of Tides has been solely a celebration of the Thalassarian's harmony with the sea and, if there are candidates, the Stormcaller's Rite."

He was too shrewd. If I said more, he might guess what I *wasn't* sharing. There was more to Rowan of Estmere than he had revealed thus far and switching topics was in my best interest. "Why has the Aetherian king chosen you, a human, for this mission?"

"As I've mentioned, I traveled with her to be reunited with the king. Mev is my friend."

That explained it. At least, in part. "How did you come to travel with her? What is she like? Is it true she was kidnapped by Prince Kael?"

"It is. Princess Mevlida is... insatiably curious about our world. She is determined, and quick-thinking. And quite beautiful."

"You like her."

"Very much." He cocked his head to the side as if attempting to understand my question more completely. "But not in that way."

I raised my brows, uncertain if I believed him.

"You know already the princess was taken by Kael of Gyoria. But it seems the rest of that story has not yet reached the shores of Thalassaria yet."

"The rest of that story?"

Rowan's slow smile made my insides feel as if a school of fish had stirred beneath my ribs.

"They are partnered."

My wine glass nearly slipped from my fingers. *Surely not.* "Prince Kael, of Gyoria? And King Galfrid's daughter?"

By way of a response, he continued to grin.

"He hates humans. And Aetherians."

"But loves Mev very much. She has changed his thinking on both, although I never truly believed that Prince Kael inherited the same vitriol for humans, or Aetherians, from his father. You'll remember his inheritance was stripped for attempting to save a human's life."

"An inheritance of title and land. The only inheritance that truly matters is not Balthor's to offer."

"Which poses an interesting conundrum, now that Kael has pledged his loyalty to Mev and her father, if he ever proves to be more skilled than his father..."

Rowan let the question go unasked.

"History tells us the sons or daughters of kings and queens often do inherit their parents' powers," I said.

"Indeed."

"If Prince Kael ever proved more powerful than his father." I took a sip of wine. "I cannot imagine what might happen then."

"Perhaps it will not matter. They say Prince Terran is more skilled than his brother."

"Do you believe it to be true?"

Rowan sighed, appearing to think on my question. "I do not know, even though I've seen them battle."

I sat up straighter. "You have?"

"We intercepted Prince Terran on the way to Aetheria. Mev had already fled north with Lyra." He paused. "Whom I believe you know?"

"I served on the Council for a short time," I said, but it seemed Rowan knew as much already. "So aye, I know Lyra well."

"She traveled with Kael and Mev, later taking the princess safely to her father while Kael prevented Terran and his men from following them."

"Men? Prince Kael is powerful, but not more so than his brother, especially if he was accompanied by Gyorian warriors."

"No," Rowan agreed. "He is not, but he convinced his brother to return to Gyoria."

"Rumor told us that the princess had been taken by Prince Kael, who later returned her to King Galfrid. I had no notion of the extent of their bond. That will certainly complicate matters for King Balthor."

"It certainly will."

Rowan had revealed more than I expected, but there was much he held back as well. I did not need to have the power to read emotion to tell as much. Though I did wish for the power to control my own emotions a bit better. I would endeavor to avoid looking directly into his eyes, which drew me into their depths with every glance.

"You cannot tell me why you are here on King Galfrid's behalf? Or how Queen Lirael might aid him in reopening the Gate?"

He looked directly at me. So much for avoiding his gaze.

"No, I cannot."

"Why?"

The question seemed to surprise him. Rowan placed his wine glass on the table and leaned forward, his elbows resting on his knees. He was a handsome man, this human. But a mysterious one, too.

"Some truths are dangerous," he said finally.

I knew it well.

Better than he could possibly imagine.

7

ROWAN

Two days, and still no summons from the queen.

Each morning had started out the same. Being escorted to the palace hall to break my fast, a tour of the palace, and then a respite that Nerys knew I did not need, but gave me anyway to tend to other responsibilities. To end each day, the evening meal.

Spending my days, and nights, with Nerys was nothing to complain about. Although we'd avoided further talk of politics, at each opportunity, I asked Nerys more about her upbringing and shared, as much as I was able, my own. It was the first time I truly understood my grandfather's warning when I had begun to question why so many of the Keepers went unmarried.

"It is a rare man, or woman, who will give themselves fully to a Keeper knowing, or at least suspecting, they keep secrets."

We took many vows, but none were as important as our vow of secrecy. The rule was a simple one. Only those with Harrow blood, or married to one with Harrow blood, knew of our existence. Scattered throughout the kingdom, some Keepers were nobles, others in less-esteemed roles, but all existed, at least partially, in the shadows.

Never once had I been tempted to share these secrets with anyone outside my family.

Until now.

When the knock came, I was resolved to have Nerys send a message to the queen, but her appearance erased thoughts of the Tidal Pearl and my mission. I'd seen her elegantly dressed, the gowns she wore to supper each evening taking my breath away. But today, the simplicity of her attire was somehow even more striking. Once again, I was forced to calm a quickened pulse I seemed unable to easily control since arriving at the palace.

Nerys wore a tunic the color of fresh seaweed, paired with fitted trousers in a soft, sandy beige that allowed ease of movement. A silver belt cinched her waist, with a small pouch at her side. Her boots were simple but well-made, and Nerys's typically loose hair was tied back, strands framing her face, a soft glow of determination lingering in her eyes.

With the quiet confidence of a woman accustomed to navigating the world with poise, her attire suggested a readiness to act when needed.

"I thought perhaps you might wish to visit the training yard."

I had not seen my weapons since arriving, and would indeed be glad for a training session.

"There has been no word from the queen?"

Nerys admitted she saw the queen infrequently as she typically interacted most often with her inner circle, of which Nerys was not a part, and took her meals in a private chamber.

"None. I sent a message this morn, reminding her of your presence."

"Thank you," I said, closing the door behind me as we walked into the corridor. "I was planning to ask if you might do as much today."

"I am certain she will not keep you waiting much longer. She already knows it concerns the princess. I would think Queen Lirael would be most anxious to learn the truth of her return."

The queen would not know of my ties to King Galfrid, nor of the true nature of my visit. Before I could respond, Nerys paused and spoke to a servant, asking him to fetch my sword and bring it to the training yard.

"Do you wish to break your fast first?" she asked.

"Not unless you do." Nerys had already admitted to me it was her least favorite meal of the day. She said, when not assigned to me, she skipped it most mornings in favor of a walk along the sea.

Without responding, she headed in a direction of the palace we'd not ventured through yet. After a multitude of twists and turns, passing countless shallow pools, fountains and waterfalls, we appeared to be leaving the palace building and heading downward. When we finally emerged, the shores of the Marevean Sea were before us.

Here, Thalassarian warriors were already engaged in training, though none used swords. Instead, it consisted of arm and hand movements as they manipulated the ocean waters. I'd seen water magic performed before, but never by so many at once.

"Are there not rules against me being here?"

Nerys seemed surprised by my question.

"Should there be?"

I watched as a man created a tunnel of water, like a mini-cyclone, and dragged it over the sand. He seemed surprised when it fell apart and landed at his feet.

"Thalassarians are normally so guarded."

Nerys began walking to a nearby structure. Like much of the palace, it seemed to be erected from the sands, its cream color blending seamlessly with the sand on which it sat.

"They are apprentices who have received special invitations to train with Stormcallers. Some from noble families, as a favor.

Others who show promise. But all wield basic magic. There is nothing proprietary about their skills."

As I looked closer, the truth of her words revealed itself. There were even two children among the young ones, Elydorians who had not yet reached one hundred years of age.

As we approached the structure, its thatched roof like many of the huts along the shores of Thalassaria, a man around Nerys's age greeted us. Behind a driftwood counter, weapons of every kind stared back. The presence of tridents and spears, along with what appeared to be healing potions, reminded me of an armory back home.

"Has a sword been brought—"

Before Nerys finished, the man produced my weapon from beneath the counter.

"Fine morning, Nerys," he said without looking at me.

"Indeed, it is. And Caelum?"

"There." He pointed toward the sea.

"A sword for him as well?"

By the time I worked out what was happening, I had my weapon back and we were striding toward a group of three who practiced water-wielding; only one doing so successfully.

"Caelum is an old friend and a trained swordsman," Nerys said, explaining as we approached. "An Aegis Commander of the palace."

He said something to his pupils, who scurried away.

"So this is your human?"

"He is not my human, Caelum."

I'd been about to say the same. Instead, I bowed to the warrior, who did the same back to me. "Sir Rowan of Estmere," I said.

"Master Caelum of Thalassaria," he said, watching me carefully.

Tall and lean, his dark hair, unusual for a Thalassarian, was tied back. With sharp eyes and an angular jaw that looked permanently set, as if the weight of the world had hardened him, Master Caelum would be a formidable training partner. By the look of him, though still haranya, he had many, many decades on me, perhaps multiple centuries.

"No magic," Nerys said.

Caelum looked at her as a father might. Kindly, with enough reproach that only the recipient could decipher its true meaning.

"How many years of training do you have on me?" I asked him.

Lifting his sword, Caelum said nothing but inclined his head, as if acknowledging his advantage.

Nerys backed away, but she was the only one. Before the first strike, most of those who previously were training had moved toward us. Blocking out the sun, the sound of waves crashing and of the cheers that were raised as we sparred, I relied on my training, hearing my grandfather's words.

The fight begins in your mind, Rowan. If you hesitate, you've already lost.

My father's words.

Move with purpose, not just strength. The blade follows where your mind leads.

And my uncle's, one of the greatest swordsmen in Estmere.

A sword is an extension of yourself. When you wield it, let your heart guide its edge.

With every parry and strike, more cheers filled the air. Beads of sweat dripped from my forehead into my eyes, but I ignored them and everything around me but learning this man's fighting style. Few Elydorians bothered to learn the skill of swordsmanship, their magic much more powerful. Those who did, however, typically were worthy opponents.

Caelum was no exception.

We sparred for some time until, remembering Nerys was watching us, I used a move my uncle showed me once, an unpredictable lunge followed by a swift withdrawal. In response, Caelum stepped back so I did the same.

"You wear no armor," he said. "Our weapons are not blunted."

Both facts I was well aware of.

"I didn't expect to find myself here, with such a worthy opponent," I added as the crowd dispersed.

"Where did you find such a human?" Caelum asked Nerys, who stepped forward and took his sword.

"He found us. Rowan is here to speak with the queen."

Caelum didn't appear surprised by the fact which meant he already knew as much.

"This is about the Aetherian princess?" he guessed.

"It is."

"They said the Gate remains closed."

"It does," I said, glancing at Nerys. She nodded, so I continued. "Princess Mevlida coming through seems to be uniquely related to her standing as King Galfrid's daughter. What confuses me most," I said, having admitted as much to Nerys already, "is that your queen must know this. And she also knows my presence here is related to the incident. And yet she does not grant me an audience."

"She will," Caelum echoed Nerys's words. "Otherwise, you'd not have been admitted to the palace. As to the delay..." He shrugged. "Who can know the mind of a queen?"

Both Nerys and Caelum knew more of Queen Lirael's mind than they shared, of that I was certain.

"Nerys."

All three of us turned to face the shore as the same servant who'd fetched my sword earlier ran toward us.

"Yes, Eoin?"

If he were human, I'd say the boy had not seen fifteen summers. But most likely, he had been alive longer than me.

"The queen has summoned you both."

Finally.

Caelum reached out his hand. Since we were in Thalassaria, and not Estmere, the parting was one of deference to me. I shook it, grateful.

"Until we meet again," he said.

"I look forward to it."

"Your swords." The boy, Eoin, reached out both hands. Though reluctant to hand mine over, I did so. Watching him walk off with it, I was about to ask Nerys how he'd fetched it so quickly when she spoke first.

"Come quickly. The queen does not like to be kept waiting."

"The queen sounds less and less appealing each day," I murmured for Nerys's ears only. She pretended not to hear me, just as I pretended not to be staring at her as she walked in front of me. But just as I'd done with Caelum, I vowed to put everything else out of my mind. I was here for one purpose only, and it was not to become enamored with my escort.

The fate of Estmere, of Elydor, rested on the shoulders of those of us who knew what was needed to open the Gate. Whether I liked her or not did not matter. I needed—we needed—the Queen of Thalassaria's aid.

And it was time to find out how willing she would be to give it.

8

NERYS

"Are you ready?"

Rowan gave me a slight nod. He'd changed clothing, as I had, from training. He looked every bit a nobleman now, his deep-green tunic emblazoned with the heraldic emblem of Estmere: a cracked stone tower under a golden crown, the crooked key behind it symbolizing their origins. With Rowan's square jaw set, the seriousness of his countenance was unusual enough to be slightly disconcerting.

I gestured to the guards, who simultaneously opened the great throne-room doors.

The first time I entered this room, my reaction was far more animated than Rowan's. He stood stoic, head held high, his gaze fixed on the queen with a composure I had never seen before. I, on the other hand, was young when my parents first introduced me to Queen Lirael, and the memory still lingered: the queen seated on her throne of coral, a sheet of water cascading silently behind her until it struck the surface far below, flowing out to sea. Everywhere we looked, scenes of sea battles and creatures from their depths were etched into the walls. I knew each of the stories intimately, my knowledge of Thalassarian history necessary before entering the Stormcaller's Rite.

As we walked toward the queen, I was surprised by the lack of guards. Typically, Queen Lirael was surrounded by members of her cabinet in addition to at least two guards, yet even the ones that opened the doors were gone.

She wore an aquamarine silk gown that, if she stood, would flow behind her in waves. As always, she wore elaborate jewelry made from pearls and sea glass.

Without the queen's usual entourage to introduce him, that duty fell to me.

"My queen, it is my pleasure to introduce you to Sir Rowan of Estmere. He is—"

"You may rise," she said to Rowan, who had entered a deep bow, befitting her station.

"I will be directly outside," I began, but Queen Lirael stopped me once again.

"You may remain."

The queen, though not quite thaloran, was at least four hundred years old and spoke with all of the authority that came with her age and experience. As always, I tried not to bristle at her tone. It was simply... her way, to speak as such.

"I was given leave by King Galfrid and Princess Mevlida to share my information with your majesty alone," Rowan said, his voice steady and firm, but kindly, as always.

Her eyes darted from Rowan to me.

"You will remain."

The queen had no special love for me. Thinking quickly, I could only assume she required me to stay as a demonstration of her power. Or perhaps she wished to gauge my reaction to Rowan's words.

"My message is for the queen's ears alone," Rowan pushed back.

I tried not to wince. Perhaps I should have warned him that the queen did not take kindly to having her decisions questioned.

"Nerys is a trusted member of my court," she said. "As I am certain you've learned already."

What did that mean? Had she deliberately delayed this audience as a test of my loyalty?

"I have learned," Rowan responded, looking to where she sat above us, the queen's throne perched on a dais four steps higher than where we stood. "She is a capable and intelligent escort, and I thank you for her care."

Spoken like a true diplomat. My parents would have liked him.

"Your message?" she prompted, leaving Rowan with a choice. He could either share with us both or not share at all. That the queen would wish me to remain, when she'd never shown an interest in having me be a part of her inner circle, was curious. Especially given she had cleared the throne room, obviously anticipating the sensitive nature of his audience.

Rowan showed no annoyance, only patience. Neither did he spare so much as a glance at me.

"As you are aware from my earlier missive," he began, clearly resigned to my presence, "I come on behalf of the Aetherian king and his daughter, who has returned to Elydor by way of the Gate which had previously been closed for nearly thirty years. I had an opportunity to assist in escorting the princess to her father—"

"Since the Aetherian Gate," the queen interrupted, her thin lips pressed together between speeches, "is in Aetheria, that she needed escorting *back* to it was because of Prince Kael of Gyoria, was it not?"

"Aye, it is true Prince Kael abducted the princess for the

purpose of taking her to his father. He changed course, however, and she is safely ensconced in the palace with her father."

If there was one thing that annoyed Queen Lirael more than being questioned, it was the Gyorian king. Most of Elydor had that in common.

"Do continue," she said.

"As you may have heard, Princess Mevlida and Prince Kael are now partnered."

She knew already. The queen did not appear a bit surprised.

"He has pledged his support to King Galfrid's cause, which is, as it has been for these past years, to reopen the Gate."

The queen's brows raised. "Is it not reopened?"

"No, it does not appear to be so. Princess Mevlida, it seems, is an anomaly."

The queen did not react to that news.

Rowan hesitated for the first time since we'd entered the throne room. He looked at me and then back up to the queen.

"As you and very few others in Elydor are aware, the Gate was both opened, and closed, with the use of each clan's most revered artifacts."

What did he just say?

I tried not to react, but struggled.

For her part, the queen's nose flared in annoyance.

"King Galfrid formally requests use of, when it becomes necessary, the Tidal Pearl in reopening the Aetherian Gate."

Impossible. How could the Tidal Pearl have been used to open the Gate? The queen would never have allowed its use by anyone but her. Even if she had, it was well known King Balthor closed the Gate, and the only way he could have gotten it...

"No king in Elydor will ever again make use of our Tidal Pearl," she said, the queen's voice as steely firm as I'd ever heard it. Her gaze darted toward me, her eyes narrowing. "It was stolen from us once. It will never be taken again."

Stolen.

King Balthor stole the Tidal Pearl to close the Gate.

It explained everything. Including my parents' death.

A rage like I'd never felt before consumed me. I could not see. Or think. Or even breathe.

The Pearl had been stolen which was why, when the seaquake struck, Queen Lirael was not able to quell it. All sensed it had been coming, yet she couldn't stop it. At least, not without the Tidal Pearl amplifying her power. But instead of telling her people it had been stolen, she claimed to have used it, to no avail.

I cannot stay here.

Before thinking it through, my feet had begun a forward motion and even my queen's command did not stop them. I fled the throne room, pushing open one of the two heavy doors, and ran and ran. Ignoring curious stares and my name being called, I ran until I was outside of the palace. Only then did I stop, contemplating my direction, and bolted toward the sea.

Once on the beach, I continued to run toward a spot that few visited. On the other side of a rocky outcropping, it had been a haven of mine for many years. Sitting in its entrance, I didn't dare allow my mind to consider what I had just done. Fled the palace. Ignored the queen's command. Suddenly, I was no longer the daughter of two nobles, a Stormcaller who had received an appointment in the palace. I was Nerys, the woman who lost her parents and had difficulty controlling her magic. An orphan, afraid of her own skills.

I stood, walked slowly to the water's edge, and lifted my hand.

9

ROWAN

"Your majesty. I've spent my life bridging worlds: between those who wield power and those who serve it, between duty and what's right. Galfrid sent me here because he knows I fight for something larger than myself. My people have suffered for many years and still hold out hope that they will one day be fully accepted as Elydorians."

"I am not without compassion for the humans," she said. "Which is why you were granted an audience."

I was granted an audience because the queen wished for information about Mevlida, but I smartly kept that thought to myself.

"A fact that is much appreciated," I said instead.

"But I cannot help you. The Tidal Pearl will never again be used by anyone but the queen, or king, of Thalassaria."

I was prepared for such a statement.

"When the time comes, and King Galfrid is positioned once again to reopen the Gate, I will escort you myself to it so that you may be present for the Gate's reopening. It will pass through no hands other than your own and, briefly with you as witness, the Aetherian king's."

Her eyes narrowed shrewdly. "Even if I were to agree, Galfrid will never have use of the Stone of Mor'Vallis."

"The return of King Galfrid's daughter has changed things. The Gyorian prince is now pledged to him. When the time comes, if the Tidal Pearl is the only artifact remaining needed to open the Gate, will you answer King Galfrid's call?"

She hesitated. And would deny me again. So instead, I asked for something less than her pledge.

"Will you consider my request?"

I would point out to her that denying it would not endear her to Aetheria, but the queen knew as much already. Waiting, I thought of Nerys. I wondered why she became so upset. I expected her shock; the information she learned today was known only to a handful across Elydor. But why did news of the Tidal Pearl's theft by King Balthor send her from the throne room?

"You may stay until the Festival of Tides. I will render my decision then, and it will be final. Since your escort has abandoned us, a guard will take you to your chamber."

It was the best I could hope for. Bowing, I thanked her as Queen Lirael lifted a coral staff beside her, banging it twice against the floor. Immediately, the doors opened behind me.

"Thank you, your majesty."

With a final frosty stare, Queen Lirael lifted her chin. It was the last thing I saw before retreating.

"Escort him to his chamber," she called as I passed from the throne room into the corridor.

"I will take him." Caelum must have been standing close by, waiting. Neither guard objected, but neither did Caelum allow them the opportunity to do so. "Come with me."

He said nothing while we walked through the watery corridors of the palace. There was something to look at around every corner, but my concern was not with the beauty of this place at the moment.

"Do you know where she is?" I asked, certain Caelum knew that, and more.

"I am taking you to her."

It was only when we reached the lower floor and had left the palace that Caelum spoke again.

"Word spread quickly of her retreat from the throne room. I can guess her whereabouts but thought to fetch you first."

"Why?"

We walked along the shore, the palace on our left, sand and surf to our right. I could easily become accustomed to this place.

"I served with her father in diplomatic circles. He was a good man, but too protective of her. By the time he and her mother perished, Nerys should have received a position at court, but he shielded her for much too long. I'd have taken her into my home if Aneri hadn't done so, and Nerys benefited from her training as a healer. I was not surprised she was eventually chosen to perform the Stormcaller's Rite, nor when she was brought to the palace."

"Why were you not surprised?"

Caelum hesitated.

"She is... extremely powerful."

"Why do you tell me all this?" I asked.

"Because I know Nerys well and can easily see the trust she so quickly placed in you. I would not be surprised if she has told you much of this already."

I did not deny it. Evidently, he did know Nerys well. My first instinct, that he was somewhat of a father figure to her, had been accurate, it seemed.

"Nerys has long believed, as her parents before her, and as I do, that Thalassari's future lies in strengthening ties with our northern neighbors, including humans."

I stopped walking. Caelum did the same.

I'd been trained as a spy. Trained to understand what wasn't said. To see what wasn't visible. And that's how I knew Caelum's escort was more than it seemed. His revelations, not knowing for certain Nerys had opened up to me already, were not just unusual for a Thalassarian. They were unheard of.

"What are you not telling me?"

In response, he moved closer to the water, so I followed. From this vantage point, I could see her. Nerys had been shielded by a rock outcropping that stopped just short of the waves which crashed against it. Behind them, as the water ebbed and flowed along her bare ankles, she waved her hands. In response, funnels of water rose above the sea and then crashed back down.

She did it again and again, the sea itself responding to her will. With a single sweeping motion of her hand, the water in front of her stilled, unnaturally, eerily calm. Then, with a sharp flick of her wrist, the calm shattered. A towering column of water erupted from the surface, twisting and spinning into a perfect spiral that defied gravity, reflecting the sunlight in a kaleidoscope of shimmering blues and greens. With her arms outstretched, she turned slowly, her movements fluid, almost like a dance. The spiral followed her lead, coiling tighter and tighter until it exploded outward in a rain of droplets that sparkled like diamonds.

Never in my life had I seen anything like it. Chills ran along my spine as my mind raced, unable to decide if her movements were beautiful or terrifying in their intensity.

Both. They were both.

I turned to Caelum. "I've never seen a Thalassarian do such a thing."

His secret smile told me why Caelum had brought me here. "And you never will."

Our eyes met. I knew the question to ask. And frankly, I knew the answer already too.

"Can the queen do that?"

Caelum shook his head, the movement barely discernible.

"Does she know what Nerys is capable of?"

He sighed. "To what extent, I am not certain. Nerys would never do as much"—he gestured to her as Nerys continued to manipulate the sea before her in awe-inspiring ways— "in front of the queen, or anyone, for that matter. With a few exceptions."

"Who does she trust to show that?"

Who can I trust?

"Me. Aneri. Marek. And a few others."

I did not know Marek, but that was a question for another time.

"How will she feel about me seeing this?" I asked, still uncertain why Caelum had allowed it.

"Ask her for yourself."

Turning my attention back to Nerys, I realized she had spotted us. Arms now at her sides, she hardly moved at all.

"Go," he said. "Speak with her."

Caelum wasn't coming with me. I stepped forward.

"And Rowan?"

I turned back to look at him.

"If you betray her, I will kill you."

Bowing his head, as if he'd not made that statement but instead had told me to have a good day, Caelum retreated. I didn't doubt his words, but neither did I worry. I had no intention of betraying Nerys, but I did intend to get some answers from her.

10

NERYS

I could not have been more surprised to see him.

That Caelum had taken Rowan to me was more than a little out of character for him. When my parents had died, it was he and Aneri who had lifted me up, but they did so in very different ways. Aneri, as kind and loving as my mother, and Caelum, more stoic and relentless than my father had been. I could never guess what he was thinking and only once, in a quiet moment after training, had he admitted wishing for that rare thing only a small fraction of Elydorians experienced.

A child.

I'd already known I was like a daughter to him, but that conversation had confirmed it. Since then, he'd never truly opened his heart again to me, but once had been enough. Now, with each step Rowan took toward me, I tried to understand why he'd allowed a stranger to him, a human, to see me this way.

If you wish to practice such skills, do so here where you cannot be seen by the palace.

Remembering his words the first time Caelum had taken me to this place, I watched as Rowan removed his boots, tossed them onto the sand, and made his way across the rocks. His movements were agile and effortless, the words he'd spoken to Queen Lirael still playing in my mind.

"Why did he bring you here?" I asked without preamble. Though the tempest inside me had somewhat settled, it hadn't yet been replaced by the calm I needed to return to the palace.

"He said that he believes you put your trust in me. If that is true, your trust would not be misplaced, Nerys."

I turned to the sea, watching as the waves rolled in, one after another.

"Some believe it is Thalassa, the sea goddess who created all we see before us. But how is that possible, when Elydor was all one before the clans were created?"

"I cannot claim to know any more than you, with certainty, of Thalassa, or Zephyra or Terranor or my human god."

"Hmm."

Rowan moved closer, facing me. Waiting.

"It is true, I had begun to put my trust in you, but it is also clear there is much I did not know, including your true purpose here."

"That was not my story to tell, but King Galfrid's and his daughter's. But I am glad Queen Lirael asked you to stay. You know the truth of it now."

I turned to him. "Why you?"

Rowan's smile faltered. "Another story that is not mine. If it were, I would share it, Nerys. Surely you know, at least, we want the same for Elydor. It is my fervent wish the Gate is reopened, my people who never intended to remain able to return and be reunited with their loved ones. I believe, as you do, we are stronger working together, all four of Elydor's kingdoms united."

"Too many still do not see Estmere as a legitimate clan."

"Perhaps because we continue to call it a kingdom."

That did make me smile. It was a minor detail, but highlighted an important difference between us. "You have assimilated but still keep many of the human ways."

"As do all the king... clans... in Elydor."

"True," I said, feeling calmer with each passing moment. A distraction to my thoughts was needed, it seemed.

"You are troubled."

"As evidenced by my fleeing from the throne room, ignoring the queen's command?"

"As evidenced by your expression." He grinned. "And your fleeing, too."

Could I trust a man who admitted there was more he could not, or would not, tell me? As an ally, perhaps. Though there was a part of me that wished for more, if I were being honest with myself.

"None know the Tidal Pearl had been stolen. Or if they did, the queen kept the circle of knowledge small. We knew the seaquake was coming. There were signs, and the queen was the only one powerful enough to stop it. But she was unable to do so. Afterward, there were many questions about how, with the Tidal Pearl amplifying her power, the queen had failed to harness its strength to calm the waters."

Understanding dawned on Rowan's face. "She did not have it. That quake occurred not long after Balthor closed the Gate. Some believed the two occurrences were related."

Further words refused to escape my mouth. I could remember learning of it, rushing to the water's edge and falling to my knees, surrounded by wails and shouts of disbelief. Not since the War of the Abyss had so many Thalassarians perished at one time.

His arms were around me before I could stop him, though I would not have tried. Lying my head on his chest, I relished

Rowan's embrace as I might a lover, but he was nothing of the sort. This man was a human. A near stranger. And yet nothing in recent memory had felt more natural than slipping my own arms around his waist.

He smelled of sea salt and cedar, like the ocean meeting the shore. The warmth of his body against mine steadied me, as if I no longer felt adrift.

For a moment, I allowed myself to forget the questions and secrets. In his embrace, everything faded into the background except the sound of sea meeting surf.

"I am sorry, Nerys," he whispered above me. "For the loss of your parents. For the queen's deception. And for learning about the latter from me."

It was not his fault, and though Rowan likely knew as much, I told him by pulling him tighter, unwilling to let him go just yet.

We stood that way for longer than was proper, but suddenly, I did not care about propriety. Or my duties. Or even hiding, something I'd gotten very good at doing these past years.

"I am stronger than her," I murmured.

It was treason to speak the words aloud and not challenge her. Thalassarian law, as with the other clans, was simple. The most powerful among its people was crowned king or queen. It had been so since the first days of Elydor, before the clans even existed.

"I know," he said. "I believe Caelum wanted me to see it for myself."

Reluctantly, I stepped back, inadvertently looking at his lips, wondering what it would be like to kiss him. As if we needed that further complication.

"He wants me to challenge her."

"As you should. Is that not the main purpose of your Festival of Tides? One which it seems I will witness, as your queen denied my request but agreed to reconsider, giving me her answer on the day of your festival."

"Unfortunately, I expected as much. And aye, that is the purpose of the Festival of Tides," I acknowledged. "But we've gone for so long without a challenge to the queen..."

Rowan's gaze was shrewd. "The challenge is its primary purpose."

He wasn't wrong.

"Do you think she suspects?"

"That," I admitted, "is an excellent question. I do not believe so but she knows there is someone more powerful courtesy of the Tidal Pearl."

Little by little, each clan's key artifact becomes less amplifying, a sign to the current ruler one has been born that will replace them.

"Will you?"

"Challenge her?"

I shook my head. "I am no queen."

"Nerys, if you are truly more powerful than Lirael—"

"I should have said, I believe I am more powerful. None can know for certain without a direct test of our skills. If I were to challenge her, and lose... I cannot risk it. Maybe in the future, but not now." Not giving him a chance to argue, which I was certain he was about to do, I moved toward the water. "Let me show you something."

I stepped to the water's edge, the cool spray of the sea misting my face as I extended my hand. Kneeling, my palm hovering just above the surface, I closed my eyes. The water stilled, unnaturally calm, as though the ocean was holding its breath.

A faint glow spread from my fingertips and the water responded, rippling outward in delicate, synchronized patterns: circles, spirals, and symbols. Slowly, the designs rose from the sea, droplets forming into glistening sculptures that danced in the air.

I didn't stop yet.

With a whispered command, the sculptures transformed into living images: a pod of dolphins leaping joyously, a towering wave frozen mid-crash, and finally, a majestic figure cloaked in flowing robes, her features too ethereal to belong to any mortal.

"Thalassa," he breathed, recognizing the image of the Eternal.

I stood. "This is not just water. It is memory; the sea holds fragments of what it's witnessed. Few of us can summon it, and even fewer can shape it," I added, in case Rowan was not clear about the meaning of this demonstration. "I should not have witnessed their last moments, but was unable to stop myself. Nor is it a "gift" I wish to share with anyone, its burden too great to bear."

"Then let me bear it with you."

11

ROWAN

I sat up in bed, an odd sensation waking me. It was as if I could feel others' emotions, a tangled web of them, even though I was alone. How could I be sensing emotion when there was no one around? My bedchamber was still dark, but I made a quick sweep of the room, confirming that I was alone. Standing back in front of the window, as the sky began to slowly lighten, a figure seemed to take shape. Impossibly, it was well out into the sea, as if standing on the water.

The figure was female. As she waved her arms, water rose and fell in a delicate dance that felt important, somehow. The figure spun toward me.

Nerys.

Blinking, I looked again, but she was gone.

Squeezing my eyes shut, I willed whatever madness had taken hold of me away. Instead, a humming filled my ears. What was that sound? Opening my eyes, I strained my memory, attempting to place it, but I couldn't.

No. It could not be.

Watching as the rising sun began to lighten the world outside my window, I grasped my mind for Grandfather's words.

It felt... as if my very soul were shifting, aligning with something I didn't understand. When my time is ended, the new Keeper won't need to search for a new chosen one. They will know and spread the word.

I stumbled back, the humming resonating in my chest, as if every heartbeat carried the weight of something far older than myself.

"Grandfather," I whispered, my voice breaking.

He was gone.

The knowledge hit me like a physical blow, my knees buckling as the truth settled in. He'd died, and with his death, The Keeper's burden had been passed to me.

The hum grew louder, filling every corner of my mind. It wasn't just a sound; it was a presence. A legacy. A duty.

I was no longer a Keeper. I was now *The* Keeper.

I stayed there on the floor until the humming passed. It was replaced with trepidation, but not my own. Trepidation and something else... excitement. Hope. Desire.

I stood, remembering more of my grandfather's words.

Your own abilities will heighten, and you will need to re-learn how to hone them. Along with them, the visionary abilities of our forefounder, the first to pass through the Gate, will begin to manifest. I cannot explain how since some, like myself, already had the Sight. For me, it was a strengthening. For others, this new skill will be another burden to carry.

My vision of Nerys on the water. It was a glimpse of the future I didn't yet understand or know how to control so I couldn't be certain of what it meant.

A knock at the door interrupted my thoughts.

I went to it, asking, "Nerys?"

"Yes," she replied.

"I will be just a moment."

Dressing as quickly as possible, I joined her outside my door.

"Apologies," I said, realizing the emotions I'd felt were hers. It seemed I no longer needed to be close to someone to read them. Thankfully, it seemed my ability to block them out remained intact.

She was dressed casually, her tunic-style top a gentle seafoam green and cinched at the waist with a braided kelp cord. Deep-navy, form-fitting breeches and her hair tied loosely back completed a look that spoke of quiet elegance.

In short, she was strikingly beautiful, as always.

"I thought perhaps we might get away from the palace today."

"Have you been given leave to do so?"

Nerys's good humor seemed to be restored. "I haven't yet spoken with the queen, but she did send me a message saying I was to continue as your escort. I'd expected more of a reprimand, which may be coming still."

"When you are not escorting me, or another guest of the palace, what are your duties here?" I asked as we walked.

"Like my parents, my role is mainly as a diplomat, although they traveled more often beyond our borders. Endless council meetings, disagreements about trade agreements... that sort of thing. That said, the queen has increasingly, over the years, reduced our trade with other clans. I help train new recruits to the palace and am sometimes used when the palace healer becomes overwhelmed."

He is gone.

As soon as the thought popped into my head, I forced it out. I could not grieve or dwell on the responsibilities that had been placed on me as the new Keeper. Questions as to why I was chosen or how my new abilities would manifest would have to wait.

Even if I trusted her. Even if I wished to tell her, the code of the Keepers strictly forbade it. Especially now.

"Do your duties align with how you wish to spend your time?"

We made our way out of the palace and toward the same entrance where I first met Nerys. She greeted people as we walked by, though none appeared familiar to me.

"What do you mean?"

"Your ideal life," I asked, the same question my grandfather had when my father began to train me. There were two types of Keepers: shadow and lore. Lore Keepers were also noblemen and women, laypeople, blacksmiths... members of the Estmere kingdom but also descendants of the Harrow family who kept its secrets. Shadow Keepers were the trained warriors, the most skilled also serving as spies, who not only kept the family's secrets but actively pursued a better life for all Harrows, and humans, in whatever capacity was necessary. My father assumed I would be the latter, but it was my grandfather who asked what I wished for my life.

I was uncertain at the time and told him as much.

"My grandfather asked me once," I told her as we moved through the palace gates, "when I closed my eyes and watched myself living my ideal life, what it looked like. I told him and began my training that day as a knight."

It was not a lie. I'd been knighted by an earl who had no knowledge of my family's history. But attaining knighthood was not truly the goal of my training. Gaining information, aiding whatever human's cause was most needed—in my lifetime reopening the Gate—was my true life's purpose.

"My ideal life," Nerys murmured.

"Or lives. You live many, which I suppose changes the equation."

"In that respect, you're right," she said as we apparently reached our destination.

A stream that ran through the palace walls had opened up, wide enough for narrow boats the Thalassarians called scapha. We walked down a set of stairs toward a holding area where many of them were stored.

"Yet my mother often told me to live as if I might die. I'd always thought it was a morbid sentiment, but I understand now she meant it to be the opposite."

We walked onto a wooden dock, Nerys untying and preparing a bright-coral scapha as if she'd done so thousands of times.

"Come," she said, "we will take this into Serenium Square. The markets are today."

I stepped into the boat and sat behind her. With a flick of her wrist, our scapha began to move forward just as another passed on our right to dock where we'd pushed off.

"I've seen the scapha before and wondered how they move simultaneously in different directions."

"We guide the currents, not unlike a rider directing their horse. The water beneath us is alive, responsive to intention and touch. But it does take some skill, which is why young ones do not travel by scapha."

As the palace walls shrunk behind us, Nerys and I glided away from the elegance of Maristhera through intricate canals toward the center of the city.

"My ideal life," Nerys said. "I've thought only of goals I wished to achieve. Making my parents proud, and later, honoring their memory. Showing Aneri she was not foolish to take me under her wing, that I could become something, as my parents had before me. Performing the Stormcaller's Rite."

"All very worthy goals."

"But my ideal life?" she continued. Nerys somehow turned

halfway toward me but managed to steer our boat with nothing more than a few flicks of her wrist. "I suppose it would be with a partner, someone to wake up to each day and love. Together, we would see Thalassarians thrive in a united Elydor, where our own happiness was not wrought at the expense of those less fortunate."

What surprised me most about her response was how similar it was to my own, even at a young age. I saw my own happiness as very much tied to the world in which I lived.

"Have you been partnered before?" I asked, using her word for our human concept of marriage.

"I have not. There have been lovers, but none with whom I wished to spend an eternity."

Of course she had taken lovers. Immortals saw their relationships much differently than us humans. They partnered less readily, with good reason. As in Estmere, separating from a marriage was not taken lightly, but their "forever" lasted much, much longer than ours.

She turned more fully toward me.

"Do you have a partner, Rowan?"

Her words were nearly drowned out by the waterfall we passed. Nerys's hands were so quick, I'd have missed the movement if I had not caught the unnatural redirection of the water away from our boat. She did it so that we did not get wet. Or more accurately, so I did not get wet. Everything a Thalassarian wore, from their tunic to their boots, resisted water.

"Or a wife, as you call it?" she clarified.

"I do not."

Nerys turned back around just as the city came into view.

It wasn't until she navigated us toward one of many docks in Serenium and we were back on land that Nerys and I finished our conversation as we walked toward Serenium Square.

"Did you ever come close?" she asked, watching me. "To marrying?"

I couldn't explain that marrying was more difficult for me, especially now. The secrets The Keeper held were a weight that some might call a burden. It would be a rare woman that would be able to share it with me. So nay, I was not likely to marry.

"I..."

And that's when it happened.

A flood of emotion, not only Nerys's but all of those who walked near us. It was like being brought back to my childhood when my abilities first began to manifest. For a moment, I thought Nerys was reaching for my hand until I realized it wasn't actually her but a vision of her. Hazy, like the one of her on the water. She was smiling, about to say something.

As quickly as it came, the vision dissipated and was replaced by a very real, very concerned-looking Nerys.

"Rowan?"

I took a deep breath, held it, and released... clearing my mind. Eventually, the flood of emotions went away.

"I'm fine," I said, trying to convince myself as much as Nerys.

She, of course, was not convinced at all. Refusing to move, she crossed her arms and looked at me as if I were a young child. I'd have laughed at her expression if we weren't interrupted.

Out of nowhere, a man picked up Nerys and spun her around. If not for the vision, I'd have seen him coming.

"How could you possibly be more beautiful than the last time I saw you?"

Laughing, Nerys slapped him on the shoulder. They obviously knew each other well. Was he one of the lovers she'd mentioned?

A corsair by the look of him. Everything about this man said "Thalassarian sailor". From his tanned skin and sun-bleached hair to his loose, linen shirt and leather belt with daggers hanging from it, this was a defender of Thalassarian waters if I ever saw one.

"It's been much too long," she said as he finally put her down. "I'm glad you're back."

He noticed me.

Nerys looked between us, swatted him again on the shoulder and said, "Behave." Which told me, he typically did not.

"Rowan, meet Marek. My..."

I steeled myself for it.

"Best friend."

12

NERYS

"Best... *friend*?" Rowan appeared skeptical. Not surprising, given Marek's flirtatious nature. He simply couldn't turn it off. Even with me.

"We met during Marek's early naval training," I explained.

"I charmed her with my irreverent humor and sharp wit."

Ignoring him, I said, "Marek challenged me to a sailing competition and won."

"I'm surprised how readily you admit it." Marek pulled a dagger from its sheath and flipped it over in his hands. He excelled at many things—sailing, commanding his men, turning impossible situations to his advantage—but being still was not one of them. Rowan, unfortunately, likely took it as a threat. He watched the dagger carefully.

"Because you would tell him anyway. Is there a person in Thalassaria who does not know you bested me?"

"Pardon." Marek stopped an elderly thaloran on her way to the market. She was at least a middle-tier noble by the quality of her dress and cane. "Do you know my friend Nerys?" he asked.

"She once lost a sailing competition to me many years ago. I wondered if you'd heard the story."

The woman looked from Rowan to me and then landed on Marek. "You must be quite skilled," she said.

I tried not to laugh lest the woman think I did so at her expense.

"He likes to believe so," I said. "Do enjoy yourself at the market. That is where you are headed now?"

"I am," she replied. "Good day to you all."

In response, Marek bowed with a flourish only he could manage without insult. If she were a few hundred years younger, the woman may have blushed. If her smile were any indication, she did not mind the interruption.

We watched as she passed us, her movements slow.

Having known him for many years, I could guess what Marek would do, and was not at all surprised when he took a step toward her.

"Apologies to you both for being denied my presence. Until we meet again, Rowan."

Rowan had no time to respond before Marek had caught up with the woman. Linking her arm with his, he began to walk her toward the center of the city.

"That was... surprising."

I laughed. "Which part, precisely?"

"All of it."

"Marek is unique, for certain. But he has a good heart, though many don't see past his roguish ways."

Rowan's brows lifted, his expression insinuating.

"Not with me."

"No?" he asked, clearly disbelieving me.

"No, though not for his initial lack of trying. And he may have succeeded. As you can see, he is quite handsome."

We began to walk once again.

"What prevented it?"

Smiling at the memory, I breathed in the salt air as a murmur of voices and the smell of spiced fish and baked kelp bread reached us.

"Not what, but who. I'd been at the docks, having finished one of my first royal duties, overseeing a diplomatic mission on behalf of the palace, when he ported. He overheard me being complimented on my sailing skills and, as he told you, I found myself in a friendly competition, not knowing of his reputation. Even then, as a corsair, before he earned the title of Navarch in the Tidebreaker fleet, Marek was quite skilled."

Rowan whistled. "Navarch. And with the Tidebreaker fleet? Impressive."

"If you know of the Tidebreaker fleet, you must also know that they aren't officially a part of the Thalassarian navy. They operate independently, often bending the rules to achieve their goals. It is a perfect fit for him, but not an easy position to obtain."

"As I've heard. But I'll admit, I'm most interested in how you avoided becoming one of his conquests."

I could not help laughing at Rowan's very accurate assessment of our first meeting. "It was a narrow escape, I can assure you. After he won, Marek suggested a drink at The Moonlit Current, a tavern popular with sailors. And one of my personal favorites. We'd just sat down when a human woman, a beautiful one at that, marched up to our table and slapped Marek across the face. She didn't say a word. Not before, or after. The woman left and although I invited Marek to go after her—he clearly wanted to do so—he remained. He said only that he deserved the slap. It was the only time I'd ever seen him so defeated."

"I can understand how that might change the dynamic between you."

"It did. We never spoke of it. Not that day, or since."

"Never?"

I shook my head as we approached the town square. The occasional call of seabirds overhead began to mix with vendors calling out their wares.

"That day, I could sense he didn't wish to discuss it. There were times, in years since, I brought it up, but Marek would only mumble his well-used mantra: that love isn't worth the pain. Marek isn't shy about his uninterest in love. Women? They are another story entirely."

We arrived at the center of the city. Brightly colored stalls with woven seaweed canopies transformed Serenium Square. Everything from shimmering shells and rare pearls to intricately carved coral and trinkets infused with water-based enchantments were being peddled.

I picked up a large, aquamarine pearl. "Marek's mother is a pearl diver," I said to Rowan, who stood at my back. "This is beautiful," I commented to the vendor.

"It was harvested from the Bay of Serenium," she said, pride in her voice. "A rare find, meant for someone with the sea in their heart."

Putting it back down, I thanked her and walked to the next table. We moved from vendor to vendor, Rowan asking questions about various items and Thalassarian culture. We ate spiced fish as he garnered more than one curious, and appreciative, glance.

"It's rare for Thalassarians to be with humans," I teased him at one point. "But I believe if you wished to do so, you would have your pick of women here."

When Rowan didn't respond, I turned around. He'd been right behind me moments earlier. Spotting him nearby, I called

Tide of Waves and Secrets

his name, but Rowan didn't reply. Something was amiss. I'd felt it earlier, but was convinced now. Blinking, he finally focused on me.

"What is it?"

"Nothing. I—"

"Rowan," I said, more firmly. "Let me take you to Aneri. I only possess a fraction of her skill as a healer."

Rowan looked into my eyes, as if seeing me for the first time since he lagged behind.

"She cannot help me."

My heart skipped a beat. Something *was* wrong. "Are you ill?"

He looked around us, as if unwilling to say any more lest we be overheard. "Is there somewhere we can go to speak privately?"

I thought quickly. It would take us a bit to get there, but I had no other duties at the palace other than as Rowan's escort. No one would bother us there.

"There is. Follow me."

13

ROWAN

"Wait until you see it when the sun sets."

I'd been in many inns and taverns in my day, but none quite like this. As we approached, it became clear its regular patrons included seafarers and sailors. Sitting so closely along the coast, the building seemed in imminent danger of being swallowed whole by the sea. It was also remarkably clean and well-kept. Even from the outside, it was clear the innkeeper took great care of the place.

Two stories tall, the most striking feature was a rounded section, complete with rounded windows. As we walked inside, not one person turned to look at us, a sign its patrons valued discretion. Although the sun hadn't yet set, flickering candlelight and a two-story fireplace in the corner invited us in further. Driftwood accents and shipwreck remnants lined the walls as the strum of a lute played soft music, further lulling us inside.

"Will this do?" Nerys asked, gesturing to a small table in the corner.

"Perfectly," I said, sitting and surveying the room for threats. Being without weapons in a clan of immortals had set me on edge all day. Aware, even with my sword, I could do little in a room of Thalassarians, I turned my attention back to Nerys.

"Your sword," she guessed.

"How did you know?"

"Your hand moved to your hip many times today. I did attempt to regain it for you, just for today, but was denied."

"Even when I am not in the palace?"

"The queen takes no chances. You have intimate knowledge of the palace, having stayed within its walls, and we plan to return at day's end. It makes little sense to me, but..." She shrugged. "Her kingdom. Her rules."

Now that I knew Nerys better, it was easier than ever to pick up on her resentment, one I began to understand. Outside of Thalassaria, the queen had a reputation of being closed off, a fair monarch but one concerned with her people alone. Inside her own kingdom, it seemed Queen Lirael's reputation was even more of a mixed bag.

"It seems I've heard of this tavern once before," I said as a woman made her way toward our table.

"Since that first day, Marek and I have made The Moonlit Current a regular haunt. As you can see, it is a popular spot for men, and women, of his ilk."

"Of his ilk?"

Our server's brown hair was darker than many in Thalassaria, but her piercing green eyes marked her very much as one of them. She was older, perhaps halfway to thaloran.

"You can only be talking of Marek."

"Indeed," Nerys said. "Nerithia, this is Rowan. Rowan, meet the innkeeper, or tavern keeper, if you will."

"Nerithia. I am certain we have not met before, but there is something familiar about you."

Nerithia locked eyes with me and did not look away, as if searching for something.

"The winds remember the first crossing, and the stone keeps their weight."

She was a Keeper.

"What did you say?" Nerys asked.

Thankfully, Nerys was focused on Nerithia and didn't notice my surprise at the innkeeper's words.

"A phrase," she responded. "When you are told you look familiar. A way to say that we are all connected, and 'tis likely the reason."

Aye, she was a Keeper for certain. All knew that phrase, to identify another Keeper they may not have met. But, just as importantly, they were prepared with an explanation on why they used it, avoiding suspicion.

"I've never heard that expression before."

When Nerithia smiled, the corners of her eyes wrinkled, further revealing her age. A perhaps three-hundred-year-old Keeper, living in Thalassaria. If he knew of her, my grandfather would have told me of Nerithia before I left for this mission.

Grandfather. My god keep your soul.

It was difficult to comprehend I now lived in a world without him. He had tried to prepare me, but like most in my family, his lessons on becoming the next Keeper never fully penetrated. I never actually imagined it would be me. Our network had grown large, and there were many just as worthy.

"Rowan?"

Both women were looking at me.

"Seafood? Or land-based?" the innkeeper asked. "Human, and all."

It was a clever way to hide her connection to us. "I will have the same as Nerys."

"Fish stew and a Tidal Kiss?"

"Perfect," I said as Nerithia walked away.

"What is a Tidal Kiss?" I asked.

"You've not had one before? It's rum-based, with lavender and sea salt, always served in a shell-shaped glass."

There was another type of kiss I could not help thinking of, since we were on the topic. I was best to avoid considering that too deeply.

As darkness began to fall, the reason for The Moonlit Current became apparent. With a wall of windows, many of which were open, the soft glow of a full moon bounced off the waves outside the inn, casting a silvery reflection across the floor.

"Spectacular," I said, of both the moon's reflection and my companion.

"I remember the first time I came here—"

"With Marek."

Nerys paused. I hadn't meant for the words to slip out, and certainly not as acidly as they had.

"Apologies for my tone. I suppose you do not need to have my human intuition to sense my envy of him."

"Envy? Why?"

These visions, the unwanted flood of emotions, had taken their toll. There was so much I could not tell her; I would at least offer honesty in this.

A servant put our drinks in front of us, and just as Nerys predicted, the glasses were shaped like conch shells. I took an extended sip.

"When I read your emotion that first day, and I told you that you were not alone in your desire, I was being honest, Nerys. In truth, I am as drawn to you. I don't say that to make you uncomfortable. On the contrary, I know relations between Thalassarians and humans are rare for your kind. I say it only because there is much I cannot tell you, such as what happened to me in the marketplace. I would offer you honesty, however, where I am able."

Nerys took her own sip of rum, her long lashes peeking out from under the glass.

"You have me at a disadvantage, being able to know my emotion at any time."

"Yet I do not use that ability with you. I made that promise and intend to keep it, when I am able."

"What does that mean, Rowan? When you are able?"

"At the market... something did happen. But there are things about me I cannot share. Even if I wished to do so."

Nerys was the embodiment of calm. Like the ocean to which she was so tied, she had the ability to make those around her feel at ease, as I did now, even revealing what I had. But the power inside her, the storm that simmered beneath the surface... I thought back to what I'd seen her do at the water's edge.

Before she could respond, Nerithia arrived with our food.

"Pardon me," Nerys said, standing. "I'll return shortly."

I watched her walk off, part of me wishing to follow, not wanting her to come to any harm. But the other part of me able to admit, Nerys was much, much more powerful than me. She didn't need a protector and was more than capable of attending to her needs alone.

"Why are you here?"

Nerithia asked the question in a whisper so low, I almost did not hear her.

She knew the code. Was a Keeper. The familiarity I sensed must be tied to one of my new abilities.

To her, I could be honest. "To seek the queen's aid in helping King Galfrid reopen the Aetherian Gate. How did you know?"

"My ability. I can sense other Keepers. My father was human. My mother, Thalassarian."

I pulled the stew toward me, smelling it as if we were discussing the food. "My grandfather said nothing of you, yet knew of my mission here."

"I've hidden myself well these many years and, like the queen, remain out of human affairs. Rowan of Estmere. Your grandfather is The Keeper."

"No longer. He has passed, last eve," I said, for the first time aloud. "I am The Keeper."

Her eyes widened. "You are certain?"

"Aye. I was trained well to recognize the signs."

Nerithia swallowed, looking behind her, presumably for Nerys.

"My condolences on the loss of your grandfather. The pain of losing my father, though it has been many, many years since he left us, is not one I'd wish to endure again. It is for that reason I do not involve myself in human affairs, but there is Harrow in my blood. If I can be of service in any way, you know where to find me, Sir Rowan."

She said my name with more reverence than I deserved. I may be the new Keeper, but I'd not yet earned the title.

"I wish to get word to the others. They will not know yet, and I'm needed here still."

"Consider it done. Nerys," she said, standing aside as my companion rejoined us. "your human is more affable than most."

"He is not mine, Nerithia," Nerys said, a smile in her voice.

Winking, the innkeeper replied, "Not yet," as she strolled away.

Neither of us commented on that.

With the low murmur of voices around us, we ate, mostly in silence. A compatible silence broken only periodically. I wondered if it was coincidence, a concept most of my people did not believe in, to have found myself in the single place in Thalassaria where I might get a message back home. More likely, I was meant to be here.

More accurately, I was meant to be here... with her.

It had been less than a day, but I did not need to be The Keeper to know these visions were of Nerys and her destiny. One, I was now convinced, that I'd been brought to help her claim.

Which meant my feelings for her were nothing more than that. I desired her. Wanted to kiss her. Wanted to be with her in every way possible. And yet, Nerithia was a reminder why Elydorians so rarely married humans. The inevitable heartbreak was, for most, too great a price to pay. Perhaps Marek was onto something, as bleak as his "love is not worth the pain" motto might be.

More importantly, this was not just any Thalassarian. Tonight, I shared a meal with the future queen. Caelum was meant to take me to her. To show me firsthand what she was capable of. What he did not realize was that, because of my new role as The Keeper, a reminder of Nerys's destiny was not necessary. We could not ever be together.

"What are you thinking?" she asked, pushing her finished bowl of stew away.

Unfortunately, Nerys wasn't quite ready to accept the destiny I knew awaited her. So I offered another truth instead.

"That I've never felt so at peace with another before."

A small sigh escaped her lips as Nerys reached for her drink. "I feel the same. Which is remarkable, given the circumstances."

"Such as?"

"That we both find ourselves at the mercy of the queen. I await a reprimand, and you, an answer. An important one at that."

That's when it hit me.

If Nerys did challenge Queen Lirael and won, she would be the new queen of Thalassaria. Use of the Tidal Pearl would be her decision alone.

This was a problem.

I didn't wish Nerys to question my motives in pushing her to challenge the queen, yet I couldn't reveal my visions without breaking my oath as a Keeper. As *The* Keeper.

"Wielding battle," someone yelled near the door.

One moment the tavern was filled. The next, every single patron was on their feet, rushing toward the door. Including Nerys.

"Where are you going?" I asked, resisting the urge to grab her hand and pull Nerys back to safety.

Her wide grin was the only answer I needed. But she responded anyway.

"To see the battle, of course. Hurry, or we'll miss it."

14

NERYS

"What happened?"

Thankfully, we could see everything from here since they'd moved closer to the water's edge. I could see why immediately. The younger one had some difficulty summoning water. He was likely the one who had taken the fight outside.

"They're fishermen," someone said. "On the same vessel. One apparently summoned the other's ale... directly into his face. I don't know the cause."

"Ooh," Rowan said as the older fisherman hurled a small wave at the other, knocking him off his feet. In response, he brought a wall of water up in front of him.

"An impressive skill," I said. "If he can..." the water came crashing down on top of him, "...hold it."

Rowan chuckled as a fog enveloped them. "I can't see you," he said.

"One of them must have heated the water with a spark of elemental energy to create the fog. A more useful skill when its direction can be controlled."

As quickly as it came, the fog dissipated.

Cheers erupted from the crowd as one of the fishermen—I couldn't tell which— turned the sea into a tempest. It would have been amusing if he could have controlled it. Instead, onlookers were drenched.

Nerithia appeared next to us, clearly not amused. "Nerys, will you stop them, please? My patrons are getting wet. And the younger of them is my nephew. I've no wish to embarrass him."

"Of course," I said, unable to see either of the fishermen's identities from my vantage point.

With a flick of my wrist, the water suddenly receded, leaving both men momentarily confused. Before either could react, I pulled the tide forward as two towering columns of water rose like serpents, one behind each man. Gasps rippled through the crowd as the shimmering liquid wrapped tightly around the fighters, hoisting them into the air.

With another flick, the serpents tossed both men into the waves, eliciting more cheers and chatter.

"I can't guarantee your nephew will not be embarrassed anyway. But that should end it."

Nerithia laughed. "He is rash, with much to learn."

The crowd began to disperse. I attempted to pull coins from the leather pouch at my side. "I best not be here when he emerges from the sea."

"Nay." Nerithia stopped me. "There is no need. Thank you for your assistance."

Unless I was mistaken, a look passed between Rowan and Nerithia, one I couldn't decipher. She walked away, Rowan and I doing the same in the other direction.

"It isn't a short journey, but if we walk along the coast, we can get to the palace this way."

"I would be pleased to walk this way," Rowan said.

With the sea on our left and soft glow of the city above us to the right, somehow the beauty of Thalassaria continued to amaze me. I stared out into the sea, its closest floating lanterns remaining in place despite the power of those waves: a testament to Thalassarian magic.

"How did you learn to do that?" Rowan asked suddenly. "The serpents?"

"Have you heard of the Deep Archives?"

"In Ventara? Aye."

"My mother had a close contact there, so growing up, I accompanied her often. I was enamored with the clifftop village and spent many hours in the Archives there while she worked. For anyone curious enough, every skill throughout our history has been recorded there. I read about that particular wielding technique from accounts of one of the first kings of Thalassaria who ruled not long after The Great Sundering."

"Elydor's first war."

"Aye. Though I supposed our separation was inevitable. It was then as it is now. Aetherians have always believed their mastery of the skies symbolized enlightenment, making them natural leaders, while Gyorians prioritized stability and connection to the land. Early Thalassarians, meanwhile, flowed with innovation and adaptability but demanded independence. We were likely meant to be separate, though connected still by our ties to the same land."

"And the humans?"

"I do not believe even King Galfrid understood how they would influence Elydor. I know it unsettles you to be without your weapons, to know those around you can wield the magic that imbued our land from its inception, but you and your kind have more influence than many realize."

"Our abilities are different than most, but I agree, humans do wield power here, even among a land of immortals." Rowan stopped and squatted down to the sand. He picked up a shell, glowing faintly a light teal color. Turning it upside down, he inspected it. "It's not bioluminescence. How is this possible?"

I took the shell from him. "The waters of Thalassaria hold memories of every tide, every storm, every life. Some objects, like this shell, absorb that magic over centuries. It's not uncommon in the depths of the seas around us, but it is for this shell to end up here, far from the deep currents. Keep it," I said, handing it back, our fingers brushing as I did. "It is a rare find."

"Should I not leave it where it belongs?"

"It belongs on the depths of the sea, but since it found its way here, perhaps you are meant to have it."

Rowan slipped the shell into his pocket.

"As for the sea serpents," I said, returning to my story. "This early king not only considered them a favorite bit of magic, but he recounted how the spell was performed. It took much practice, I will admit, and has little practical purpose."

"You've not used it to stop a wielding battle at The Moonlit Current before?"

"Nay, I have not."

We walked in silence for some time, lights falling away as the cliffs to our right rose higher and higher. I closed my eyes, breathing in the air that gave my clan life. When I opened them, Rowan was watching me.

"You hold as many mysteries as the sea."

"Not as many, but..." I could tell he wished to say something to me but struggled to do so.

"Tell me."

"My grandfather... died last eve."

We stopped talking. The pain on his face was real.

"I cannot tell you how I know, but the knowledge does not put you or Thalassaria in danger."

A telepathic link of some sort, not unheard of among humans. Yet most had only one skill and Rowan had revealed his already. More importantly...

"I am so sorry, Rowan."

"I'd have told you earlier but was uncertain if I could, or should. I know you have many questions—"

"None of which matter."

It was odd to not see him smiling. I went to him, without thought, and found myself, for the second time, in Rowan's arms. Like before, neither of us spoke. What was this bond between us? I simply could not stay away, nor did I wish to. Closing my eyes, cradled into his chest with his arms around me... it should not have felt as right or natural as it did. But instead of questioning it, I welcomed the comfort, even though my intention was to comfort him.

"He was the best of men. He had my father's patient nature, but a sense of humor too. I have not known a wiser man alive and will miss him dearly."

I opened my eyes and watched the waves beside us that carried my tears from so many years ago but also sustained me and my people.

"The tides carry away what we love, but they always leave behind the memory of their touch. Your grief is the ebb, Rowan. In time, the flow will return, and with it, the strength to honor him."

"You cannot know," he said quietly, "what that means to me."

Rowan pulled back slightly, looking down at me. I thought he might kiss me. Instead, he had that same expression as he did in the market.

"Rowan?"

He blinked. Something was wrong. Very wrong.

"Rowan, please tell me what is happening."

"I..." He took another step back and then turned away. "I wish I could."

And just like that, the moment was gone. Just like that, we went back to being strangers.

"I'm fine," he said, and began to walk once again. "It has been a long day."

He was not fine. But whether the news of his grandfather, however it had been received, or something else, bothered him, I could not know. Because Rowan would not fully let me into his world.

"You will attend your first Festival of Tides, then?" I asked, stepping back, changing topics. It was all anyone spoke of; the twice-yearly festival was an exciting time for Thalassarians.

"It seems so. Will you tell me more about it?"

As we walked, I shared past festivals and our traditions, explaining to Rowan what he could expect. One thing I did not tell him was how badly those close to me wished for me to challenge the queen. The truth was, as brave as I pretended to be, inside, I was afraid.

Afraid of the queen's reaction. Afraid of what people would say. Afraid of failing. If I challenged her and was not successful, I could not continue my work at the palace. Queen Lirael was many things, but overly forgiving was not one of them.

As we turned a corner, the palace came into view well ahead of us. It was a spectacular sight, built partially over the ocean and partially on land, its lights glistening like the reflection of moonlight on the water.

"What if you succeed?"

Realizing I hadn't heard the whole of Rowan's story, I asked him to repeat it, admitting I'd been lost in thought for a moment.

"I was reminded of the first time I was given a steel sword. I asked my grandfather what might happen if I failed to defend myself. Would I be mortally wounded? He said that instead of being so concerned with failing, that I should ask myself instead... what if I succeeded? It is a question that resonates with me still."

"Do you remember what you said to him?"

Rowan smiled, whatever had bothered him seemingly forgotten. "That I might live to see another day, and be proud of it."

"Did you wear armor?"

"We did, but I was young and hadn't realized the difference yet. But that was typical of him, to offer such advice rather than giving a more direct answer."

"Which would have been?"

"That between the padded gambeson I wore and our blunted weapons, there was little chance of me being mortally wounded."

What if you succeed?

It was a question I rarely asked myself, the answer more far-reaching than I could imagine. What would happen if I succeeded in challenging the queen? The queen and I thought very differently on Thalassaria's future, how it related to the other clans. And according to Aneri, more believed as I did—as Caelum and Marek did—than ever before.

What would happen?

Everything would change.

But also...

"Rowan?"

"Nerys?"

I loved the way he said my name.

"Something just occurred to me."

"You finally realized I am the most charming, handsome, intelligent man you've ever met?"

That too.

I stopped, grabbing his arm.

"What is it?" he asked, concern, rather than laughter, now etched into his expression.

"If I challenged the queen..." I dropped his arm, realizing I still clutched the fabric of his shirt. "If I won..."

He waited.

"I could give you the Tidal Pearl. King Galfrid and the princess could reopen the Gate."

Of course, he was not surprised. This would have occurred to him already.

"They still need the other artifacts, but aye, we would be one step closer to reopening it."

He took me by both arms, his grip firm. Steadying.

"Listen to me, Nerys. There are few people in Elydor who wish the Aetherian Gate to be reopened more than me. Namely, the king and his daughter. Even so, that alone is not a reason for you to challenge the queen."

"Is it not?"

"No," he said, his voice firm. "It isn't. I thought of it, of course. And would dearly love to bring that Pearl, or the promise of it, back to Galfrid and Mev. But not at your expense."

I lifted my chin. "You do not believe I should challenge her?"

"I believe," he said, "the choice is yours, and yours alone to make."

"My magic is more powerful than hers, Rowan."

"I do not doubt it. But the question is... do you?"

15

ROWAN

Dressed for the day, I waited for Nerys by the window, though no visions came to me this morning. After we returned last eve, I had difficulty sleeping. Grandfather was gone. For some reason, I was now The Keeper, a responsibility no amount of training could have prepared me for. And then there was Nerys. She'd realized what I had: that more than the future of her own people was at stake in her decision to challenge the queen. If Lirael did not plan to offer Galfrid and Mev use of the Tidal Pearl, the future of Elydor remained in peril.

Eventually, I had fallen into a fitful slumber, my dreams of a very different variety.

Twice now, I'd held Nerys in my arms. Twice, I'd not wanted to let her go. It was more than desire, more than lust, although more than once throughout the day, I'd imagined what it would be like to strip every bit of clothing from her and bring Nerys pleasure.

Her knock came at a most unfortunate time. I forced my mind to wander to less erotic thoughts, but it was still a moment or two before I could comfortably make my way to the door.

Opening it, despite that Nerys could have easily done so since she had a key to my chamber, I groaned.

"Nerys."

I turned away and headed back into my chamber. Sitting on my bed, I took a deep breath, appalled at my own lack of control.

She came inside and stood in front of me, genuinely confused.

"Have I done something to offend you?"

She truly did not know how she affected me. I took in the fitted, sleeveless and legless training tunic, the black and seafoam green making her eyes shine brighter than usual. Black boots covered her legs, up to mid-thigh at least, her gloves doing the same for her arms. A decorative, belt-like piece rested at her hips, adding a touch of sophistication. She looked like a warrior of the sea, prepared for battle, though not the kind of battle to which I was accustomed.

"I've never seen such a garment before."

Nerys looked down, as if seeing herself for the first time. "Likely because this is for training—surprisingly warm too given how little it covers."

"The other day, when the young ones were training..."

I let my voice trail. Though on purpose. Being "speechless" held more meaning than ever before. Turned out, it was not merely hyperbole.

"They trained for the morning. I plan to be at the water's edge all day and do not wish to be encumbered. Which is what I've come to ask you. Would you prefer to remain here—"

"I am coming with you."

Her eyes widened. "There will be naught for you to do but watch me."

"I can think of no more pleasurable activity than watching

you." I stopped short of saying, *in that*, but was fairly certain the actual words were unnecessary.

Nerys cocked her head to the side, clearly doubtful. And then, the worst possible thing that could have happened, did. Her eyes darted from me to the bed. Groaning, I stood, needing to move. Unfortunately, I startled her, standing so abruptly that Nerys stumbled backward.

I caught her by the elbow as our eyes met.

Her lips parted, and not for the first time, I wanted to kiss her. Wanted it so badly that I pushed aside every reason not to. Nerys's destiny and mine might have crossed paths, but both those paths would diverge. Mine as The Keeper in Estmere. Hers here, potentially as the next Thalassarian queen.

Even so, I did not move away.

"The heartbreak," she whispered, "of falling for a human is one I would avoid."

I released my grip on her elbow but still did not move. "I would not dishonor you by taking advantage of our proximity, knowing I am not long in Thalassaria."

There it was. Our reasons for not leaning into one another and taking what we desired. For there was no doubt that Nerys and I desired the same thing.

One of us had to step away.

There is no greater honor than to be chosen to carry and protect the secrets of our ancestors. To see our future and guide humans toward their rightful place in Elydor.

I could hear my grandfather's words as if he stood there and spoke them aloud to me. It was his strength, and not my own, that allowed me to take a step, and then another, away from her. With a firmer resolve than before, despite the most enticing vision in front of me, I asked the obvious question.

"What do you train for?"

In response, Nerys walked toward the very window I'd been staring out of since coming here. Though I joined her, I was careful to put enough distance between us as not to be tempted to reach out. To touch her again. To pull Nerys into me.

To take what we both wanted but neither could afford to have.

With a flick of her wrist, a silencing mist formed all around us.

"It was not far from there," she said, pointing into the distance. "Where a fishing vessel overturned. Some storms, even the strongest Thalassarian cannot calm. None worried for the men aboard, as all were experienced water-wielders and they were close to shore. One by one, they rode waves back to that dock. Except for one."

Nerys's hands balled into fists.

"What happened?"

"He was young, had not seen fifteen summers yet. The others returned to the shore, thinking they'd all made it back, but the young one's abilities were no match for the storm. He hung onto a piece of debris as the ship's captain debated whether or not to save him."

She was becoming angrier as the story unfolded.

"Why on Elydor would he not save him?"

When Nerys looked at me, though anger still lingered, there was resolve in her expression too.

"Unfortunately, the queen was on the dock, preparing for a voyage to Aetheria. She forbade it, saying that the sea was a trial, and if he couldn't master it himself then it wasn't for anyone to take the burden from him. You see, she believes in balance. That Thalassarians must master the sea without relying on others, or they weaken themselves. But it wasn't about balance that day."

"What was it about?" I asked, almost afraid of the answer.

"He was half-human. And though born with the Thalassarian abilities of his father, he struggled to master the sea as quickly as he might have otherwise."

"And you believe that was the reason she did not want him to be rescued?"

Nerys frowned. "Some believe so, aye. I do not think it was so straightforward as that. The queen is well known to take such a stance. For us to rely on no others, we must be strong. And though I do value independence, neither do I believe seeking aid is a weakness. The queen would disagree, however."

"Did he survive?"

Nerys smiled for the first time since she began her story. "He did. The captain, in defiance of the queen, rescued him. And would have been punished for it if there was not an uprising that found Queen Lirael more at odds with her people than ever before in her reign. At least, that is what I am told."

"You were not there when it happened?"

"No. But the story has haunted me. Last eve, when you spoke of your grandfather and said, 'He was the best of men,' I thought of the boy, clinging to life on a piece of driftwood. Of you, and the other humans I've met. Good people who do not deserve to be locked inside a bedchamber because of the queen's fear."

I hadn't thought of it before, but her words made sense. "Gyorians, Aetherians are not locked inside, as I am?"

"No," she confirmed. "It would do little good as they would be able to easily escape. There are ways to... subdue their powers. But it is considered unseemly to use them, unless in battle."

I glanced about my chamber. My prison. "In some ways, your queen is no better than King Balthor."

Nerys's laugh was harsh, not at all one of joy. "In *many* ways, though hers are more subtle. And of course, closing the Gate after kidnapping King Galfrid's partner cemented him as the ultimate villain of Elydor in terms of his hatred of humans."

My gazed wandered from Nerys's face downward. How could I not possibly notice how enticing she looked this way? I imagined her with naught but those boots, beneath me on the bed...

"As to the reason I tell you this story."

My head snapped back up, and though I didn't believe she caught me staring, I couldn't be certain. I would tell her there was so much more to her allure than simply Nerys's beauty, that the resolve in her eyes, the love Nerys had for her people... Instead, I remained silent, knowing naught could come from such words.

"You asked what I train for today."

Somehow, I'd forgotten the question. With Nerys, it was easy to forget, if even for a moment, the pain of losing a man I loved and admired, the mission that brought me here... all of it.

"I have known for some years that my power exceeds the queen's. And I supposed it was my hope she would put out the call, knowing there is one among her more powerful. But she has not, and I've delayed the inevitable, afraid for myself. Having you here"—she sighed—"I am more afraid for our future under her continued rule and know, if naught else, I would lead with more compassion than she. My parents would will it for me. For all of us."

"You train to challenge the queen."

It was not a question, and there was no need for Nerys to respond.

I wanted to tell her of my vision. That her decision had already been foretold. Instead, I offered all that I was able.

"I will aid you in any way that I can. And when you are queen of Thalassaria, together, we will forge a new path for our people that strengthens us both."

"Perhaps our paths were meant to cross, for this purpose,"

Nerys said as she strode across my chamber with purpose and determination.

"Perhaps," I whispered, knowing our respective roles also meant we were destined never to be together. "Nerys?" I asked as the mist faded and she reached the door. "The young one, who nearly drowned. What became of him?"

Her secret smile made me even more curious.

"Think on it. I am certain you know the answer already."

16

NERYS

I do not doubt it. But the question is... do you?

It was never my abilities I doubted, but my willingness to challenge the queen. But as I attempted an advanced sea-bind, and failed, Rowan's question swirled in my mind.

He'd said nothing but sat patiently watching me. Though we'd broken our fast before coming to the cove, it was well past time for a midday meal. I disliked stopping now, but a break was in order. For us both.

My arms had begun to ache from holding them in the air for so long. It felt good to stretch them, dropping them by my sides for a rest. Like this morning, when he first opened the door, Rowan's expression hid nothing. I will admit, knowing he watched me with such admiration had made this training session different than most. I wanted to please him even though the approval of a man was something Aneri had long warned me not to covet.

"I'm glad to see you still smiling after so long a session," I said.

Rowan stood from where he'd been sitting on a flat rock, watching me.

"I have every reason to smile, and none to frown. You are magnificent, Nerys."

There was something in his voice that gave me pause. A sincerity that stopped me from offering a glib reply, as I might have had Marek offered such a compliment. The two men were equally as handsome, in different ways. But when I looked at my friend, I saw only someone who cared for me. Not since our first encounter did Marek look at me the way Rowan did now. Nor did I wish him to.

Rowan, on the other hand?

I'd have let him kiss me this morn, and it would have been a mistake.

I curtsied, not in jest, but in honest reverence to his sincerity. And to give thanks, not just for his compliment, but Rowan's patience.

"It is I who should bow to you, the future queen of Thalassaria."

"Not if I am unable to sea-bind at will. It is a skill Queen Lirael performs well, and one revered by my people."

Making my way to the sack I'd placed beside Rowan, I took out the leather pouch.

"Have you eaten yet?"

Rowan shook his head. "I waited for you."

"That was most chivalric of you," I said, only half-teasing, handing him a seaweed wrap.

"So tell me of the challenge. How and when will it happen? And I've been wondering. Can the queen summon sea serpents?"

"I've not seen her do so, but my guess is that there is nothing I can do that the queen cannot." I took a bite, sitting on Rowan's rock, glad to not be standing. I had not realized how much time had passed. Seeing his confusion, I explained. "There may be minor skills that the queen can perform and I cannot, or the opposite. But mostly, those will be performative, but lacking substance. The ones that will be tested are those which save lives, and protect them. Such as sea-binding, which she excels at."

"What is sea-binding?"

"It is the art of holding the water still no matter how wild it becomes: an essential skill for calming storms or redirecting tidal waves. As to how the challenge will happen: on the last day of the festival, the queen or her council asks for challengers."

"Which she's never had— Nerys? What is that?"

I stood, taking another bite of seaweed wrap, and looked in the direction of Rowan's pointed finger. When the pelagor emerged, I dropped my wrap and ran to the water's edge. It had been many years since I'd seen one and knew well its perceived significance.

"A pelagor. They are an extremely rare species, so rare, most are unlikely to see them in their lifetimes. We can ride it if we get closer. Hurry."

Making my way deeper into the sea, I dove headfirst into the water and, holding my breath, stayed there long enough to allow the pelagor to feel my presence. Willing it not to leave, I finally emerged, surprised to find Rowan swimming beside me.

"I was uncertain if you'd come."

He swam surprisingly well, for a human.

"This is madness. It's more likely to swallow us whole than give us a ride."

We headed out even further and then treaded water, waiting. "It would never eat us." I thought about that more deeply. "At least, it would not eat me. Perhaps it knows the difference between a Thalassarian and a human."

Only because Rowan appeared genuinely concerned did I drop the ruse. "I am jesting. They— look!"

It was coming toward us.

"Stay here."

"As if I have anywhere else to go."

Diving beneath the waves, I angled myself toward the pelagor and watched. It was, indeed swimming toward us. Closing my eyes, I envisioned it gliding under Rowan and me.

He is human; tread carefully.

Emerging once again, I laughed at Rowan's expression. "He knows you are human. When you feel him under your legs, just allow yourself to sit and float upwards."

"Nerys—"

Whatever he was about to say had to wait. The pelagor was under us now. It moved through the water so slowly, I was certain it had heard me.

"Steady," I called, as we were raised above the water. Moving myself to kneel beside him, the back of our pelagor slightly concave and four times wider than Rowan's bed, there was no need to hold on, even if we wished to do so.

As we moved, I watched Rowan marvel at the mosaic of blues and purples that made up the unique coloring of the pelagor we rode. It was my second time seeing one, the first not nearly as large or magnificent, but just as awe-inspiring. They were gentle and intelligent creatures that humans likened to whales in their world, though pelagors were much larger. Their size could be intimidating, as evidenced by my wide-eyed companion.

"It is... magnificent."

Running my hand along the slightly rough back of the pelagor, who seemed intent on taking us further out to sea, I was rewarded by a deep rumble of contentment.

"He likes it," I said, reaching for Rowan's hand, placing my own on top of his and showing him the circular movements these creatures were said to enjoy.

When the pelagor made the sound again, Rowan smiled as if he were a young one. It was the smile of innocence and unadulterated pleasure. I removed my hand, or attempted to. Rowan reached across and put it back in place.

Our eyes met.

Whether or not Rowan felt it too, the warmth and connection that was becoming increasingly difficult to deny, I could not be certain. But I wasn't surprised when he flipped his hand upside down and curled his fingers through mine.

It was beautiful, and natural, and no part of me wanted to pull away.

"Look." I turned his attention to the clear, blue-green sea beside us as a school of marisol swam by, their fin-like frills giving the effect of ribbons.

"Incredible."

Rowan's hand tightened around mine as we rode further away from shore. Though he appeared calm, I sought to reassure him just in case.

"The pelagor is one of Thalassarian's oldest creatures, their memory and lifespan longer than any Elydorian. He will deliver us safely back to shore."

"I am not worried."

He must be. Rowan was human, after all. And we were well beyond sight of the shore now on a creature very few even spotted much less rode.

"Not even a bit?"

His gaze was steady. "I've watched you all morning, Nerys. There is not a Thalassarian alive I feel safer beside in the sea than you."

While it was true I could deliver us safely back to shore if anything were to happen, I appreciated his confidence in me.

Rowan trusted me with his life. I wanted to remark upon that fact, but instead said nothing. There were no words that would do this moment justice, so I simply offered a reassuring smile and looked to the horizon.

In fact, neither of us spoke for the remainder of the ride. Instead, deep in our own thoughts and companionable silence, we accepted the ride we'd been offered.

When the pelagor finally turned back and delivered us to the very spot where we began, dipping below the surface and depositing us back into the water, I thanked him, grateful for such an experience.

Grateful that it had been offered to Rowan, too.

When we made our way back to the shore, I thought to explain to him the true significance of what just happened. Except, no words came from my mouth. Instead, I simply stared, my feet sinking into the sand at the water's edge, as Rowan casually removed his linen shirt and wrung it out.

His back, his shoulders, were that of a warrior. One who spent a good portion of his time wielding the heavy broadsword we'd taken from him. Rowan's muscles rippled as he moved, glistening as brilliantly as the school of marisol. I had seen many warriors train. A man's form was not new to me, and yet...

This was Rowan.

He turned and caught me staring. I didn't move. But he did.

Rowan's steps were measured, determined. And in that moment, I knew—whether it was a good idea or not—my longing for his kiss would soon be fulfilled.

17

ROWAN

I had every reason in the world not to do this.

The same refrain that had held me back before simply had vanished. The only thoughts that ran through my mind now were of seeing Nerys at my chamber door this morn. Of watching her train. Of Nerys's smile while we rode the pelagor.

Of the way she looked at me now.

I knew well how to practice restraint. To keep the secrets that would allow Estmere to thrive in a world to which we hardly belonged. To put my family's legacy before myself, and certainly that was more important now than ever.

And yet...

"Rowan," she whispered, a clap of waves against the rocks behind us punctuating a moment that was about to become an important one in my life. Why did that fact seem so certain? I would explore later.

Reaching for her, I meant to be gentle. To cup her face, look into those bright-green eyes and take in the sight before me first. Instead, when my hands reached her, Nerys's lips parting in anticipation, all thoughts of pausing fled my mind. Instead, our mouths crashed together, our tongues exploring each other almost instantaneously. Slanting my head for better access, I drank from her, relishing in a kiss that was so much more than that.

It was a joining of two people who were connected from the moment they met.

It was wave after wave of the kind of electricity, a term I'd heard from the most modern humans in Estmere but had never experienced myself.

When Nerys's hands lay gently on my shoulders, I held her head still, groaning at the pure pleasure of the moment, never wanting it to end. Our mouths were made for each other's, fitting perfectly together, the rhyme of our kiss so natural that not doing it seemed absurd.

"This is not the kind of training that will see you best the queen."

The deep voice startled me in a way I couldn't remember being startled before. How many years had it been since someone had come upon me in such a way? I was trained as a damn spy and had been actively blocking Nerys's emotions and therefore hadn't sensed him.

I'd have expected Nerys to jump back, startled, and maybe even embarrassed.

She was neither.

"Your timing," she said as we put space between us, "is not ideal."

Marek's knowing grin was not at all apologetic.

"How did you know I was here?"

Spying the wraps Nerys had brought, Marek strode to them. Taking a new one out of the satchel, he sat and began to eat as if he had no care for anything but that seaweed wrap.

As the modern humans among us might say... he was a real piece of work.

"There was talk on the docks of an incident at The Moonlit Current, something to do with sea serpents?"

Smiling at the memory, I made my way with Nerys toward where Marek sat.

"Not surprising, I suppose," she said with a sideways look in my direction.

It was difficult not to notice the fullness of her lips and imagine I was still kissing her.

"I tried to find you, to hear the story." He shrugged, and then took a bite of his wrap. Finishing chewing, he said, "But I will admit, I did not expect to find you lip locked with your human."

"Rowan," I said, still trying to determine if I liked him or not. If it weren't for Nerys, and the promise I made to her, I'd open myself up to sense his emotion.

As the thought crossed through my mind, it came to me anyway.

Curious.

It was all I could gather, but being able to sense it while blocking Nerys... I hadn't known such a thing was possible. And it might not have been, before now.

"Your jest hits its mark," she said. "I actually was training and plan to challenge her."

Marek's hand froze midway to his mouth. Dropping his wrap onto his leg, propped casually on the rock in front of him, Marek glanced back and forth between us.

"It has been years since the last challenge, so I could be mistaken, but I do not recall the ability to kiss well one of the skills needed."

Despite myself, the corners of my lips tugged upward.

For her part, Nerys rolled her eyes. "We've been here since sunrise."

"What changed your mind?"

Whether or not she realized it, Nerys darted a glance in my direction.

Marek noticed. "Him?" he asked, incredulous.

"I had naught to do with her decision," I said, unwilling to come between them.

Marek's smile faltered for the first time. "Something changed her mind. I've been begging her to do this for years," he said to me.

"Excuse me," Nerys said. "The 'her' you're speaking of is right here."

Marek didn't appear the least bit apologetic. He leaped from the rock and bowed deeply.

"Pardon, your majesty. I meant no offense." He sat back down in as exaggerated a manner as he stood. By rights, Marek was wholly unlikable. And yet, I could see his appeal too... why she would be drawn to him.

Thankfully, as only a friend.

Because as Nerys marched over to Marek and swatted the back of his head as an older sister might to her wayward younger brother, my own thoughts were anything but brotherly.

Without warning, as the two continued to verbally spar over Nerys's reversal on her decision to challenge the queen, a shape formed loosely in front of me. I turned toward the sea, as if distracted by its beauty.

This time, knowing the vision was coming, I was able to harness it using the same methods I'd learned years ago to sense and filter emotion. Blocking out everything—including Nerys and Marek's conversation—I could see the figure more clearly. It was the seafarer himself, Marek on the deck of his ship, yelling orders. He appeared to be battling a brutal storm, and I could sense he was terrified.

But not of the storm.

He was terrified for a woman's safety. Nerys?

A hand on my shoulder interrupted the vision.

"Rowan?"

Her touch was featherlight. Before I could stop it, that concern flooded into my senses. I'd not meant to read her emotion and immediately blocked it. I knew from my grandfather it would take years of practice to manage the merging of my old and new abilities.

For the first time in my life, I seriously considered the possibility of breaking The Keeper's code. I wanted to tell her. Confess everything and work with her openly, as our goals were the same.

Our eyes met.

Not yet.

The voice was my grandfather's, likely my own conjuring what he might sound like, whispering into my ear. And yet, if I could imagine what his advice might have been, those weren't the words I would have imagined.

"I'm sorry," I said, hating to mislead her. "I was deep in thought."

A partial truth.

"Let's see your sea-binding then," Marek said.

I wanted to kiss her again. To tell Nerys everything. Instead, I simply watched as she walked forward until she was ankle-deep in water and lifted both arms.

Raising her chin, Nerys took a deep breath, pressed her hands together and moved them slowly outwards, both palms down. Her shoulders dropped, and nothing seemed to be happening at first. Little by little, though, the waves began to calm.

Dropping to her knees, as if the weight of the water pressed down on her, she continued to hold her arms outright. Little by little, as far as the eye could see, the ocean's waves began to dissipate. Where moments ago, they crashed along the rocks, the sea was now placid.

I looked at Marek. He looked at me.

I had no idea how Queen Lirael's abilities fared against Nerys, but one thing was clear: Marek was in awe too, and unlike me, he had likely seen similar skills performed many times before.

Nerys had calmed the sea.

I opened my mouth to ask about it, but no words seemed adequate. Instead, I opened myself up to him and felt his reverence.

Without warning, Nerys stood and shot her arms into the air. All at once, the waves returned with a vengeance that even I could feel, as if they'd been bound and were now set free. Her shoulders sagged, the effort of such a skill clear, and Nerys turned to us.

Her gaze found mine, weary but resolute. The truth struck me with the force of her unleashed waves: Nerys wasn't just destined to be Thalassaria's queen.

She already was.

18

NERYS

Rowan opened his bedchamber door. He looked like a prince, or at least a high-ranking nobleman.

"You received my message, it seems?" I asked.

"I did."

Since this afternoon, when Marek returned with us to the palace, we hadn't yet spoken alone. Although they seemed initially at odds, Rowan and Marek had warmed to each other on the walk back. I'd remained mostly silent, exhausted, confused, and more than a little excited. I'd never been able to calm such a large portion of the sea before. Since sea-binding was my weakest skill, the idea that I truly may prove more skilled than Queen Lirael had taken root. The responsibility that went along with such a fact weighed heavily on me.

And yet, it wasn't the possibility of becoming Thalassaria's next queen that kept me so silent.

There was no doubt the kiss I'd shared with Rowan was not some simple lovers' exchange that could be enjoyed and forgotten. Falling for a human? I'd never considered the possibility before. Now, however, I couldn't think of anything other than how it felt to be in his arms. The ease with which we came together. If not for Marek, we may have not stopped. At least, I would not have been the one to stop us, certainly.

I hadn't expected Marek to walk with us all the way back to Rowan's chamber, but apparently, he wished to speak with me alone. Even after I attempted to explain my reasoning, why I'd decided to challenge the queen, he had continued to prod. Finally, I reminded Marek that his understanding of the situation was less important than the fact that I did, indeed, intend to follow through.

My parents would approve.

It was the last thought he'd left me with when Eoin found us, giving me the queen's message. The presence of both myself and "the human emissary" were requested at this evening's meal. Was it to finally reprimand me for ignoring her command? Or worse, had she somehow guessed my intentions? My training grove was well-hidden, but even so... being summoned was not a regular occurrence.

"That is a beautiful gown."

If I were being honest, I'd have told him it was one of my favorites and that I'd worn it specifically for him. A deep teal along the hem lightened as it made its way upward, the neckline nearly white. A swirling pattern, reminiscent of waves, highlighted my breasts, its deep V cut almost approaching my waist. Although I normally disliked the formality of dining in the main hall, this eve was an exception. If it weren't for the queen's summons, I'd have thoroughly enjoyed a reason to wear this gown... to dine with Rowan... to have him look at me this way.

"Thank you. Aneri had it made for me many years ago, when I was first brought to the palace."

Would he mention our kiss from earlier today?

"Nerys." His jaw flexed, Rowan's penetrating gaze knowing.

Tide of Waves and Secrets

Though a part of me wanted to discuss it, I was suddenly feeling more shy than I had a right to be. I'd lived for many years and could navigate the after-effects of one simple kiss with a human man, could I not?

"We should go. I am rarely summoned by the queen, and the meal will begin soon."

"Of course."

Taking my hint, Rowan closed the door to his chamber and we made our way to the hall. When it was full, the palace hall could hold well over two hundred. But this eve, as most days, there were less than thirty in attendance.

When Rowan offered the crook of his arm, I took it as if striding through the tables together was something we'd always done. A warmth spread through me, as if I'd just jumped into a hot spring. None took note of it, the formality of Queen Lirael's court one I'd never particularly appreciated until now.

"The tiles." Rowan was looking at the far wall where schools of fish and coral reefs were depicted. "How is that achieved?"

It was a feature of the dining hall that I particularly adored.

"They are enchanted with bioluminescence, capturing the shifting light of the deep sea. Does it not look almost real?"

We'd reached the table where I sat most days.

"It does," he said, pulling out my seat. "As if we are under the sea."

Rowan sat across from me, and thankfully, our small table was thus far empty.

"Look up," I told him, and he did. "The ceiling is meant to resemble the underside of a wave frozen in time. The seashell chandeliers, if you look carefully, are interspersed with pearls enchanted in the same way as the fish scales on the wall tiles."

As Rowan continued to peer at the vaulted dining hall ceiling, I studied his expression. Seeing things through his eyes reminded me of my early days at the palace. I had been in awe of everything around me, often wishing I could have served here at the same time as my parents.

"Thank you," I said as wine was served and Rowan turned his attention to me.

We'd ridden a pelagor today. I calmed a larger portion of the sea than ever before, emboldened by a sign that may be nothing more than legend. One I hadn't yet had a chance to tell Rowan about yet. Come to think of it, I'd not even shared the experience with Marek. And it was not because of what I'd done or the impact of my decision to challenge the queen.

The simple fact was, despite all that was happening, it was our kiss that I could not get from my mind.

"May I join you?"

The quiet question came from a man who rarely dined in the hall. A vaelith named Thalon whose long beard was braided and adorned with pearls.

"Of course," I said as he sat.

Thalon's gaze, so often distant as if the historian were lost in thought, was sharper this eve than most.

"There is talk," he said to Rowan, "that you plan to remain for the Festival of Tides."

The cup bearer filled Thalon's glass, though he did not seem to notice. I thanked the servant for him.

"I do. I am Sir Rowan of Estmere and pleased to meet you—"

"Thalon," I provided. "He has resided in the palace for centuries and knows more of Thalassarian history than most. Do you remember," I asked him, "when we first met? In Ventara?"

"Nerys," he said to Rowan, "could be found in the Deep Archives more than any other in Thalassaria."

"Not more than Thalon," I argued. "Though I'm unsure why as he must have read every tome in its depths, more than once."

The old man sighed, though did not disagree. "So tell me, Sir Rowan of Estmere, why are you here?"

Rowan was spared an answer as another of the palace inhabitants sat beside him, a beautiful woman, no more than twenty years older than me. Carys was a sharp-tongued Thalassari diplomat with light-brown hair, streaked with unnatural shades of red, and eyes like polished turquoise. It was rare for anyone to change their hair coloring, Thalassari highly valuing nature's own contribution to how they appeared.

We sat together for meals often enough for me to know our energies did not align well.

"He is on a mission from King Galfrid," she said, abrupt as always.

That earned her a look from Rowan that was one I did not often see from him. He had a right to be wary. Carys had long desired the queen's attention, and received it, as one of her favorites. But that ambition had made her few friends at court.

"Indeed," he said smoothly, "I am. But it seems you are at an advantage, knowing much more about me than I do you."

If I didn't know him better, it would seem Rowan was flirting with her. Somehow, I knew he was not. But Carys, as sharp as she could be, did not seem to realize it. Her painted red smile lacked any warmth.

When she did not offer her name, I provided it.

"Carys," I said as a clam soup was placed in front of each of us. I looked to the dais, which was still empty. Odd. The first course was never served before the queen arrived.

"A human," Thalon said, twisting one of the pearls in his beard, "on a mission for the Aetherian king? It would seem the return of his daughter has initiated some interesting alliances."

To anyone watching, Rowan would not have appeared bothered in any way as conjecture around his presence swirled.

Placing his spoon to his lips, he seemed more concerned with the soup in front of him than the discussion.

When he finished, Rowan responded casually. "I have met Princess Mevlida. She is every bit the woman one would expect of King Galfrid."

If the others noticed he didn't answer Thalon's question, or respond to his observation, they forgot it quickly. Both asked him question after question about the princess, how she came through the Aetherian Gate, her father's reaction and more. Some questions, he answered. Others, he evaded, telling them even less than what he'd told me.

But many additional questions remained. Why did Galfrid send Rowan on such an important mission? Though Rowan had admitted there were things he could not tell me, he had never hinted at what those things might be. The more I got to know of him, the more certain I was that Rowan held back more than he shared.

When the main course was served, I finally interrupted their questioning.

"The queen is not attending the meal?"

Thalon did not appear concerned. After all, the queen missed as many meals as she attended. That she'd summoned Rowan and I to be here, though, was exceedingly odd.

"We'd not be eating already if she was," Carys said.

There was something about her tone that suggested Carys might know more than she let on. As a part of Queen Lirael's inner circle, I would not be surprised if she knew precisely why the queen summoned us.

Rowan and I exchanged a glance. I attempted to communicate my concern without allowing Carys to see it and might have been too subtle. He simply smiled and continued to eat his meal, praising its flavor and Thalassari cuisine.

When dessert was served, still with no word from the queen, and after more questions from Carys than would be deemed polite, my suspicions grew. And were confirmed when she asked Rowan if he was looking forward to the festival.

Rowan had not told her for certain he was staying until then.

His response was calm, effortless. "Very much. I've heard of the Festival of Tides, of course, but never thought to witness it myself."

Carys's smile faltered, the polite curve of her lips thinning as though she'd expected more. She swirled the wine in her glass, Carys's gaze lingering on Rowan in a way that made me tighten my grip on my glass.

As the final course was cleared, she rose, her movements deliberate and poised. "Enjoy your stay, Rowan," she said, her tone sweetly sharp, like a dagger wrapped in silk.

Rowan inclined his head, his easy charm unbroken. "Thank you, Lady Carys."

I said nothing as she left, Thalon following not long afterward.

"She summoned us," I said, keeping my voice low, "and yet she doesn't appear."

Rowan lifted his gaze to the empty dais. The sharp planes of his face were steady, but his eyes betrayed a flicker of curiosity. "Carys is close to the queen?"

"She is," I confirmed.

"Perhaps she wanted her court to ask questions for her." Rowan's eyes flicked to mine, and for a moment, the queen's motives didn't matter. Earlier, outside his chamber, I wanted to forget our kiss, knowing it was something we should not repeat. But when Rowan looked at me that way, I forgot to care about all the reasons the two of us wouldn't work. "Then let's give her something worth watching," he said, his voice low.

Heat rose to my cheeks. "You're far too comfortable with this game."

"You're far too quick to assume I'm playing."

Oh, he was playing. If nothing else, this dinner told me as much. King Galfrid had sent Rowan of Estmere on this mission for a reason. And I was beginning to work out at least part of that reason: Rowan's charm hiding his slyness.

Whether we admitted it or not, liked it or not, we were already part of her game. And I wasn't sure if Rowan would prove my greatest ally—or my undoing.

19

ROWAN

"This isn't the way to my chamber?"

"No, it's not."

Unlike the keeps that dominated Estmere's landscape, like the one in which I was raised, which were built in perfect squares and rectangles, the palace was a mass of twists and turns that made little sense architecturally.

Nerys walked briskly ahead of me. Neither of us spoke as we descended a set of stairs and turned at least four more corners.

"This way."

As we approached a curtain of cascading sea vines, Nerys twisted her hand, fingers outstretched, and the vines parted. I froze at the sight before me. It was the vision I'd had in the market, a place I hadn't known even existed then.

The grove hummed with the energy of Elydor's magic. It was a sanctuary of gently swaying flora that cast a soft glow into pools of water in hues of gold and green. Tiny, luminescent creatures darted between branches of trees that could only be found in Thalassaria. It was unlike anything I'd ever seen above the surface, a sanctuary that felt alive.

"The Garden of Luminous Tides," Nerys said, urging me forward. With another twist of her hand, the vines closed behind me. "It was created by King Aldrion, a Thalassari ruler known for his diplomacy and magical expertise. Reading about his feats, I have no doubt he was one of the strongest Thalassarians that ever lived."

"I've heard of him before. He was king during the War of the Abyss?"

"He was," she said, sitting on a stone bench at the edge of the water.

I wasn't ready to sit yet. The shock of seeing this place for the second time, realizing my visions were at least partially accurate, and the beauty of this grove...

"It's remarkable."

"This is my favorite place in the palace. There are few of us that are able to enter, and no silencing mist is needed here."

"I don't understand." Kneeling, I tried to get a better look at one of the tiny creatures that left a trail of light in its wake but it darted past me too quickly.

"The king, wanting a sanctuary where he could not be disturbed, made it accessible only to those who could unlock its magic. He was killed, as you likely know already, in the war. With him, knowledge of how to enter was lost until it was rediscovered by the man we dined with this eve."

That this place had gone unused for so many centuries was sad, and surprising. "Why did King Aldrion not give others access? How did it thrive for so long unattended? And what are these tiny creatures?" I stood, giving up. They apparently did not want to be truly seen.

"The king was a deeply private ruler and apparently created the garden as a private sanctuary. The magic he used on it was extraordinary by any standards, its balance protected by the elemental spirits." She smiled. "Or as you call them, tiny creatures. As to why they are elusive, I cannot say."

This felt like a more important question: "How were you able to enter?"

Moving to the edge of the pool, about to dip my finger into the water, I looked up, realizing perhaps I should not contaminate it. But in my vision, I was crouched down at the water's edge, my hand wading through the water.

"Go ahead," she said, Nery's expression telling me something would indeed happen. With the first swipe, a light appeared beneath my fingers. Moving it back and forth, light trailed behind in the water's wake.

I glanced up.

"When I first discovered that I was able to come inside, I spent many hours as you are right now. There is nothing quite like it in all of Elydor."

I suddenly wanted to know more about this king.

"I was in the Deep Archives, not long after I began working at the palace, when Thalon also happened to be there. He apparently stumbled on a passage that offered a clue about the ancient incantation the king used to protect the garden from intruders. From that day forward, we were able to enter, although Thalon does not come here as often as me."

"Surely others know as well by now?" I thought of the vines on the other side of the door. "It isn't very well hidden."

"They do. But thus far, only Thalon and I have been able to enter. I sometimes wonder if the king's magic allows Thalon entry because he found the scroll that contained its secrets, though I'm uncertain why entry extends to me."

"And the queen?"

"As you can imagine, is displeased at her inability to come inside, though both Thalon and I have downplayed its beauty."

"Why doesn't she come in as your guest? Or his? Surely, you're able to bring anyone inside, as you did me."

The way Nerys looked at me then... she was about to say something important. I stood, holding her gaze and slowly walked toward the bench.

"Nerys," I said softly, sitting too far away to touch her knowing what would happen otherwise.

"I had no notion if you would be able to enter with me. I've tried many times, as Thalon has, to bring the queen here. I've long wondered if she suspects I, or both of us, deliberately misuse the spell necessary for entry. But the same thing happens each time either of us attempts to separate the vines while we're in the company of others. Nothing."

"Why me?"

I wanted to tell her about my vision. About all of it. My family's history, the Keepers, my role as The Keeper... but I was sworn not to do so unless we were wed.

"The pelagor," she said, folding her hands neatly onto her lap, as if unsure where to put them. I understood. My own wanted to wrap around her, pulling Nerys into me.

"The pelagor?" So much had happened since, I nearly forgot about a ride that, had it been any other day in my life, I'd have thought of little else. The feeling of freedom, and acceptance, riding with Nerys atop such an intimidating but awe-inspiring creature had been unrivaled.

"Do you remember how rare I told you it was to see one? Never mind actually ride a pelagor, as we did?"

"I do."

"Long before the rise of King Aldrion, the waters of Thalassaria were ruled by an ancient, primal force known only as the *Pelagor*. It's said the creature is an embodiment of the oceans themselves, a living force of both creation and destruction. Its body, composed of shifting waves, its eyes glowing like the stars in the darkest part of the night sky, and its voice resonating like the echoes of the ocean floor... all evidence of such a myth, if legend is to be believed. It is said that the pelagor only reveals itself to those destined to be its successors."

Destined to be its successors.

My heart beat wildly as I thought of that first vision. If only I could have seen the outcome and not just the battle itself.

"I did not know," she continued, "if you could enter with me. But when the pelagor not only appeared but allowed you to ride him, I wondered... I'd have taken you here directly if we were not summoned by the queen."

Was it somehow related to my being The Keeper? "What does it mean, do you think?"

"As I said on the beach, I believe that we are meant to work together."

Could it mean more than that? I left the question unasked, guessing the answer already.

"I feel honored, both for today's ride and being allowed in here."

"You are clearly worthy of both."

Wanting to lighten the mood that had been much too heavy since we were summoned by the queen, I teased her. "You believe so, do you?"

Nerys rolled her eyes. "You don't fool me with that false modesty, Rowan. I've gotten to know you better than that."

"I am your humble servant," I pushed back. "Modest in all things."

"Hmm. If you are modest, then Marek is painfully shy."

An untruth if ever I heard one. "I'm surprised to find myself liking him more than I'd have expected to do so."

"Please speak to Aneri on his behalf, and mine. Even after all these years, he's been unable to fully charm her."

"I would have to meet her to do so," I hedged.

"We will go to her tomorrow, so I can tell her of my plans to challenge the queen."

"Good." I adjusted myself on the bench, closing a bit of the distance between us. "Speaking of the queen..."

Nerys sighed. "I can only guess she wished for Carys to question me. Or you. Or both."

"I thought the same. Do you believe she suspects your intentions?"

"I'm uncertain. I've attempted to keep the strength of my skills somewhat hidden, but over the years..."

"Word of sea serpents tend to spread?"

"Something like that, aye."

Our eyes met. It suddenly seemed ridiculous not to mention it. "That kiss," I began, unsure where to go from there.

Twas incredible. Let's do it again. If Marek hadn't come along, I'd have wanted to take you on that damn beach.

"I do not wish to dishonor you," I said instead.

Her eyes fell to my lips.

I want it as much as you, dear Nerys. Maybe more.

"You could never dishonor me, Rowan."

It warmed me to hear her say as much with surety.

"I would never willingly do so. Now tell me something of yourself I do not know."

Nerys hesitated, but then seemed to make up her mind. "There's something I've told very few about my past... not even Marek. But now seems like it might be the right time to share it."

20

NERYS

"In their roles as diplomats, my parents traveled more often to Estmere than any other region of Elydor. They would often say that humans were special. While it is true you may not have elemental magic, or immortality, your intuitive gifts and intimate knowledge of another realm, according to my father especially, reshaped Elydor in ways we could not."

"And your mother?"

I swept away the heaviness that always came from thinking too deeply about the work my mother never finished. "She thought humans were the missing piece of something greater. All know King Galfrid opened the Gate because he was obsessed with the human realm. But my mother believed that it was meant to happen. That the human presence would someday bring us together in a way we've not seen since the clans were formed."

"Do you believe that?"

"I believe that working together can only make us stronger, so yes. I do. I also believe strongly, after today, you are special to..." I hesitated. "To Elydor."

And to me.

Rowan waited. When I said no more, he stared into the pools, alive with Elydor's magic. I watched as he reached into a pouch at his side. Then turning to me, Rowan opened his hand.

In the center of his palm lay the aquamarine pearl I'd spotted at the market. I stared at it for a moment until he extended his hand toward me.

"For you."

It was a beautiful pearl, the color my favorite. "How?" I asked, unsure if I should take it even though he offered it to me. "I was with you the entire time."

"I worked quickly," he said, not taking his eyes from me. "Please accept it as a gift for all you've done for me."

I picked up the pearl, allowing my fingers to brush along his palm, wanting to touch him again even if that touch was brief.

"I've done little—"

"That is not true," he said as I swirled the pearl around in my hand. "You accepted me from the start, shown me more of Thalassarian culture than I've ever known... offered a path forward for my people even when your queen refuses to do so. That pearl is but a small token."

"It is beautiful." I closed it within my hand.

"Fitting, as its owner is too."

My shoulders rose and fell with every breath, an awareness of him, of us, like nothing I'd ever experienced. In a short time, everything about my life would change. If I proved to be the strongest water-wielder in Thalassaria, I would be immediately named as queen. Lirael would retire to Nymara, and a new era would be ushered in. One where the hopes and dreams of my parents, of Aneri and Caelum and Marek and so many others, would be realized.

With it, every move of mine would be scrutinized. Discussed. Dissected.

And Rowan would be leaving.

"Everything will change soon."

Rowan did not deny it.

"There is a hopeful part of me that looks forward to such a change. But if I could have this day again, even for a short time, I would do so."

"If I could have the past few days for any length of time," Rowan said. "I would do so."

"Open your senses to me."

A flicker of surprise crossed his features.

"Nerys—"

"Please."

Still, he hesitated.

"I am not prepared to be the queen of Thalassaria. That thought has prevented me from challenging Lirael these many years. But I'm no longer willing to let that fear prevent the inevitable. Even so, I am scared," I admitted. "Not only of the duty and responsibility that comes with such a challenge, but of the scrutiny that will be placed on me."

I left the rest unsaid, but I could see that Rowan understood.

I could tell when he'd opened himself to me as Rowan's expression began to change. I would not look away, even as my longing for him was now exposed.

Suddenly, his head snapped toward the entrance. "Someone is there," he said, all traces of tenderness gone. "Someone is there," he said again, "trying to reach you."

When he shot up and headed toward the vines that marked the entrance, I followed.

"How can you be certain?"

His jaw flexed, as though Rowan was agitated. He positioned himself between me and the door. "You should open it." His hand moved toward his waist. I hated that Rowan was not allowed his weapon in the palace. While I understood the reasoning, it was clearly so much a part of him that Rowan struggled without access to it.

"I will need you to step aside to do so."

He moved to the side just enough for me to reach out. When the vines parted, no one was there. Confused, Rowan stepped through into the corridor. I followed, the entrance closing behind us.

"I thought..."

He looked up and down the corridor.

Nothing.

"Rowan, will you please tell me—"

"There you are." Caelum turned the corner, all but running toward us. "I've been looking for you. More importantly, the queen has been looking for you."

"Why?" I asked, aware Caelum was likely not privy to such information.

"She summoned me to ask of your whereabouts. I've only just returned to the palace this eve and told her as much. I do not know, but..." Caelum flicked his wrist, and a silencing mist settled around us. It was a dangerous thing to do in such a public place. Anyone walking by would question its use. "I spoke to Marek."

"I'd have told you myself but could not find you this morn."

"I was on an errand for the queen, one that could have been avoided with a simple marisol message." Caelum frowned. "Go to her, but tread carefully. Say as little as possible."

Something was bothering him.

"I can't shake the feeling Queen Lirael may make challenging her difficult."

"More difficult than being the most powerful water-wielder in Thalassaria for the last hundred years? I spent the morning sea-binding, but even still... she will be more than a formidable opponent."

"There are other ways she can challenge you," Rowan said. "Before the festival even begins."

"This is not Estmere," I told him. "It is a simple and straightforward test of our abilities, as it is with all three clans. We've not had a true succession crisis in our history."

"No, but Gyoria has. And my people have, in their own realm, many times before."

"I fear Rowan may be right," Caelum interrupted. "Or it could be simply my overactive mind, coupled with the queen's increasingly isolationist policies, that has me fearing the worst. I've no doubt you are more powerful, as I've been saying for many years. But why has she not already called for a challenge? I dislike the games she plays."

Knowing we were on borrowed time, I said quickly, "And she did summon Rowan and me to the evening meal and then never attended. I suspect she planted Carys to interrogate us."

"We must assume she suspects you plan to challenge her." With another wave of his hand, the mist disappeared. "I will take Rowan to his chamber. Go, speak to the queen," Caelum said.

"No."

Such a simple word but, the way Rowan said it made it seem like a king's command.

Caelum's brows rose.

"I'm going with her."

Both men looked at me.

What had Rowan sensed before we'd been interrupted? And how did that impact his decision to remain with me? Questions I would ask him later. For now, Caelum was right. We needed to hurry as the queen did not take kindly to being denied.

"He comes," I said to Caelum as we began to walk. "Will you find Marek and tell him to meet us at midday tomorrow?"

"Of course. Remember, Nerys, speak less than necessary, for the more you say, the more you give others the power to twist your words."

I nodded, each step toward the queen's chambers heavier than the one before. Perhaps it had been foolish to think my path forward would be an easy one. I would give anything to go back to the garden to finish our conversation.

Being with Rowan would have to wait.

I had a queen to placate first.

21

ROWAN

For fear she may somehow be listening, an increasing inevitability given what I'd learned about Queen Lirael thus far, Caelum and I discussed everything except Nerys. As we waited for her to emerge from the queen's chambers, he asked questions about Estmere. About the lost princess and my mission. I told him what was public knowledge, but made no mention of the Tidal Pearl or the exact nature of my mission.

"And what of you?" I asked. "How does one become an Aegis Commander to the palace?"

"Do you know of King Tyreos?"

I knew of all the clans' histories. It was required of me as a Keeper.

"I do. His murder is the reason I am escorted at all times here." I patted my waist. "And why I've been mostly without my sword since arriving."

Caelum made no comment, but he had the decency to wince.

"After his death, swordsmanship was taught to all palace commanders. In time, however, the skill was once again lost, in favor of water-wielding magic. The queen, knowing her history well, sought me for the appointment."

"Because you are an expert swordsman," I finished, remembering our introduction.

"It was an appointment I..." Caelum stopped, his expression laced with loathing, telling me how he felt about it. He'd not been a willing recruit, and I began to suspect the reason.

Think on it. I am certain you know the answer already.

"You were the young one that Nerys told me about." And the reason Caelum had taken to me so easily. "You are half-human."

"Correct, on both accounts. Which is why I know well the dangers of immortal and human partnering."

I ignored that second part. "And you knew Nerys's parents well? Were a friend of her father's?"

"We performed the Stormcaller's Rite together. He was the most powerful water-wielder I knew until..."

Until Nerys.

The rest, I had to infer and did so quickly. "This," I said of Nerys, "has been a long time coming."

Caelum's slow smile was my answer. "She had to decide for herself. Pushing someone toward their fate, however inevitable it might seem to others, is not the way."

No, it was not.

"He must have been an extraordinary man, her father. As yours must have been too."

"He, and her mother, were exactly as you would expect."

If I was not mistaken, the hardened warrior's eyes softened as he said it. Whether for their memory, or pride in Nerys, or both.

"My own?" His grin, so uncharacteristic of Caelum, told me all I needed to know. "He was the bravest, most loyal man to have ever walked Elydor."

"And you? Have you partnered with a woman?"

It was a personal question, but Nerys made no mention of it and Caelum did not seem to take offense. "Once. Many decades ago."

He said no more, and I did not press him.

When the door opened beside us, all thoughts of Caelum's family history were momentarily forgotten.

Nerys glanced briefly at us both, and then to the guards who had been inside the chamber with her. As they closed the doors, one looked pointedly at me. When we'd first arrived, he'd initially forbade my presence until Caelum had claimed personal responsibility for me.

Both Caelum and I followed Nerys through the corridor, and when a vision suddenly appeared, I was not only able to process and understand it; I could also make it fade. It was, as my grandfather would say, "A vision of naught and of everything all at once." Some visions had implications for our entire kingdom. Others, like this one, were seemingly innocuous. It was of Nerys leading Caelum and I through the palace, though we wore different clothing than we did at this moment.

"We leave you here," she said, turning to Caelum. "Tomorrow at midday?"

Which meant she did not wish to share what the queen had said until then.

Caelum nodded, but it was not the kind of nod that said, "*Very well.*" It was deeper, and more reverent. The kind one might give... a queen.

My vision. It was of a future time when Nerys, Queen of Thalassaria, led us through the palace corridors. Except, that was impossible. I would be gone when she became queen.

There were few roaming the corridors at this time, but those we passed always had a smile for Nerys... and a wary glance toward me.

When we arrived at my chamber door, Nerys remained with me on its threshold.

"How did you know Caelum was looking for me?"

"I would break a sacred vow, to my family and my people in telling you."

I'd disappointed her. It was the first time in my life I wished to be a regular human, a blacksmith's son. Someone, anyone, other than a Harrow.

"I would not ask for you to break a vow," she said, surprising me. "But will admit I am very curious."

"There is a way that I can tell you," I blurted, and then immediately stopped talking. Had I gone mad? The only way to tell her was to make Nerys a Harrow by marriage. And that would never be. The Keeper could not live in Thalassaria, and the queen of Thalassaria certainly could not reside in Estmere. Even if the problem of my mortality did not bother her, which it did.

I said no more, and thankfully, Nerys did not press the matter.

"What did you feel from me?" she asked. "Back in the garden?"

"A much easier question to answer." I glanced at my bedchamber door. "And even easier to show you."

Our eyes met, and held.

You could never dishonor me, Rowan.

Her meaning, and emotions had been clear. We would be temporary. A fleeting affair. And as much as the heaviness in my chest told me that wouldn't be enough, my mind argued the point. It was that, or nothing. Given those choices, and what Nerys offered, I would take it.

Nerys's delicate fingers swirled, and with the movement, my chamber door opened. Before I could move toward it, she stepped inside.

I followed.

22

NERYS

You're going to break your own heart.

I ignored the warning.

Pushing aside my conversation with the queen, and an instinct that told me this was a bad idea, I walked to the windows. Rowan followed. But instead of standing beside me as I looked beyond the iridescent pools and lights scattered throughout the palace grounds to the sea beyond, he stopped behind me.

Rowan gently moved my hair to one side, placing it in front of my right shoulder. I waited. Anticipated. Sure enough, his breath on my exposed neck told me what Rowan intended. At the first touch of his lips, I closed my eyes. His lips were warm, his hands laying on my hips as if to keep me in place, like I would dare move.

A second kiss, and then a third, and Rowan was just below my ear.

"Do you want to talk about it?" he whispered.

"Later," I said, preferring to delay the inevitable. "The queen interrupted us once. I'd not have her do it again."

Wordlessly, Rowan kissed just below my ear. It was rare for a

Thalassarian to get cold, our climate remaining temperate. But nevertheless, I shivered.

Turning my head to look at him was my second mistake of the evening. Where a moment ago, his movements promised a slow and steady seduction, now, his eyes blazed. Spinning me around to him, Rowan captured my mouth, though I was a willing captive. In a tangle of tongues, we melded together like before. But this time, a promise of more hung in the air.

We stayed that way for some time, Rowan's low groans and my own whimpers the only other sound beside running water. I'd been in others' arms many times, but never been so consumed by a kiss as this.

My hands dropped to the hem of his tunic, but when I tried to tug upward, our bodies got in the way. In response, Rowan broke off the kiss and all but ripped the tunic from his body. Wanting to see him again, I fumbled with the buttons on his linen shirt.

"You are well-formed."

"For a human?" he teased, helping me with the buttons.

"For an Elydorian," I said. "Human or otherwise."

With his shirt off, I wanted to explore. Touching his chest, both palms splayed across muscle that tensed deliciously beneath my fingertips, I licked my lips. His eyes dipped down to my chest. Without a second thought, I spun back around, presenting him my back. "There is a zipper," I said of the human invention, one of a few that had been brought to Elydor.

The pressure of his fingers at my back was followed by the loosening of its bodice. Pulling my arms from each sleeve, I let the gown drop to the floor, stepping out of it. Tossing off the heels that I so despised, I wore nothing but undergarments which matched the gown itself, though made from the finest lace in all of Elydor. Rowan lifted it and carried my gown to the trunk at the foot of his bed. As he draped it carefully across the top, I followed.

"This is dangerously close to the bed," I said as I sidled up to him.

"Is it?"

In response, he lifted me up by the waist as if I weighed as much as a piece of sea coral. Holding on as he stalked toward the bed, I only let go as he placed me onto it.

"Yes," he said, quickly unlacing his boots and tossing them aside. "It is."

One moment, Rowan was joining me. The next, he was removing my linens, the soft fabric made of fine Thalassarian seaweed fibers tossed onto the floor.

"Look at you." Rowan positioned himself between my legs. Spreading them wide, his thumbs pressing into my thighs, he smiled as if privy to a private jest. It was quintessential Rowan, and I was reminded of when we first met. "I've lived only one lifetime," he said, his thumbs now circling gently as his hand inched upward. "But long enough to know you will enjoy this."

I did not doubt it.

"You seem confident in your abilities, Sir Rowan. From experience, no doubt?"

Reaching my upper thighs, he stopped. Grinned.

"You will enjoy this because I intend to worship you, Nerys, as you deserve. I've never kissed a woman and had the feel of her lips linger all day. Or held someone, never wishing to let go. I sometimes forget you are the most powerful water-wielder in all of Elydor, because to me, you are my escort. Someone I can talk to as easily as I might those I've known my whole life. But then I see what you are capable of, and I'm honored to be in your presence. You are extraordinary, Nerys. And deserve no less than to be revered."

With that, his finger found me. Rowan didn't look away. His gaze held mine as he unraveled me. "How should I make you come first? With my fingers or my tongue?"

He was brazen, "my" human.

How many times had I said, he's not my human? Yet right now, it felt as if he might be. As I was his, at least for this night. And maybe a few more. Until it was time for him to leave.

"The thought of your tongue on me—"

I hadn't finished the thought before Rowan's head was between my legs. At his first touch, I melted. His fingers opened me to him, and whether Rowan admitted it or not, he clearly had experience in this area. I gripped his sheets as Rowan's tongue circled and then plunged inside as if I were a feast and he was a starving man.

"Rowan," I pressed into him, both wanting to close my eyes and keep them open. A sound escaped my lips: part sigh, part moan. I both wanted more and for him to stop, the building sensation threatening to have it ended too soon.

"Mmmm," he murmured as my eyes whipped open. He looked up and licked me from one end to the other. Then with a devilish smile, he began to flick his tongue against me, likely knowing that I was so close to exploding.

"You are unbelievable," I managed. Even if I wanted to hang on, I couldn't. But Rowan did not stop. Not as I screamed his name. Not as my legs shook.

He did stop when I finally caught my breath.

Leaping from the bed with the grace of an Aetherian, he removed his belt and breeches. Relaxed in the after-effects of release, I was still able to take in the thick, muscled thighs and a readiness for me that was most impressive.

He was above me in a heartbeat. Leaning down, Rowan captured my mouth in a searing kiss as his hands explored. I did the same, wanting to touch every bit of him. When his thumbs ran across my nipples, hard and ready, I arched up, telling him I wanted this now. Instead of granting my silent request, he had the audacity to chuckle against my mouth, playfully circling my tongue with his.

In a mass of tangled limbs and fervent kisses, we explored each other until finally, mercifully, Rowan pressed one finger inside me. Finding it slick with need for him, he replaced it, the head of Rowan's cock now where his finger had been a moment earlier.

But instead of pressing into me, he pulled up. Halted our kiss. Implored me with his eyes, though said nothing. If he were waiting for me to stop him, I'd not do it. When he finally guided himself into me, my head fell against the pillow. By the time he was fully buried inside me, I had no inclination to move slowly. Apparently, neither did Rowan, because a few quick thrusts later, he was filling me so completely and without abandon that I wondered how this time could be so different than any other.

But it was.

Our pace matched each other's perfectly. It wasn't a soft or gentle one, but one born from frantic need. I held onto his shoulders as Rowan's hand moved between us, finding the sensitive spot that assured I would come again. Already, it was building, the sight of him, when my eyes peeked open, reminding me that he truly was as perfectly formed as I remembered.

We kissed, his tongue matching the rhythm of our lovemaking.

You are extraordinary, Nerys. And deserve no less than to be revered.

That was the reason it felt so different. Rowan promised to worship me, and that was exactly what he did. With his mouth, his body, and the care he took in pleasing me.

"Please," I begged, tearing my lips from him. I wanted to see him. Look at him. "Rowan…"

"Go ahead, Nerys," he said, my name on his lips just one more sweet pleasure. "Let go. Give me all of you."

That's precisely what I wanted to do. I held back nothing, my fingers squeezing his shoulders, telling him I was close.

"I cannot wait to release myself inside you, Nerys."

That was all it took. Thrusting my hips into him, I held on and looked into his eyes, showing Rowan how right he was about enjoying this. In response, he buried himself full hilt, his mouth opening as we called each other's names.

It had been frantic and wild, perfect in every way. As I shuddered around him, holding on tight, I tried to catch my breath. Rowan collapsed on top of me, holding himself back enough as not to crush me.

I buried my face in the crook of his neck, sighing against it. In response, he did the same, clearly contented, as I was. And despite the afterglow, shivers running from my shoulders down to my toes, I knew one thing for certain.

This had been a mistake.

23

ROWAN

"There it is."

We stood in front of a water-smoothed stone house adorned with carvings of waves. Arriving in Maristhera by canal and scapha boats, Nerys and I had avoided another summons by the queen thus far today. But after what she told me last eve, I expected one sooner rather than later.

Last eve.

When everything, and nothing, changed. She'd left late into the night and this morning, when Nerys came to my door, though I'd been tempted to pull her into my bedchamber, I took my cue from her. When she'd asked if I was ready, I'd said simply, "Aye," and followed her from the palace.

No mention of the night before.

As soon as we'd left the palace walls, Nerys told me what the queen had said. Since then, we had spoken of nothing else but that topic.

Before we could approach the door, it opened.

Aneri was exactly as Nerys had described. Halfway between thaloran and vaelith, her many years on Elydor were etched in fine lines on her face. The kindness in her eyes offset the severeness of her gray hair, pulled back into a tight bun.

"Your friend is inside already," she said to Nerys. "With luck, this one does not have so high an opinion of himself."

"Marek adores you," Nerys said, defending him.

"Not as much as he adores himself. You are the human Marek told me about."

"I am," I said, bowing in the Thalassari way. "Sir Rowan of Estmere."

Nerys hugged her as we walked inside.

"I already like him more," she said as we made our way through to the sitting room.

Aneri's home was modest yet inviting. Wide windows let in natural light, casting shimmering reflections from the nearby canal. A polished driftwood table was surrounded by cushioned seats, while shelves displayed hundreds of seashells, weathered books, and vials of liquid. We walked through a kitchen with pearl-inlaid stone counters, the scent of citrus lingering.

She led us into a back courtyard, a fountain centered around water plants in pots and shallow pools creating a tranquil retreat. Aneri's home was clearly a place of warmth and belonging.

"Your home is lovely," I said, trying to imagine Nerys outside in this courtyard. She'd told me once that she'd spent many hours practicing water magic on that very fountain.

As Marek did now. He was toying with the water, making it leap and fall with small splashes.

"Thank you." Aneri eyed Marek warily.

"Caelum will be arriving any moment," Nerys said. Before she'd even finished, Aneri disappeared back into the house, apparently to fetch him.

"I thought you were exaggerating," I said to Marek.

"Unfortunately not," he said, still toying with the water. "She tolerates me but..." He shrugged.

I looked to Nerys for an explanation.

Sighing, she glanced back to the door where there was no sign of Aneri.

"Aneri does not agree with some of his"—she nodded to Marek—"trade ventures."

"Ahh," I said, understanding better. "You are a smuggler?"

Marek shot Nerys a look. "I would not call it as such."

Nerys laughed. "What, then, would you call it?" she asked him.

Marek's easy grin told me he was unbothered by judgment, even from Nerys. "I'd call it... creative trade negotiations," he said smoothly with a hint of mischief in his tone.

Nerys arched a brow. "Creative trade negotiations that happen to bypass official routes and involve contraband?"

"Contraband." Marek tsked. "I prefer to think of it as the redistribution of goods."

"So." I crossed my arms. "Smuggling?"

Marek placed a hand over his heart in mock offense. "I am a Thalassari Navarch, not a criminal."

"Aneri would disagree," Nerys said, her eyes flicking to the door again before returning to me. When our eyes locked, it brought me immediately back to last eve. Nerys, in my bed with her atop me, the second time we made love. Hair spilling around her, Nerys's full breasts above me as she moved—

"Ahh, by the tides. Really Nerys? A human?"

The spell broken, we both turned our attention to Marek.

"I'm jesting, of course," he said to me. "I actually quite like you." Uncharacteristically, his smile faded and Marek looked at Nerys. "I like you together."

"Soon, all will change," Nerys said in response. It was the

same refrain I'd heard from her more than once last eve, as if reminding me of the temporary nature of our relationship. Not that I needed reminding. Just this morn, upon waking, I had another vision. This one, I could not untangle. It was a group of people, none of whom I could make out, sitting on stools in an unfamiliar place. We raised our glasses, toasting, as I was among the group.

These visions came every day now, and they would continue to do so because I was the new Keeper. I had a destiny of my own to fill.

Aneri returned, then, with Caelum. After a shuffle of seats, Caelum wasted no time.

"What did she say?" he asked Nerys.

She explained his question to the others, telling them first of the queen's summons to the meal and then again last eve.

"It is my belief," she said, "the queen knows I plan to challenge her. I am uncertain how she learned this since none beyond this courtyard have been informed."

"The queen is not a stupid woman." Caelum stretched his legs out in front of him, crossing his arms. "She knows you are more powerful than her. It is the reason she brought you to the palace. To watch, and monitor."

"If you are more powerful, which I believe you are," Marek added, "then the Tidal Pearl has been losing its effectiveness for some time."

"Yet she did not call for the challenge," I said.

Aneri sighed. "Some give up their rule more willingly than others. And tides have turned in recent years. There has been a growing sentiment that we are too isolated, and it has not made Thalassaria stronger for it. She knows this."

The explanation was made for me, I realized. That she'd accepted me so readily into this inner circle was surprising. I ignored a pang of guilt for keeping my own secret when I was welcomed into their fold.

"What, precisely, did she say?" Caelum asked.

"She asked how the human emissary had been occupying his time and what more he'd told me of his mission."

I avoided Nerys's gaze, not wanting to make the same mistake I did with Marek by unwittingly revealing too much of our relationship.

"Why do you believe she knows?" Marek asked.

This was my least favorite part of the story and one that cemented my dislike for Queen Lirael.

"She said, 'Keep close watch on him, Nerys. It is your duty. One which you are uniquely qualified for, as your parents were before you. Thalassaria is lucky to have you... as a Stormcaller and diplomat.'"

Aneri's grey brows furrowed. "That is all?"

Caelum answered her question. "I know the queen, as Nerys does. It was not a compliment but a warning. She was reminding Nerys of her role and not to reach too high above it."

"That was my belief as well," Nerys said.

"A subtle warning," I added, "but one Nerys will not heed."

"No," she confirmed. "I am committed to challenging her. And should have done so long ago."

As I looked at the faces of those around me, those closest to Nerys, who cared the most for her, I made a decision. "There is another reason the queen may be suspicious."

Nerys's head snapped in my direction. If Nerys trusted those gathered around us, I would as well.

"I am here on a mission from King Galfrid and his daughter, Princess Mevlida. Since she slipped through the Gate, which, as you know, has been closed for many years, there is renewed hope it might be permanently reopened. To achieve that end, they need the Tidal Pearl. I am here to receive it, or at least promise of its use, when necessary."

Everyone began speaking at once. I answered their questions, or those I was able to answer. While I did so, Aneri never took her eyes from me. It was as if she could hear what I did not say. See me in a way the others could not.

Did she know Nerys and I had been together, perhaps? She had lived for many, many years and was perceptive in a way I could never fully understand. It was easy, at times, to forget how very different we were. Immortals and humans.

Perhaps I was thinking too much on the matter, but behind her kindness was a wariness too. One I could understand if she suspected there was something between us.

"Do you think the queen believes Nerys will challenge her so that she can give you the Tidal Pearl?" Marek asked. "Is that why you do it?" he added to Nerys, as if an afterthought.

Nerys raised her chin. "I do it because the most powerful among us has a duty to challenge the current ruler. I do it for our people and our future. And aye, I do it for Rowan and King Galfrid and Princess Mevlida, and for all humans, because the Gate should be reopened."

Her words were like a challenge themselves.

None took it nor disputed her words.

Grateful, knowing already the Gate's reopening played a part in her decision, something inside me stirred as I looked at Nerys. Knowing she was scared to claim the role of queen and rule a kingdom, as anyone in her position would be, and yet spoke with such assuredness and conviction...

Dammit, Rowan.

I knew better than to fall in love with an immortal. Every human knew better and guarded their hearts against it. And yet, I'd done it anyway.

24

NERYS

I approached Rowan, who sat at the entrance of the alcove, but Marek was nowhere to be found. Wading through knee-deep water, I stretched out my arm and bent back fingers that had begun to cramp after so many hours.

After the meeting when it was decided Rowan and I would remain as far from the palace as often as possible from now until the festival, Marek had joined us, training with me for a spell. He was between voyages, and with the Festival of Tides approaching, none were imminent as all of Thalassaria halted for the twice-a-year festivities.

"Where is Marek?" I asked.

"He apparently had an 'assignation.' His word, not my own."

"He is incorrigible."

Rowan approached, holding out his hand. "Let me help."

He took my hand, the first time we'd touched since last eve. Massaging one finger at a time, he gave no hint of the man who had elicited from me more calls for his name than I could count. Until he was finished with my fingers and moved to my palm, rubbing circles which became increasingly slow and methodic, the exhaustion I'd felt moments earlier left my body completely.

"This is so very dangerous," I said, my mind warring between knowing that fact and not caring if it were true or not.

Rowan dropped our joined hands to the side, closing the gap between us.

"Why?"

My heart raced as he peered into my eyes for an answer I was certain he knew already.

"Because this is no assignation."

"No," he said, leaning into me. "It is not."

When our lips touched, it was as though they were meant to fit together. One moment, we engaged in a simple kiss at the end of a long day of training. The next, our kiss deepened and Rowan's hands held my head in place, as if I needed a reminder to stay put.

There was nowhere on Elydor I wanted to be more than on this beach with him. And that was the problem. Instead of admitting it, or moving away, I wrapped my arms around him, pulling Rowan closer to me.

If we could have remained that way all eve, I'd have been glad for it. But as the sun began to set, it occurred to me Rowan hadn't eaten since Aneri had served us fresh fish before we'd left her house. I needed sustenance, as did all immortals, but Rowan needed more.

"You've not eaten," I said, reluctantly pulling back.

"If you're asking me to choose between standing here with you or a meal, I choose the former," he said, brushing my hair to the side and kissing the skin at my collarbone. Then lower, he kissed, his tongue taunting. I moved my hands to his backside and let them roam, no longer caring about sustenance.

In truth, I did about guarding my heart, and that was still necessary. Even so, I could not, would not, stop him.

"Shall we stay here and forgo a meal at The Moonlit Current?"

At the reminder of our plans, Rowan asking earlier if we could return, he lifted his head.

"As much as I would enjoy that, perhaps we should finish this later?"

There was something about his tone that piqued my interest. A lack of casualness that was so characteristic of Rowan. With a reluctant sigh, he stepped back and took my hand, and I cursed whatever madness had possessed me to remind him about the tavern.

As before, we walked along the shoreline, Rowan asking about my training methods. Once, when a sound behind us revealed nothing more than a startled seabird, when his hand moved to the hilt of a non-existent sword, I apologized again.

"Humans will not be treated as such when I am queen."

"I and my kind are thankful for it. When did you first know, Nerys? How powerful you'd truly become? That you might be stronger than Queen Lirael?"

"In a training session, with my father."

"That long ago?"

"Aye, though at the time, I believed it was just a father's wishful thinking. But even as a young one, there was talk of my skills. For some, their abilities are in direct relation to their parents, or bloodline. They say Prince Terran and Prince Kael, for instance, are nearly as powerful as their father."

"I've witnessed both fight and can attest to that fact as truth."

"You have?"

"I have." As we approached town, the beach became less desolate, though none paid us mind as we walked by. "As you'll recall, I mentioned on our journey to Aetheria, Prince Terran attempted to stop us, stop his brother, from escorting Mev to her father. Their battle lasted for some time, though I believe Terran may be even more powerful than his brother."

"And Mev, as you call her? Is she powerful, like her father?"

"I believe so, though she was still learning as I left to come here."

"It is rare for a child of a powerful immortal, especially sons and daughters of kings and queens, not to be so. But when a union does not bear children, as it most often does not? I mean to say, my parents were skilled, but none could have predicted I would be the product of their union. It took them as much by surprise as anyone. And yet, if they were alive today, I do not believe they'd be surprised at all, that I find myself in such a predicament. If that makes sense?"

"It does. Although I would not call your situation a predicament, but an opportunity. Thalassaria will benefit from your rule, Nerys."

As a young one ran by, looked at us and giggled, I realized we still held hands. Reluctantly pulling mine from Rowan's, we continued toward the tavern. I wanted to reach for his hand again. I wanted to fall into his arms again. I wanted to be his again.

But every step we took toward town meant more scrutiny, and with it, the knowledge that I would have little anonymity soon. As we walked inside, I imagined what it might be like, me as queen, holding Rowan's hand. Would they accept it? A Thalassari queen and a human?

Perhaps. But even so, what would happen as Rowan aged? We would march toward his death, and my undoing, year after year a reminder of the certainty that I would someday live without him by my side. Because... there was no doubt... I enjoyed having

Rowan by my side, if I could keep him there, if he would have me.

We entered the familiar tavern.

"Nerys. Sir Rowan. Welcome."

The innkeeper greeted us the moment we walked inside.

"Good eve, Nerithia," I said.

"With luck, I'll have no need of your sea serpent services, this eve." She escorted us to the same table as before. "And of course, your meal tonight is on me."

"I've done nothing to deserve it, but will not turn away a meal," Rowan said good-naturedly to the innkeeper.

Nerithia held Rowan's gaze for a moment longer, as if she wanted to say something more. Instead, she assured us a servant would be along to bring our drinks. It was Nerithia, though, herself who brought our food: two trenchers of fresh fish and vegetables. She seemed to take extra care in handing Rowan's to him before moving away.

"I could become accustomed to the food here. Actually, I could become accustomed to most things in Thalassaria."

"Even me?"

It was out of my mouth before I thought better of it. What had possessed me to say such a thing? Laughing, as if I'd made a joke, I instead asked Rowan what he thought of Aneri. Rather than answering, he simply looked at me.

"Nerys?"

He said my name so deeply, it was as if Rowan spoke directly to my soul. I looked up from my nearly empty trencher of food.

"Especially you."

At that very moment, the moon moved into place, streaming its light through the windows in a way that gave the tavern its namesake. Though we couldn't hear the sound of the ocean's waves from inside, I could feel the tide as it shifted, a gentle pull against the edges of my consciousness, as if it whispered secrets only the water could know.

Do not, Nerys. There is no hope for it.

"Open yourself to me."

This time, unlike the last, he didn't ask if I was certain. Instead, Rowan stopped eating. Stopped drinking. Seemed to stop breathing as he stared at me. His nostrils flared, Rowan's lips parting, as if he would speak.

But he said nothing.

I waited.

"I wish you had my ability to sense emotion," Rowan said finally. "And could feel mine too."

The gentle hum of voices, of glasses clanging together, of merriment and camaraderie, surrounded us. It was the sound of Thalassaria, of joy. It wrapped me like a warm current, or perhaps it was Rowan doing that to me.

"You could tell me," I ventured.

"I do not need to say it aloud, Nerys. Doing so will only..."

He either could not, or would not, continue.

Will only cause us both more pain later. Rowan didn't need to say the words for me to know the truth of them.

"Could it..." I started, but then stopped.

Nay, Nerys. You've said enough.

"Could it what, Nerys? Ask me your question."

"Could it... could we..." The words refused to form.

"Could we be possible?" he asked for me.

I didn't confirm that was my question, but neither did I deny it. Rowan looked as if he would be ill. Nay, not ill. Sad. Immeasurably so.

Of course we could not be possible, for so many reasons. I should not have asked.

"As much as I would wish it, no. I do not believe we could."

25

ROWAN

One truth, and it all came tumbling down.

And while I'd not have lied to Nerys, telling her that it was somehow possible for us to be together, that truth had cost me everything. Though she attempted to pretend otherwise, a budding hope shattered and Nerys's mood with it.

We opted to return by canal, our conversation stilted. Every time I thought to discuss it, words escaped me. Without being able to tell Nerys the full truth, how could I explain that if my presence wasn't needed in Estmere as The Keeper, the answer would be yes? That if she believed her people would accept a human king, and despite the challenges which immortal and human relationships presented, we would find a way beyond them? But not one vision of the future, thus far, showed Nerys and I together.

If not for our respective roles, could we be possible? She had reservations, valid ones, about my mortality, but if she could accept it, I would forgo my life in Estmere. Except I couldn't. The Keeper lived among their own. There were just too many obstacles between us.

"There is an eeriness about the palace this eve," Nerys said, echoing my own thoughts as we headed toward my bedchamber.

"The hour is late," I said. "But there are fewer about than usual."

In Aneri's courtyard, we'd discussed the possibility of Nerys being watched more closely. If the queen truly did suspect Nerys planned to challenge her, coupled with the knowledge that at least one of her inner circle had been apprised of my purpose here, we had to assume Carys was not the only threat.

Opening myself to our surroundings, but blocking Nerys, I sensed nothing.

"Can I open myself to you?" At her look of suspicion, I clarified. "By blocking you, I am able to sense less," I whispered.

Our footfalls the only sound in the empty corridors, Nerys's "aye" echoed.

I regretted it immediately.

Her sadness flooded my senses. I shifted my focus outward, still unsure of this newfound ability to sense what was not directly in front of me.

There!

Unseen, but undoubtedly present, a... hesitation. And also, the feeling of anticipation. Yet, I could not tell where it was coming from.

Putting out my hand, I stopped Nerys. Needing a distraction, I whispered, "Trust me."

And then kissed her.

She allowed it.

The Keeper's visions do not come on demand. When you're ready to receive them, they will find you.

So instead of attempting to force a vision, I lost myself in Nerys's kiss. It wasn't a difficult feat, her lips soft and inviting. Before long, the ruse was not a ruse at all.

That's when it came to me. A shell, large and luminous, on the palace wall. Its most unusual feature was its colors. Unlike much of the decor in the palace, this was not only shades of blue and aquamarine, but also pink and purple and yellow.

I pulled back, whispering, "A shell, of every shade. Where is it?"

Nerys's eyes widened. But she didn't hesitate.

"This way."

Instead of turning right, toward my chamber, we turned left. As we did, a hooded figure spun and fled in the opposite direction. I ran, the figure bolting. The chase was on, and I meant to catch the culprit.

Gaining on him, certain it was a man, I caught him on a turn, grabbing onto his wrist. The figure spun, his clear, blue eyes narrowing as he used his other arm to channel water from some unknown source into my face.

Reaching for a sword that wasn't there, another blast of water attempted to loosen my grip. Instead, I held more tightly. One moment, the figure thrashed in my hold. The next, I was thrown backward as he fell onto the floor in front of me.

Turning, I saw Nerys just before she sent another line of water, perfectly formed and targeted, in our direction. Though it kept him down momentarily, he quickly regrouped and ran. I stood, intending to follow, when a voice stopped me.

"What is happening here?"

One of the palace guards came from nowhere, staring at the flooded corridor. Nerys stood behind me, looking every bit as fierce as she had the night she summoned those sea serpents. She took a step toward the guard.

"Precisely what I would like to know myself," she said, her voice strong. Unwavering. "Is there a reason why a guest of the palace is being watched? And attacked for little more than attempting to discover the spy's identity?"

The guard swallowed. He turned to look in each direction, but we were alone. The spy, gone.

I opened to him. He felt hesitation. Hope. Judging from it, and by his expression, I wondered if perhaps he was not as loyal to the queen as his position might dictate.

"Say it," I prompted, opening my senses and knowing we were alone. "He is long gone."

Nerys visibly relaxed. "Aelois? Do you know something more about what happened here?"

Again, the guard swallowed heavily, and this time, I felt his nervousness.

"I... Lady Nerys..."

"Speak plainly," I prompted him, suspecting what he might be about to say.

"There is rumor, among very few of us, that you... that you, perhaps..."

As I thought.

"There is no need to say it," Nerys cut in.

"We hope that you will. Perhaps tonight's attack was related to that? All know you are close to him." He nodded toward me. "And that he is here on an important mission that is connected to the return of the lost princess."

And so it had begun.

Rumor had spread. And the queen had revealed her hand. She would not willingly relinquish the crown, but instead would fight to keep it.

"We?" Nerys asked.

A good question.

"There are more of us than you might expect. Even among her guards—"

I put my finger to my lips. He stopped talking, immediately understanding. Clearing his throat, Aelois stood straighter, as if remembering his role in the palace. "Were you able to identify your attacker, Sir Rowan?"

"I've not seen him before, and it was difficult to get a good look at him as he was hooded."

"I will clean the corridor," Nerys said. "If you would be on the lookout for any other strange occurrences, we would appreciate it."

"Of course," the guard said, bowing to Nerys before he left.

Making good on her promise, Nerys sent the water below our feet back to an unknown source. We headed back in the direction of my chamber. As we passed the shell that I saw in my vision, I asked Nerys of its colors.

"This is the shell of the Sea's Embrace, a symbol of our kingdom's protection and unity. The colors represent the different elements we hold dear: blue for the ocean's depth, pink for the tide's nurturing power, purple for the wisdom of the ancients, and yellow for the promise of new beginnings. The shell is a reminder that we are all connected, like the ocean's currents, and that no one stands alone in Thalassaria."

Nerys's sideway glance warned of her question to come.

"How did you know of his presence here? Just as you knew the queen had summoned me?" Before I could respond, she laughed, though it was not a sound of joy. "A silly question. You will not tell me."

"If I could, Nerys—"

"Aye, I know. If you could, you would."

"Nerys." I reached for her arm, stopping us both. "I want to tell you. To explain."

"Then do so," she challenged.

"I cannot."

Her eyes narrowed. "You ask for my trust, but do not offer yours. When I asked of your abilities, you said naught of having the Sight, but clearly you do so. What else have you lied to me about, Rowan?"

I did not lie. When I said that, I did not have the Sight.

When I remained silent, Nerys pulled her arm from my grip. "I will leave you to your chamber," she said, apparently intent on walking me to it and leaving me locked inside. Without her presence. Not that I blamed her, but tonight, of all nights, I did not wish for her to wander the corridors alone. I was being watched, and likely she was too.

But there was no hope for it. I had nothing more to offer except the memory of one night together and a handful of kisses. So when she opened the bedchamber door, I stepped inside wordlessly. Nerys closed it behind me without looking back.

I stared at the closed door, cursing my family legacy. Cursing the Thalassari mistrust of humans. Cursing everyone and everything until realizing doing so achieved nothing.

Slipping my hand inside a hidden pocket of my tunic, I took out the missive Nerithia had given me when she handed me my meal. Unsurprised at how quickly she was able to send, and receive, a message to the Keepers, I unfolded it.

And read.

26

NERYS

It was the first time since he'd come to the palace I left its grounds without him.

After sending a meal, and message, to his chamber, I began the day training at the alcove that, in the past, had been my safe haven. But now, unless completely engrossed in water-wielding, I looked for him, wishing to find Rowan watching me from behind.

By midday, I decided to give up and return, guilt at leaving him locked away gnawing at me. On the way back, it occurred to me that Rowan did not have to be locked away. I'd never given him the option, and was almost embarrassed to do so now, so many days later. By the time I changed and stood outside his chamber, my cheeks flushed with embarrassment.

If you will be queen of Thalassaria, you'd best find more courage than this.

With a few deep breaths, I touched my fingertips to my face. No longer aflame, I knocked. When he didn't respond, I knocked again.

Nothing.

Fingers fumbling with the key, I imagined all sort of scenarios, most of which ended with Rowan injured... or worse. What a fool I'd been, to crave his presence more than offer Rowan his freedom.

At the sight of him, a cloth of finely woven seaweed wrapped around his waist, I froze.

Rowan arched his brows, nodding toward the door.

"You may want to close that," he said.

So much for my cheeks. I spun back around, grateful for the excuse to hide my face, and did just that. Getting myself back under control, I faced him.

Rowan hadn't moved. His hair was wet, and he'd obviously been washing when I first knocked.

"Late to rise today?" I asked. He could not have possibly just woken.

Rowan gestured toward a chair which previously had four legs. Instead, only three remained. One lay across its seat.

"It has been many years since I practiced my skill with a wooden sword. Or, in this case, a chair leg."

The admission made me feel even worse.

"Apologies for leaving you this morn. I wanted to train and just..."

"Are upset, still. Because you believe I lied to you?"

"You did lie to me, Rowan."

"I told you, there were things I cannot share—"

"You having the Sight being one of them?" His bare chest was beyond distracting.

"I do not have the Sight. Not in the way you are thinking."

"Semantics," I accused. "Do you deny knowing Caelum was looking for me? Or that you sensed, or saw, where the spy was hidden?"

"No. I do not deny it." Rowan looked up, toward the ceiling, expelled a breath, and then re-focused on me. "When I came here, I had no ability beyond that which I told you about. The others... have developed since."

That made little sense. "You developed the Sight since coming to Thalassaria?"

"What humans define as the Sight is different than what I've been experiencing. Having said as much... I am already breaking a sacred vow."

"A vow to whom?"

"My fam— my people."

"I've not heard of an Elydor-born human developing such an ability."

Once again, we were at an impasse.

"It occurs to me," I said finally, "that I should have offered you an opportunity to leave. To not be locked away and to have your sword returned to you."

"By leaving the palace until the Festival of Tides?" He'd considered as much already. "I'd considered it when Queen Lirael denied, or rather delayed, my answer."

"So why did you not?"

Crossing his arms, much like Marek might, Rowan waited for me to work out that answer myself. Instead of acknowledging that he chose to remain here, locked away, in order to be with me, I flung an accusation instead.

"You've been too often with Marek, I think."

He laughed and uncrossed his arms. "You may be right. I broke my fast with him."

"You did?"

Rowan nodded. "He came here, looking for you. I told him you'd sent me a meal and failed to retrieve me this morn. Which pleased me very little, given what occurred last eve."

Twisting my fingers, I dropped a silencing mist.

"Did you tell Marek?"

Rowan waved a hand through the air, collecting a bit of its moisture. "I did. He left to find Caelum and apprise him of the situation. We also spoke about the possibility of you staying with Aneri until the festival."

When the topic arose at her house, I had dismissed it, wishing to remain here in order to learn as much as possible of her intentions. "If we both leave now—"

"You should go. I will remain, to listen and observe."

I shook my head. "You will be given a new escort."

"Perhaps one that will reveal something to me. I like it not, you sleeping under the same roof as the queen."

Caelum and Marek had said the same, and though I didn't disagree, the thought of being separated from Rowan, even given what he said at The Moonlit Current...

He was beside me before I could respond. Rowan was like that, able to move like a shadow. Sometimes, I swore he must be part Aetherian. One finger lifted up my chin.

"You have a duty to Thalassaria, one I fear may be in jeopardy if you are to remain here. I don't trust the queen and am not free to help defend you. Take Marek up on his offer and go to Aneri's with him. It will be safer."

There was simply no other way to say it.

"I will miss you."

Rowan leaned in, kissing my lips so very softly. Reverently.

"I will miss you too."

I thought of another reason to stay. "I don't know who they will assign to you. It will likely be one of the queen's spies. Without protection, you—"

"I will be fine, Nerys. She will not have me murdered, if for no other reason than doing so would start a war with Aetheria."

"She could claim it an accident."

"Against which I've made safeguards. Ones in place before I stepped foot in the palace."

"But... you did not know she was a threat then? Even now, I do not believe the queen capable of murder."

Was Rowan even aware that, as he spoke, he'd taken both my hands in his and was rubbing his thumbs in circles along my palms?

"Nay? It was you who told me of Caelum. Surely, he is not the only one the queen thought to sacrifice for the greater good of Thalassaria."

He was right, of course. I just refused to believe someone capable of such a thing.

"If she sends a spy, even better." Rowan's eyes, now full of mischief, held my own. "I know something of spies and how they operate."

My mouth fell open. "You do? Who do you spy for?"

"I've told you more than I should have, against my best judgment, so that you will be safe. For there is nothing, not even the Tidal Pearl, I care more about than that."

I searched for the truth of his words in Rowan's gaze and found it easily.

Gaining the Tidal Pearl meant he could help the king and princess open the Aetherian Gate. It meant reuniting his people with their families. Nothing could be more important to a human spy, his network unknown but Rowan's purpose one he'd already admitted to.

Except he said that I was more important than all of that, and I believed him.

I wish you had my ability to sense emotion and could feel mine too.

He'd felt my love for him, and in saying as much, wanted me to feel his too. If I wasn't experiencing as much myself, I'd not believe anything he said to me. How could we have gone so quickly from being strangers to considering risking all for love?

But it was possible. I knew as much, because at this moment, if he asked me, I'd give up everything to be with him. And yet his admission still lay between us. We could not be together, and I did have a destiny to fill.

"I will stay with Aneri."

"Good," he said, standing back. "It's best you go now before I'm tempted to kiss you again. And this time, I won't stop with just a kiss."

"You look like this"—I waved my arm up and down, gesturing to his bare arms and chest, Rowan's tousled, wet hair begging to be touched—"and say as much?"

Rowan's eyes darkened. In a heartbeat, I would not be leaving. Or going to Aneri's with Marek. Which would be fine, except... my chest ached already with the memory of one night.

"I'm going," I said with a step backwards.

He didn't stop me. But he wanted to.

Another step.

Rowan's jaw clenched, as if forcing himself not to speak.

I would make it easier for him, and for myself too. Without another word, I turned and hastened from his chamber as if a sea demon were chasing me.

Nay, not a sea demon.

The knowledge that I was walking away from the man I loved.

27

ROWAN

It had been three days since Nerys walked out of my chamber. Three days of not hearing her voice. Seeing her smile. Finding ways to touch her or kiss her.

Three days of torture.

Making matters worse, my new escort, undoubtedly a spy for the queen, refused to bring me to the Deep Archives as Nerithia's note suggested I do. I'd asked the stern-faced guard who had informed me that first day he "had other duties to attend to." I'd also tried to get a message to Caelum, but thus far, I hadn't seen or heard from him. On the rare occasion my guard deemed me worthy to take a meal outside my chamber, I listened and watched, though my restricted movements uncovered little.

I'd considered requesting an audience with the queen, but since she'd made her presence scarce, and as far as I knew was leaving Nerys alone, I thought it best to leave it alone. I had had only one vision: yesterday as I returned to my chamber after the evening meal, but it was not of Thalassaria. At first, I thought the vision was of Kael, but when the man raised his head, speaking to someone, I realized it was his twin, Terran. The someone was his father, and the two argued. When Terran turned and walked away, the King of Gyoria called his son back, but Terran did not reply. Instead, he slammed the door on what appeared to be a throne room.

My grandfather had told his protégés, including me, that over time, it was possible to sense when the visions might take place. He said it was a feeling, one he could not teach but that The Keeper would need to learn to recognize. Thus far, I could not determine if my visions were of that very day or years into the future, making one such as an argument between the King of Gyoria and his successor less useful.

I stretched my legs out on the bed, prepared for sleep but unable to let it take me. Instead, I considered the note from Nerithia, one that was short but clear.

Go to the Deep Archives. Find Seren.

Having promised Nerys to remain in the palace to learn what I could of the queen's intentions, I had no choice but to rely on a guard who clearly disliked me at best, and who was actively working against Nerys at worst. Getting to the Deep Archives any time soon was seemingly less possible each day.

A knock on the door, at this hour, surprised me. I was even more surprised to see it open with Marek slipping inside.

"Has something happened?" I asked, every part of me suddenly prepared for battle.

"More than one something, but Nerys is fine," Marek said. "Caelum is with her." His eyes narrowed knowingly. "Humans and immortals rarely partner well together."

I could deny the thought had crossed my mind, but the denial would be hollow. I could hear the panic in my own voice, and undoubtedly Marek did as well.

"No," I agreed. "They do not."

Seemingly satisfied with my concurrence, he asked, "Caelum said you need to get to the Deep Archives?"

I was surprised the guard had told him. "He received my message?"

"He did, and would have come himself." Marek grinned. "But knows I can get you there unseen. Let's go."

"Now?"

"Would you prefer I come back in the morn for your new escort to discover you missing?"

This would not work. "I need to... speak with someone there. Breaking into the Deep Archives will do me little good at this time of night."

Marek crossed his arms. "Who said we were breaking in? And who do you need to speak with? I assumed this related to Nerys?"

As much as I wished to follow Nerithia's instructions, I couldn't lie to Marek any more than I had already. "It does not."

If he was suspicious before, Marek was even more so now. "You won't tell me the reason you wish to go there? Or who you must speak to?"

I thought quickly, weighing my options. This was likely the only opportunity, at least until after the festival, for me to get there. And while I could not tell Marek the reason, if there was any chance I could find this Seren, it was with him.

Give something to get something.

It was one of the first things I learned, being a human spy among immortals and finding myself in situations such as these.

"The mist?"

With a reluctant flick of his hand, as effortless as Nerys, Marek filled my chamber with a silencing mist. I waited for it to settle.

"Though it doesn't relate directly to Nerys, getting there may be important in helping us to open the Gate." If I had any other choice, I wouldn't continue. But fully trusting Marek was not a luxury I could afford. "In addition to the Tidal Pearl, both the Wind Crystal and Stone of Mor'Vallis are needed. As we stand here, there is an attempt to recover both from King Balthor. I don't know if speaking to this Seren will help achieve that goal, but it's possible, and I intend to capitalize on any possibility to help the king and princess of Aetheria reunite Elydor with the human realm once again."

During my speech, Marek leaned against the door as casually as if he had all the time in the world, his sharp eyes betraying an alertness that made it clear he missed nothing.

"It is Nerys's wish, as it is mine and all humans'," I continued, "to see the Gate reopened. Our contributions to Elydor are everywhere, and the cruelty of cutting ties with families who've waited nearly thirty years to be reunited, something I seek to rectify."

"I also believe it should be reopened. As do all who recognize the value of humans. But your timing sucks. I also fail to see how finding this... Seren... will help achieve such a goal."

My shoulders fell. "So you've not heard of her? Or him?"

Marek's lopsided grin was my answer. "Her. I'll admit to not spending much time at the Archives. Or reading any books, for that matter. But I know of Seren."

That, I believed.

"Get dressed."

He was taking me, and I wouldn't waste the opportunity.

It was only after we slipped from my chamber, through empty corridors and secret pathways which spilled onto the beach, that we spoke again.

"A secret entrance?"

"One few know of and ever fewer use. Be careful where you step."

We made our way around a rocky outcropping. The shore was nestled between towering cliffs with foliage spilling over its edges, creating a canopy of green that obscured the view from above. Hidden in a cove, a sleek and compact vessel. *Tidechaser*.

Wading through shallow waters, Marek approached the ship, reaching for a thick, weathered rope. He pulled it, revealing a small, retractable gangplank that extended from *Tidechaser's* side.

Climbing aboard, I took in the ship's polished wooden hull and its gleaming deep mahogany, reinforced with riveted steel accents along the bow and stern. The single mast carried a striking sail of midnight blue, emblazoned with the crest of Thalassaria: a swirling wave encircling a crescent moon.

"Do you need that?" I asked as we pushed off, pointing to the ship's sail.

"No," Marek said, placing his hands on the helm, fingers splayed against the wood. Something passed from him into the ship itself as the faintest hum beneath my feet made it feel as though the vessel had come alive.

The water around us began to churn, *Tidechaser* gliding forward smoothly, the sail slack despite our steady movement.

"I can guide her with the currents," Marek explained. "But the sail keeps up appearances. No one questions a ship traveling with the wind, especially near Estmere's shores."

I watched, fascinated, as the tide shifted beneath us, subtle swells forming to cradle *Tidechaser* and propel her forward. "You're not steering the ship," I said. "You're steering the sea."

Marek smirked, his gaze fixed ahead. "You're catching on."

I'd seen remarkable feats during my lifetime. Land split open, the strength of a Gyorian unmatched. The whispers of those Aetherians who could manipulate sound waves to speak over long distances always amazed me. But having spent more time in Thalassaria on this mission than any other time in my short life, it was with them I felt the most kinship. It was their abilities that, to me, were the most awe-inspiring. The ability to control an ocean. What could be more powerful than that?

I glanced at Marek, at ease in his position, clearly enjoying every moment, this trip to the Deep Archives one he could likely do with his eyes closed.

He winked at me, a gesture of comradeship. Of acceptance.

What was more powerful than control of the tides? The bond between two people, whether it be friendship or something more. That was the true life force, one I'd been willing to forgo for the sake of duty to the Harrow legacy.

But that was before coming here. The thought of leaving this place? Leaving Nerys?

I closed my eyes, willing my mind to quiet...

Willing my heart to forget.

28

NERYS

"It isn't necessary to stay here, dear," Aneri said to Caelum. "She can defend herself, if it comes to that. Though I do not believe the queen would be so bold as that."

I'd been about to climb up the stairs to bed. Taking a few steps back down, I waited for Caelum's predictable answer. Marek had refused to leave us, and I knew Caelum would too.

"Although I agree, it is a fact word is spreading. That Nerys will challenge her is no longer a secret."

Another fact. Yesterday, when I left for the cove to train, I was inundated with inquiries. Enough that I'd had to turn back, not willing to lead anyone to my private spot at the palace. Instead, I spoke with everyone who stopped me. And though I never confirmed it, neither did I deny my challenge, replying with things like, "I look forward to seeing you at the festival." At times, Marek, who refused to leave my side, had to step in and use his gilded tongue to say everything, and nothing, all at once.

"In addition," Caelum added, clearly reluctant, "I am not convinced that the queen hasn't already begun to send warnings her way."

I came down from the stairs completely. "What do you mean?"

Aneri and I both waited but Caelum simply frowned.

"Caelum?" I prompted.

He sighed. "There was an incident in the village yesterday," he said, folding his arms. "A young woman—some claim bore a striking resemblance to you—was found near the square. She had been hit with a whip of water. Though she wasn't grievously harmed, it did leave a mark on her arm. When she woke, she had no memory of what happened, but..."

"But what?" Aneri asked, her tone sharp.

"She didn't see her attacker, only felt the whip and fell to her knees. A voice whispered, 'Know your place,' but she did not see where it came from."

My hands clenched at my sides. "Why did no one tell me?"

"I can't speak for Marek, but I didn't want to cause you, or Aneri, any alarm."

"Caelum—"

Aneri cut me off. "We are both aware of such threats. Who is the girl? I will tend to her."

I barely listened, instead imagining a young one being injured on account of me. I honestly had not believed the queen would go to such lengths. If her antics were discovered, they would be frowned upon. Challenges were meant to be a natural part of our clan's system of rule. Undermining it would not be received well by the majority of Thalassarians.

"Will be back by morn from the Deep Archives," Caelum was saying.

My head snapped up.

"Marek is at the Deep Archives? At this hour?"

For the second time that night, Caelum appeared more

sheepish than usual. Than ever, actually. It was not his typical modus operandi.

"He is escorting Rowan there."

Rowan.

I'd attempted to put him from my thoughts, to concentrate on my training and the upcoming challenge, but my attempts were futile.

"Why is Marek escorting Rowan to the Deep Archives at night?"

Caelum shrugged. "I know only he requested to be taken there and the request made its way to me. Marek offered to smuggle him from the palace instead so as not to draw suspicion."

Unbelievable. "Smuggle him from the palace? At night? Is that not *more* suspicious?"

"Not if they aren't caught. And they won't be. It's Marek."

Marek and my human spy. But I didn't say that out loud. Instead, I marched toward the door. "I will return, Aneri—no need to wait up."

And before anyone could stop me, I whipped the door open and strode outside. I was fairly certain I heard Aneri chuckle, but Caelum was doing anything but when he caught up with me.

"You cannot think to go there now?"

"I am not thinking of it," I said, not stopping, "but actually making it happen. I want to know why Rowan requested to be taken there and why Marek thought it wise to smuggle him from the palace as a way to not draw suspicion."

"Nerys." Caelum grabbed my arm. "Stop. Please."

It was the kind of tone my father would use. Sometimes, I forgot how close the two were, but other times, I was easily reminded of it. Times like right now.

He looked at me with a mixture of admiration and concern.

"Did you not hear what I told you earlier? That attack was either meant for you or meant as a warning for you. Queen Lirael is now quietly accepting your challenge."

"I heard you," I said, Caelum's hand dropping. "And will admit my surprise at her stance and cunning. But I will not cower and hide, now or ever. It is Lirael's desire to hide herself in the palace. For Thalassaria to tighten its borders. Not mine."

He may not be pleased, but neither would Caelum stop me. "Will you at least have an escort when you are not cowering or hiding?"

"I have you, do I not?"

"You do. And Marek. And if you'll have him, the human too."

I'd begun to walk toward the canal but stopped again at that.

"What do you mean?"

Caelum looked at me as if I were a young one. "He is in love with you, Nerys."

My eyes widened. "Did he tell you that?"

"I have been alive for centuries, Nerys. And do not need to be told when a man is in love with a woman."

So he didn't tell Caelum he loved me. Of course he didn't. Why would he?

"He is a human."

"So?"

"So?" I cocked my head to the side, incredulous.

Caelum simply looked at me, waiting.

"You, of all Elydorians, should know the implications of partnering with a human." No more needed to be said. Though it happened many, many years ago, when Caelum's father took his own life, the grief of living without his mother too great, it was a shock to all.

Except Caelum.

His father was never the same, and in some ways, Caelum

once admitted to me, it was a blessing not to see his father suffer any longer.

"My father had scars that ran deeper than most, many unrelated to my mother," he said quietly. "Heartbreak is both tragic and inevitable, but avoiding love for the sake of protecting yourself is not the answer. Though I do not disagree; partnering with a human, for an immortal, is not an easy path. Especially if that immortal is destined to become queen."

Biting back tears, I blurted, "But why a human? *Why* do I have to love a human?"

"The question itself assumes love is logical, and you know it is not. Why Rowan?" He shrugged. "He is an honorable man with the same beliefs as you. He embodies qualities you admire: adaptability, optimism. And I do not believe it hurts that he is charming and pleasing to the eye," Caelum teased. "You could have chosen a worse man to love. Like Marek."

"Goddess forbid such a thing."

But he was right. Rowan was all of those things, and more. It had been as easy to fall in love with him as it had been, when I finally got out of my own way, to decide to challenge Lirael. Unfortunately, the consequences of both were far-reaching.

"Come," he said as we continued toward the canal. "If I cannot convince you to remain in the safety of Aneri's home, at least let us be done with this quest."

Changing topics, I asked Caelum about the Tidal Veil Marek had used on Aneri's house. "Do you believe Marek's Veil will work, if needed? I'll admit I thought him being overly cautious to perform it, but after that horrific attack..." I let my voice trail.

"I've no reason to believe it will not work. With luck, it is an unnecessary precaution."

Few knew of the Tidal Veil, and even fewer could perform it. I'd never even come across the protection in my studies in the

Deep Archives. When Marek suggested it, both Caelum and I were taken aback. Where had he learned such a skill? Why was it not well known?

There were parts of Marek's life he didn't reveal, even to me. And this particular ability to transform the nearly invisible mist into a raging torrent, trapping potential intruders in a sphere of water until they retreat, was apparently one of those hidden talents.

We spoke of Marek and his sometimes-mysterious nature, and of what the coming days might bring, as Caelum and I traveled by canal toward Ventara. Finally, as we stood at the massive, intricately carved door serving as the Archive's entrance, its runes glowing faintly, I wondered how Marek and Rowan planned to enter this place. Few knew the magic required to open this door, and it was only after years of studying here that I was entrusted with such knowledge.

Summing a small stream of water from a nearby fountain and watching as it spiraled on my open palm, I allowed it to stream gently into the door's runes, watching as each glowed bright blue. It had always reminded me of the runes on the Gate, when someone was entering through from the human realm, as if the same magic was used to create both.

It was not the first time Caelum had seen me perform this ritual, but his eyes widened nonetheless. It was a tricky bit of magic, and one I was proud to have mastered knowing only those who worked in the Deep Archives, along with a few others including myself and Thalon, had been granted such knowledge.

Finally, the door clicked.

Caelum pushed it open.

29

ROWAN

"It feels as if we are descending into the pits of hell."

"Humans," Marek muttered on the steps below him. "I'd have been down there by now if not for those feet of yours."

"I'll have you remember, you have feet too."

"True. But I also have the ability to summon enough water to ride down these steps. And up, too. Although that takes more skill." Marek turned to look up to me. Grinning, he added, "Skill I have, of course."

"Of course," I said with an eye roll for his benefit. "I'm guessing I have to walk back up?"

"Only way in and out, unfortunately."

"Why steps? I assume only Thalassarians, as a general rule, come down here?"

"One of the Deep Archives' many mysteries."

And just like that, Marek disappeared. A few seconds later, I joined him.

"Not the pits of hell. Below the sea's surface."

It was unlike anything I'd ever seen before. Even the

Aetherian capital of Aethralis, built among the mountains so high they reached the clouds, was not as impressive.

Walls and pillars, seemingly carved from flowing water, its blue, glowing light reminding me of the Garden of Luminous Tides. Above us, light mimicked sunlight peeking through the water. Surely, we'd not walked to a space at the bottom of the sea, but that was precisely how it appeared. There was no sound besides the gentle one of trickling water, occasionally punctuated by the echoes of splashes and distant waves.

"This place is..." I had no words to describe it.

"Only problem," Marek said, striding ahead and clearly less impressed than me. "Too many books."

As we moved forward, rows and rows of books and scrolls, encased in shimmering, protective bubbles of water, were tucked into niches in the walls. I couldn't imagine where one would start reading or how you went about finding what you needed.

More importantly, how would we find Seren? Marek admitted to never spending much time here, and though I was impressed that he was able to break in using some crystal and who knew what black magic he'd conjured, I wasn't convinced we'd get much further without some guidance.

Look down.

It was the same feeling that came over me with my visions, but instead, this was a voice. One my grandfather had not prepared us for. To my knowledge, he saw things but did not hear them. On the other hand, he often said The Keeper of each generation possessed unique skills the others did not.

When I looked down, a faint, blue line appeared. Marek, ahead of me again, didn't seem to notice. But when he took a left turn, I stopped him, pointing down. The line continued straight.

"What in the Tides is that?"

"I'm not certain," I admitted. "But maybe some sort of guidance?"

I caught up with him, Marek on high alert now. He took in our surroundings, and then apparently deciding the line wasn't a threat in any way, began to follow it. We passed row after row of "shelves," periodically punctuated by some sort of small, reflective pools. When the line suddenly stopped at a wall, Marek and I looked at each other.

"That worked well," he said, Marek's voice laced with sarcasm.

When the water that made up the wall suddenly fell to a trickle, revealing an inner chamber that looked suspiciously familiar, I smiled, triumphant.

"Aye, it did."

We stepped forward, but a voice stopped us.

"The human only."

Where had that come from? One second, the chamber was empty. The next, a figure rose from the pool of water at its center. A woman. A vaelith. She was as old as anyone in Elydor by the looks of her. At the same time, she moved with the ease and grace of a younger Thalassari. Her clothing dripped with a wetness that, with one swoop of her hand, disappeared.

Her bright-blue eyes narrowed.

"Marek. You are not ready."

"Ready for what?"

In response, she shooed him backwards. "He will rejoin you shortly. Someone comes who you must attend to."

"What do you mean, someone—"

The sound of voices carried to us then, but apparently, Marek had stepped back far enough that I wouldn't find out who the voices belonged to. The wall of water that had hidden this chamber was now firmly again in place.

"Sir Rowan of Estmere, I presume?"

Bowing to her, I said, "Indeed. Do I have the pleasure of speaking to Seren?"

When I stood, she was watching me closely.

"Good guess, my human friend. Nerithia tells me you wish to send a message back to Estmere. Is it true? You are The Keeper?"

Nerithia betrayed me.

"What do you know of The Keeper?" I asked, hoping to minimize the damage Nerithia may have wrought. Throughout our history, each time a non-Harrow family member learned of our secret, someone paid the price. Now, because of me—

"I know quite a bit. More than you, I would venture."

"Impossible," I blurted before thinking.

The wrinkles on the edges of Seren's eyes deepened as she smiled. "All things are possible. Sometimes, we simply do not like the cost of making them so."

I tried again. "Only Keepers know of The Keeper, and you are..."

Her smile deepened. Seren was one step away from laughing at me now, as if she had a secret more far-reaching than any of my own.

Nerithia was half-human, a long-lost member of our network. But Seren could not be the same. Those with human blood may gain some measure of immortality, demi-mortal as it was termed, but they did not live for more than a thousand years. And there was no doubt Seren was vaelith. If she were, my grandfather would know of her. Would have told me of her presence here. Unlike Nerithia, whom he did not know existed.

"Have you worked it out yet? Or have you forgotten your abilities?"

Of course. I had, in fact, forgotten them temporarily. Opening my senses to her, I was immediately flooded with one pervading emotion.

Hope.

But it did little to solve the puzzle Seren presented.

"I—"

"*All* of your abilities."

Still unaccustomed to the new ones, and uncertain if I could do again what I accomplished in the palace corridor, I nevertheless attempted to clear my mind. To accept what was offered. At first, nothing happened. But then I saw it. A glimmer of light, brighter than the others, from above. I looked up, watched as it moved and swirled through the water, taking shape. It was a child, a young one as the Elydorians would call her. Long, flowing hair, but no face that I could recognize. She was sitting, cross-legged on the ground, reading a book. A man came to her, scooped her up, and the girl laughed, dropping her book. A woman joined them, one as sea-born as they came. A Thalassari. But the man? His hair and skin were dark. His tunic bore the crest of...

The vision disappeared.

"What did you see?"

"There was something... different about this one," I said, realizing Seren could not, should not, know of my visions. But she did.

"Describe the difference."

"I cannot... you are not—"

"The winds remember the first crossing, and the stone keeps their weight. Now, describe it."

She was a Keeper. And yet, could not be so. But I found myself wanting to tell her.

"A light around it, as if the vision glowed. Or perhaps not a glow, precisely: an aurora."

"Of past memories."

I blinked. "That is not..." I wanted to say "possible," but she would only chastise me again. "I heard a voice," I said. "Instead of a vision. Telling me to look down. I thought that was my unique ability but... nothing makes sense."

Seren sighed. "I would tell you all, but there is a reason for you to work it out yourself. The same reason your grandfather did not tell you of me."

My eyes widened. "He knew of you?"

A reason for me to work it out myself.

That was the least difficult of her riddles. The Keepers valued discernment.

The same reason your grandfather did not tell you of me.

He knew a Keeper, a vaelith, resided in Thalassaria, but said nothing of her. He wanted me to find her myself. In doing so, I was fulfilling a prophecy. Not as The Keeper, but a Keeper. Sharpening my mind, my skills. Would he have told me if he knew I would become his successor? Likely. But the chances of it, with so many others in our network...

I digressed.

He knew. And she knew the code, which means she was a Keeper despite the fact that no human survived as long as she had. That made little sense, but was nonetheless true. And it was also true that I had heard a voice, and that vision was different than the others. Could more than one unique ability manifest in me? It seemed to be so.

"You are a Keeper," I said. "So half-human, and yet are more than demi-immortal. Which is only one of the puzzles before me, since I also seem to be developing more than one unique ability as my grandfather neither heard voices nor received memories of the past."

"Both of your presumptions are correct. What did you see?" she asked again.

"A young girl," I said. "You?"

She waited for me to continue.

"Sitting on the ground, reading. A man, human I believe, picked her up. Picked you up." It was Seren in my vision. A human father and a Thalassari mother. "And your mother was there too."

"My mother was a Thalassari scholar. She spent her days in here, the Deep Archives holding her life's work. She'd been, as so many before her, drawn to human ingenuity. Of course, she never imagined meeting one, as the Gate had not yet been opened. When it did, many years later, and my father, a human explorer, found his way to Thalassaria, they were drawn to each other, partnering a short time after he arrived. The scene you witnessed was one of many from my childhood, here among these archives."

"A Thalassari and a human. Back then, it must have been—"

"Quite scandalous, to be certain. But since my mother spent much of her time here, believing the Deep Archives held answers about her and my father's place in both worlds, it did not bother her. I was born of their union, and from the start, could sense the Archives' magic in a way no one else could, even my mother."

"Your father was a Harrow," I said, knowing he had to be for Seren to be a Keeper. She watched me, as if expecting more. What more could there be? Unless... "Impossible."

"I really must insist you stop using that word."

"Richard Harrow lived in Aetheria for much of his life, before Estmere existed."

"Not Richard," she said of the first human to enter the Gate. The first Keeper. "His son, of which he had three."

"One of which became the second Keeper. The others founded Estmere."

"My uncles did indeed, with the help of King Galfrid, of course."

My uncles.

"Your father was Caius Harrow."

She smiled.

"The history books say little of the second Keeper."

"For good reason. He lived here, and as you can see, we are quite secluded."

"But The Keeper... lives in Estmere. Among his, or her, people."

"Not always."

Heart racing, I waited for her to continue.

"The original role of The Keeper, known then as the First Harrow and the Second Harrow, and so on, was to keep the knowledge of the Gate, of The Crooked Key. And later, of the visions that were unique to one in each generation. But what are visions if humans are not fully accepted as Elydorians? That was my uncle's role, and the role of each of the Keepers that succeeded him."

My mind raced. "The voice I heard, was that yours?"

"Not in the way you are thinking. Over time, my bond with the Archives deepened." She looked around us, my gaze following hers. "I am its guardian, and in turn, its waters sustain me. I knew when you entered, knew immediately you would fulfill the prophecy. The reason, I believe, is that the Archives' magic sustains me."

She was vaelith because of her connection to this place. I'd never heard of something like it before. Elydor's magic never ceased to amaze me. But that still didn't explain the voice.

"Prophecy?" I asked, just realizing fully what she'd said.

"One I discovered centuries ago, hidden among the scrolls that have taken my lifetime to read. How did you find me?"

Her abrupt change of topic startled me. "I... A voice told me to look down. When I did, a glowing line led to you."

"The Archives aid those whose intentions are pure, though not usually in such a way. But you are The Keeper, so it does not surprise me you were led directly here. As to the prophecy... when King Balthor closed the Aetherian Gate, I searched for clues on how to reopen it. Beyond a connection to the original artifacts each clan was gifted to enhance their leader's abilities, I was unable to discover anything of more use to King Galfrid. However, like you, I was led to an ancient text. In it, a long-lost prophecy that would have meant little to me before. 'When the bridge falters and the realms fracture, a child of two paths will guide The Keeper to their destiny.' For the first time, I understood why I'd been kept alive these many years."

A child of two paths. Seren.

"What does it mean? What is my destiny?"

The hope that swelled within me was immediately dashed at Seren's expression. If she were to guide me, to restore the Gate between this world and the one of my ancestors, Seren did not know how. She was as confused as me.

"Perhaps you can tell me why you are here?"

I told Seren of my mission. Of visiting The Moonlit Current and meeting Nerithia and returning to receive her message. I told her of Nerys's plan, and as I spoke, her cool eyes seemed to warm. Opening myself to her, I felt hope, but also understanding. She'd put the puzzle pieces together, I was sure of it.

"Does it make sense to you now?" I asked. "Do you know my destiny?"

"I do," she said with a sigh that felt, to me, a long time in coming. "Sometimes, we fight what we know to be true because it is not the path we expected. Accept what is, be where your feet are, and you'll find peace, Sir Rowan of Estmere. And with luck, I will too."

30

NERYS

"She kicked me out."

Marek jumped back, narrowly avoiding being soaked, although it would only have been a temporary condition. Evaporation was advanced water-wielding, but Marek could do it as easily as me.

"Seren has little patience for those who dislike books and reading. She knows you well. Is Rowan with her?"

"He is. Guess your human likes books."

"You had no troubles at the palace?" Caelum asked.

Marek looked at him as if Caelum were a young one. "Have I ever had difficulty smug— transporting someone, or something, without being detected?"

I rolled my eyes. "I know about your smuggling, Marek, and am not certain who you believe you're deceiving."

He cleared his throat. "As the future queen of Thalassaria, it's best you know as little as possible."

I opened my mouth to argue, but thought better of it. Perhaps he was right.

"How did you get inside here?" I'd half-expected to find

Marek and Rowan on the Archives' doorstep, knowing full well he was not granted right of entry.

"Interesting story about that. I traded a moonstone shard with... a questionable character in Gyoria. He..." Marek stopped. "It occurs to me, it's best you not know that story either."

"When Nerys becomes queen," Caelum said, laughter in his voice, "how will the two of you converse?"

"I have a very legitimate business as Navarch we can discuss."

"At present, I'd like to discuss the reason you took Rowan here in the middle of the night."

"He asked."

"To be smuggled out of the palace?"

Marek winced. "Not precisely. But if he will remain there as your spy, how else do you propose to have done it?"

My spy. I wanted Rowan to be so much more than that. These past few days without him confirmed what I already knew: that he had quickly become an important part of my life.

Ignoring Marek's question, I half-listened as he and Caelum argued over the best route to smuggle Rowan back into the palace. While they did, I looked at the water wall in front of us, trying to imagine what brought Rowan to Seren. She let so few inside her private chambers... How he and Marek found it, why she allowed him inside, were just two questions I had among many.

While we waited, I wandered to a nearby shelf, looking up to one particular bubble which held a text Seren had pointed out herself to me. I had forgotten about it until now, though I wasn't sure why it caught my attention again. Perhaps it was the faint hum of its magic, or maybe the lingering memory of Seren's cryptic words when she first mentioned it. "One day," she'd said with that infuriating smile of hers. I resisted the urge to poke the bubble, if only because I could hear her scolding me in my head.

"Rowan can tell you what is inside that text, but I am not certain he will. Yet."

I spun around at my mentor's words. Seren and Rowan stood at the entrance of her chamber, one I hadn't even heard open, watching me.

What did her words mean?

I wanted nothing more than to run to him. For Rowan to put his arms around me, holding me close, telling me he missed me these past few days. To ask why he was here, why Seren accepted him. What she meant by, "I'm not certain he will." Instead, I simply stared. And waited.

"We should go," was all he said.

"Come," Seren said in that comforting way she always spoke, as if she was one step in the afterlife, a calming peace always surrounding her. As Rowan moved toward the others, I listened, resisting an urge to reach out my hand as we passed.

Cupping my face, as if a grandmother might, she looked into my eyes. "Trust him. And yourself."

"Why—"

"The next we meet, you will be my queen. I've no doubt of it, Nerys. And neither shall you. Now go before they discover him missing. He is more valuable to your cause, especially now in these precarious days before the festival, than you realize."

I didn't question how Seren knew so much. It was as if she had the human Sight, her wisdom endless. My mother had respected her above all others in Thalassaria, and for that reason, I never questioned her and would not begin doing so today.

When I nodded, Seren dropped her hands and smiled. As she leaned toward me, as if to tell me a secret, Seren whispered, "I never told you. Or anyone. Not because I was ashamed that my father was human, but because some truths lose their power when they're shared too freely."

"You are..." I swallowed, unable to comprehend Seren's words fully. How could she be? "You are half-human?" I whispered.

"Rowan will, I have no doubt, eventually explain. Now go, and do not be a stranger to these archives, even when you are queen."

She was so certain of the outcome.

I listened, not because I had no more questions, or even because I wanted to leave the Deep Archives. I listened because I knew Seren would not reveal more than she had already. And because we did need to get Rowan back.

As it became apparent the others had no idea where to turn, I stepped into the lead, Rowan walking alongside me.

"I have questions," I said, looking to see if he'd changed in three days. He hadn't, of course.

"I wish I could provide answers."

"But you cannot?"

"Not yet."

What could I say? That his lack of trust in me was disappointing on a level I couldn't put into words? How could Seren say to "trust him," somehow knowing he would tell me nothing?

Rowan will, I have no doubt, eventually explain.

Eventually. How was that even possible when he would be leaving soon? In the meantime, there was no use pressing him. Rowan had no intention of telling me why he was here, what he spoke to Seren about... or any of it.

"I've heard you do not care for your new escort?"

Rowan made a sound of disgust. "'Care for' is putting it mildly."

We walked well ahead of the others now. Far enough ahead that I could be honest.

"I wish you could tell me more, but even though you do not... even though you don't trust me with your truth, I have missed you."

"Nerys." His smile faltered. "I do trust you. Surely you know as much."

There was a part of me that believed him, despite myself.

"I've missed you too. Very much. And worry for your safety."

I turned back to the others. "Go straight until you see a reflective pool on your right. Turn left and the stairs will be in front of you at the end of that corridor. We will catch you outside."

Marek grinned. "Enjoy escorting him up the stairs." As they passed us, Marek slapped Rowan on the back good-naturedly and all but skipped ahead of us, not even noticing the look Caelum gave him.

We watched them walk straight ahead, eventually turning the corner. When they did, I was pulled into Rowan without preamble. His lips covered mine as Rowan's arms wrapped around him the exact way I'd envisioned. I held onto him, not caring about his secrets. Or about anything other than the way his tongue caressed mine. The way his hands moved effortlessly down to my waist and then upwards, cupping both breasts. I'm certain it was meant to be a quick kiss, but instead, as I released a small groan of pleasure, Rowan increased the pressure of his kiss.

When his hands moved lower, one of them slipped toward the delicate strands of braided rope that served as my belt. Loosening it, his hand dipped beneath the waistband of my fitted trousers until they found their mark. When his finger found my entrance, I groaned again, my eyes popping open as I pulled my lips from his.

"Each night when you lay in bed, without me, think of my hands this way," he said, his gaze intent. "Think of my fingers slipping into you, the wetness they find pleasing me more than you can imagine. I want you to think of this." Two fingers curled around me as they moved, in and out. "How it feels to know there is someone out there who lives to bring you pleasure. Who will champion you, love you, until his dying breath."

Did he just say... I had no time to dwell on it. Rowan's mouth remained open, mimicking my own, as he caressed me. As he moved his fingers more quickly, the pace was one of perfection. I wanted to respond, but could not.

"Come for me, Nerys. Say my name as you explode for me, as your legs buckle and I hold you up with my hand."

"Rowan." I could not hold on much longer. His words, his expression, the way he moved himself inside me. Already, I was so close.

Who will champion you, love you, until his dying breath.

This from the same Rowan who said we could not be. I didn't understand, but at this moment, I didn't want to think of the future. Only the here and now.

"Rowan," I repeated. "You said..."

He moved them just the right way. Smiling, Rowan leaned into my ear. "That's it. Come for me, Nerys. Come all over my fingers."

That's all it took. I did, and just as he promised, struggled to stand as my knees buckled. He held me up, the sounds Rowan made at the back of his throat doing nothing to help me find my footing.

I hardly noticed he pulled his hands away, but I did notice when he kissed me, hard. Kissing him back, I thought of his words. Of how he'd made me feel. Though I wished we could go on kissing forever, I thought of the others, waiting. Of the coming dawn.

Reluctantly, I pulled away, looking into his eyes.

More questions would not yield answers. Not until he was ready. When that would be, I had no notion. But I could not leave it like this.

"Will I not see you again until the festival?"

"Keeping you safe until then is the priority. If remaining at the palace might help me learn something..."

In other words, no.

"I don't understand," I admitted. "What you said... I don't understand, Rowan. Nothing makes sense."

"It will. I promise. Trust me, Nerys. Train, focus on the challenge, and trust that it will work out."

I wanted to ask if "work out" meant there was a path forward for us, but his response at the tavern still weighed on me. And there was also the matter of Rowan being human. I had Caelum's words to think about. And Aneri's guidance to offer. It was time I spoke with her on the matter as well.

"I do trust you, Rowan," I said, meaning it. "But I do not trust the queen. Not any longer. Please be careful."

"Do not worry about me. It's you she wishes to discredit."

Though part of me did not want to tell him, another part of me knew I must.

"There was an attack," I said, explaining quickly as I adjusted my belt. "They will be waiting. We really should—"

I attempted to begin walking, but Rowan was having none of it.

Grabbing my hand, he stopped me. I quickly told him of the attack, trying not to become worried at his expression. There was one word I could think of to describe it.

Murderous.

"Neither of them told me," he said, and I realized why Rowan was so angry. They didn't tell Rowan because there was little he could do to prevent it. He relied on Caelum and Marek for information. Had felt powerless since he'd come to the palace.

"I will be fine," I assured him, Rowan still looking like I'd never seen him before.

"You will," he said. "I mean to be sure of it."

31

ROWAN

Finally, my efforts began to bear fruit.

I insisted on being at every meal, to the consternation of my escort. Identifying potential allies and planting seeds of doubt about the queen's motives among the diners, I began to subtly shift the narrative, making it more difficult to discredit Nerys without ever admitting outright I knew anything about her plans. Brokering quiet alliances with those who expressed sympathies to Nerys's cause, from a discontented noble to at least one of the palace guards.

The queen thought she'd taken my weapon, and while I dearly wished to have my sword on my belt, it was not as much a loss as she might have suspected.

Two days after quietly slipping back into the palace after visiting Seren, I left a carefully folded message in the sleeve of a servant's tunic: a coded note meant for one of the discontented nobles I'd overheard at dinner. The next morn, the same servant hovered around me, clearly wanting to return a message but unable to do so. When I took his arm, thanking him for his service, it garnered more than one strange look, but also afforded him the opportunity to slip the reply back to me.

It was as I suspected. The queen had been unable to reach Nerys who, after being followed to her training spot in the cove, Caelum and Marek had convinced to remain at Aneri's until the festival. So, the queen had begun to use more manipulative tactics. Her plan, it seemed, was to spread enough rumors to discredit her before the festival. The fear and uncertainty I'd begun to feel from those at the palace meant her plan had begun to work.

"Sir Rowan." Thalon, the historian, sat across from me. I'd seen him only once since the meal with Nerys. His previously calm demeanor was noticeably absent. Opening myself to him, to the room, my suspicions were confirmed. He was nervous, rightly so if he was an ally to Nerys and not the queen, as I suspected. "These are strange times you've come to witness."

I glanced at my escort, standing with a guard and watching closely.

With the alliance of the others at our table unknown to me, I could say little.

"Strange indeed. Though I look forward to my first Festival of Tides."

"How long do you plan to stay in Thalassaria?" he asked.

It was a question I could not answer. "As long as necessary," I said, evading the question. "So tell me..."

I'd been about to ask about the festival when a burst of anger caught my attention. It drowned out all other emotions from those around me, a new sensation that could only mean this anger was important. I searched for the source. It was easy enough. A fairly young nobleman stood, two of the queen's agents next to him. None at my table paid me any attention as the movement was now the primary focus in the hall.

Tide of Waves and Secrets

A quick glance back at my escort saw him distracted by the scene.

This noble's anger was impossible to ignore. Aware of the risk, I stood and slipped away, knowing enough of the palace grounds by now, and following the man's continued rage, to find him. Thankfully, most others were at the meal, and it was easy enough to follow them to a more secluded part of the palace I'd never been in before.

Remaining in the shadows, I watched as they escorted him into a chamber. When voices came from the direction we'd just navigated, I tucked myself into the alcove, knowing my escort had likely noticed me missing by now.

I'd not have much time but needed to know why this man was so enraged.

As the voices passed, I could not see them without being discovered, but a line of vision was unnecessary. That was the queen's voice, easy enough to distinguish. Barely breathing as they moved past, I bided my time. With my luck holding out so far, there were no guards outside the door. However, it was soundproofed. I had no other option than to wait back in the shadows.

When the nobleman stormed past me, sans the guards, a short time later, I followed him. Unfortunately, he was heading back to the hall. Intercepting him before he did that was my only move. Without my dagger or sword, I had no leverage. He could as easily bring the guards down on me as not, but the chance had to be taken.

"Are you an ally to Nerys?" I said, coming up directly behind him.

The man whipped around.

"If so, come with me. And quickly."

Without waiting for him to react, I turned left with no choice but to retrace my steps with Marek. He'd not be pleased, having his secret entrance revealed, but it was that or get caught. No doubt the palace guards were already looking for me.

"I had no notion this existed," he said behind me. At least my gamble had thus far paid off. The narrow corridor we walked through twisted sharply, dim light barely illuminating the damp stone walls. The noble's hurried steps echoed unevenly behind me; his breath quickened as I pressed us forward.

We emerged into a passage so tight it felt like the walls themselves were closing in. Dust swirled around the faint beam of light filtering through a crack above, and the air carried the musty scent of disuse. "This way," I said, pressing my palm to the disguised latch Marek had shown me. The panel creaked open, revealing a spiral staircase leading into the shadows below.

By the time we emerged from the palace, my noble was thoroughly confused. He looked up, shook his head, and planted his hands on his hips. "I've been to the palace many times and had no notion that entrance existed."

Marek was going to kill me, but there was no hope for it. "Would it be too much of an inconvenience to ask it remain that way?"

"If it would not be too much of an inconvenience to ask why we are here. You are the human, Sir Rowan of Estmere?" When he stuck out his hand, our human greeting, it confirmed this man as an ally.

Shaking it, I said, "Aye. And you are?"

"Lord Gavric of Corvi."

"I've been to Corvi— a coastal trade village, is it not?"

"Known for the Pearl Market and Navigator's Guild," he said proudly. Still suspicious, though, he waited for me to explain myself. I had but one course of action here. The truth.

"I am a friend of Nerys's," I said. "And know of the queen's plans to discredit her."

His anger, still palatable, was replaced with something else, not yet fully formed. Mistrust, maybe?

"She is a friend to my clan," I explained. "And so, I would do anything possible to support her."

Mistrust turned to... curiosity.

"The queen," he faltered.

"Say it," I reassured him. "We've little time before the festival."

"The queen," he continued, clearing his throat, "attempted to persuade me to use my influence and publicly denounce her. She knows Nerys plans to challenge her, and said it was not a legitimate claim but a threat to the throne. She painted Nerys as an impetuous, misguided child too reckless to understand the consequences of her actions, let alone the fragile peace we've fought so hard to maintain."

All he said tracked with what I'd learned.

"What did you say to her?"

He frowned, his emotion shifting again to guilt. "I agreed, for fear of retribution before the festival, but I have no plans to do so. Our laws are clear, and I will not interfere with them."

"And when you do not do as she bids?"

"I will not be at the palace to learn her response."

"A good plan."

Satisfied. He was both satisfied and hopeful.

"Perhaps you should not be at the palace either. The queen will not take kindly to you having slipped away from your escort. Her fears of an assassination are well known."

"You are both lucky to have found a different sort of escort."

I'd been trained to know when someone approached, but

somehow, Marek had gone completely undetected. He was a tricky one, his emotions less evident than most.

Also, he was pissed.

"We had no choice," I said by way of explanation. "And I cannot go back, having slipped away from my escort."

He was either unconvinced I had no other option or did not care, because the look he gave me was similar to Lord Gavric when he was escorted from the hall by the queen's guards.

"Let's go."

I questioned the nobleman on the way to Marek's ship, one he very reluctantly allowed us both to board. Convinced Gavric had little else to share, and as confident as I could be that he had no plans to follow the queen's instructions, we sailed to Corvi, a courtesy, according to Marek, for his loyalty to Nerys.

When the noble walked away from us, disappearing from view on the busy dock, I waited for Marek to untie and push us off. Instead, he began to tie off ropes.

"What are you doing?" I asked, already suspecting the answer. He was securing the ship to remain docked.

"What does it look like I'm doing?"

He was still angry. Fair enough.

"I could not risk getting caught."

Marek finished, glaring at me. "He will tell others. That is no longer a secure spot for me to…"

"Aye?" I tried not to laugh as Marek screwed up his expression so it appeared less guilty. "When she is queen, you cannot continue your… less scrupulous activities. Not without putting Nerys in a difficult position."

"'When she is queen,' being the operative phrase. These past two days have not gone well. Nerys is furious, not being able to leave. Whispers of her instability spread. And if men like Lord

Gavric are giving credence to the queen's rantings, I worry her challenge will not be upheld."

I had not yet thought to ask. "Is such a thing possible? Is a legitimate challenge not within Thalassari laws?"

"Legitimate, aye. But there was a man once, well before my time, who challenged the king. All knew him to be mad and the king refused to entertain the challenge. It caused a temporary unrest, but ultimately, it was ruled that the king had been within his rights given his challenger's state. He did himself no favors by marching into the palace, claiming the king, one well-liked and respected, was an imposter, and demanded the throne as his own."

"None who know Nerys would believe the same of her."

"Hence"—Marek waved his arms—"the queen's current campaign."

"Surely, you have a plan?"

Marek stepped onto the dock, smiling from ear to ear. "Rowan, my dear human, I always have a plan. And you are the most integral part of it."

32

NERYS

Aneri's courtyard, a place that had been my sanctuary for so many years, was no comfort today. It felt more like a gilded cage as I paced around the fountain, trapped here while rumors continued to spread. Only Caelum came and went, Aneri as much a captive as me.

"You will wear a path into the ground that reaches Elydor's core," Aneri said, handing me a lemon-flavored pastry with custard. It was one of my favorites, as she knew.

Stopping long enough to take a bite, I might have moaned just a little bit. "It's still warm."

"Sit," she said. "Take your mind from the challenge."

I did, but corrected her. "My mind is on how useless I am, hiding here while the queen demolishes my reputation. A traitor and a coward," I said, only stopping to take another bite.

"A coward would not be preparing to challenge the Queen of Thalassaria, as well you know."

"Hmm," I responded, my mouth full of pastry. "Has Caelum returned?" I asked when I finally finished chewing.

"Not yet."

I knew that look. "You're worried she will discredit me before the festival?"

"Nay," Aneri said. "Marek and Rowan have been busy. While you were out here pacing, before he left, Caelum said their efforts in Corvi are bearing fruit. Marek has apparently been working the Pearl Market, meeting with influential traders and merchants, and with guild leaders at the Navigator's Guild. He said both have been holding court at The Driftwood Inn, countering the queen's narrative by emphasizing your dedication to Thalassaria's traditions, and highlighting the queen's manipulative tactics."

Rowan.

I could not think of him without recalling precisely what he asked me to remember in the Deep Archives.

"But you are worried?" I guessed, popping the last of the pastry in my mouth.

"I am worried that you do not believe yourself ready to lead."

I had not been expecting that.

She did not worry about my allies' abilities to counter the queen's narrative. She did not worry about me winning the challenge.

I said nothing, Aneri knowing me better than I knew myself. "It has been a distraction," I admitted. "My training. The queen's opposition."

"A distraction from what concerns you the most."

It was as if a dam had burst. What else could I say but the truth?

"I am young, for a queen. Neither of my parents were royalty before me, like so many of Thalassari rulers. I've made friends, and allies, at the palace, but have remained out of much of the politics with good reason, the nobles' bickering over trivial matters of little concern to me. Yet as queen, I will not have the luxury of avoiding them, or the matter of Marek's smuggling or the merchants' demands for lower tariffs—"

"Nerys?"

Without realizing it, I had stood up and begun to pace. Taking a deep breath, I sat back down.

"You are well-liked, but more importantly, well-respected. Treat others with that same respect, surround yourself, as you've begun to do, with those with similar values, and you will find your way. No one is truly prepared to be king or queen, in truth. Those who do, who are overly confident of their abilities, fool themselves, but not their subject. As for Marek, every ruler faces a reckoning between ideals and reality. Marek's methods may be questionable, but he is loyal to you. His networks and influence could be invaluable, as they've proven these past days while the queen seeks to discredit you."

As always, Aneri's advice was crucial, and I would take it to heart. But her attitude about Marek was surprising.

"You have always disapproved of Marek's more... questionable... methods. Yet you suggest I should turn a blind eye to them now?"

"Darling, Marek's father was where the young man learned such methods. With no mother to temper him, someone had to ensure he did not stray too far down the wrong path."

That we'd both lost our mothers, not a regular occurrence for immortals, was one of the things Marek and I had bonded over when we'd first met. And though his father was as charismatic and daring as the son, I understood Aneri's position.

"You warned me many times not to allow our friendship to become something more."

"Being friends with a man like Marek is one thing. Partnering with him, very much another. I quite like him, and always have, but he needs less admiration and more temperament from those who care for him."

An interesting development. "I do indulge him a bit too much," I admitted.

"As do most. And it is true, as queen, you will need to find a balance that will come only with experience. Shall we speak of another man now that you've stopped wearing a path into my garden?"

Rowan. Where could I possibly begin?

"He is more complicated than he appears," I said. "I told you of the Deep Archives, but it was not the only time Rowan has kept secrets. Each time, he asks me to trust him, but it becomes harder to do so and no wonder why he is unable to confide in me."

"He cares for you. And you for him."

It was more than that. "I love him, Aneri. I did not, do not, wish to love a human. But despite myself, I've fallen in love with a mortal man. One who is not always forthcoming, and one who has said we are not possible. But then something happened, in the Archives. I cannot explain it, but there was a shift in him."

Aneri stared at her hands, now crooked and wrinkled after so many years on Elydor. I was certain, as much as I knew about her, there were stories she'd not told me.

"I can say only one thing for certain." Her voice was heavy with the weight of years. "Love, true love, has never been simple, or easy. Especially not in times like these, when trust and secrecy walk hand in hand. His hesitation may not be a lack of trust in you, but rather, a protection of the fragile threads he weaves. Consider that he risked much for your cause. The queen has put a mark on him, Rowan's name now tied to your supposed treason. He has no hope of obtaining the Tidal Pearl from her now, if she were to somehow remain queen. Rowan believes in you, as I do."

I bit my lip, the words resonating within me. I didn't want to question my feelings for Rowan, nor the growing tension between us. But Aneri's wisdom was undeniable. If he had any doubt that I would best the queen, would he have risked failing a mission that could see the Gate closed for good?

"I only hope that, whatever truths he carries, they do not come too late."

"They rarely do," Aneri said softly, rising to refill her teacup. "But the waiting—that is where the real trial lies."

33

ROWAN

Travelling to Ventara, the same clifftop village I'd passed on my way to the palace, I never could have predicted such a chain of events. Still reeling from my vision from the day we stepped off the dock in Corvi, one that coincided with Marek's unhinged plan, one thing had become clear.

Not only was I the new Keeper, but my visions were strong and true. I would no longer doubt them but learn to harness them, as my grandfather and those before me had. But today was not about me, or Marek. His role would come in four days' time, if he was able to pull off such a scheme. Today, the first day of the Festival of Tides, I would continue to seek allies, cement Nerys's challenge and discredit the queen's increasingly unhinged claims.

In lieu of my mount, or Marek's ship, I'd paid for passage on a cargo vessel that was heading to Ventara for the festival. Paid good coin for the privilege, but it had proved a worthwhile endeavor as the ship's captain was no friend of the queen.

Making my way from the docks, I asked for directions to The Salted Gale, where Caelum had sent a message that he, Aneri and Nerys would be staying. As we sailed into port, I could see flowing banners in every oceanic hue imaginable and massive sand sculptures along the shore where some of the seaside festivities would take place. On land, the sights were no less spectacular. Bioluminescent coral sculptures, more banners, and an excitement among the swelling crowd were all evidence the festival was commencing.

"Pardon me," I asked a couple who were studying a sculpture of the goddess Thalassa. It was the largest of all the land sculptures and glowed a bright teal from within. At night, the sculpture would be spectacular. "Can you point me in the direction of The Salted Gale?"

The woman eyed me appreciatively, her partner noticing, and offered directions. I moved off without preamble, climbing a set of winding stairs that could have put those in the Deep Archives to shame. Some of the vaelith, Marek had told me, watched the entire festival from town, never making the trek down to its shores. By the time I reached the top, I understood the reason. And also why they were reluctant to move the festival elsewhere.

From here, the scene below was every bit as spectacular as Zephyria, the Aetherian spring festival of renewal held in its Sky Pinnacle, a sacred mountain where the winds were at their strongest in all of Aetheria.

But I was not here to admire the pomp and circumstance of the festival, nor even to witness its opening ceremonies where, according to Marek, the Tidecallers would conjure aquatic displays, setting the tone for the days to come.

I was here to find Nerys.

Following the woman's instructions, I navigated throngs of Thalassarians dressed in robes as flowing as the banners, most adorned with jewelry crafted from pearls, shells, and gemstones. Just as I'd been instructed, The Salted Gate, perched cliffside in perfect position for its residents to watch the festivities below, was decorated with the same banners as most other buildings. I entered the inn, serving also as a tavern, and ordered an ale.

I could not ask for her, so as not to raise suspicion. Instead, I waited for a stool to become available, sat upon it, and listened, waiting. Not surprisingly, talk was of the opening ceremonies later this eve, but also of Nerys.

"They say she is not coming until the challenge," the woman who served my ale said to a group of haranya. Like Marek and Nerys, they were neither young ones but had not reached thaloran. For nearly five hundred years, they would remain as such, appearing similar to a human who had lived nearly thirty years, like me.

"I heard she's come already. Someone spotted her at the docks but she disappeared into the crowd," one said.

"Either way, I hope she wins."

It was the soft-spoken admission of the red-headed woman sitting beside me. Her hair was an unusual color for a Thalassari. She was pretty enough, but for me, every woman would now be measured against Nerys. And every one, including this one, would be found lacking by comparison.

"Did you hear of the sea serpents she summoned at The Moonlit Current?"

I continued to listen, my head turned in the opposite direction, until their talk moved from Nerys to the queen to the next day's competition. Apparently, one of them had entered as a contestant in deep-sea pearl diving, his first time participating in the festival.

To my left, another conversation, but this one more somber. Two men, nobles by the look of them, wagered on the outcome of the challenge.

A third chastised his companions. "If there will even be a

challenge. Rumor has it the queen will render Lady Nerys 'unfit to compete.'"

The first man snorted, swirling his wine. "By accusing her of treason? The people will not stand for it."

"She's already sewed enough doubt," the first noble countered, leaning in. "Questions of her sanity have made some question Lady Nerys."

"If she's alive to make the challenge," the second said grimly.

My hands gripped the hilt of my sword, as if ensuring it was still there. Nay, not my sword, I qualified. One Marek had secured for me our first day in Corvi. My own still sat within the palace walls.

Opening myself to accept the emotions of those around me, I stared straight ahead, allowing my own anger of the noble's words to subside. She was safe, and any moment, Caelum would find me and take me to her.

Confusion. Hope. Excitement. Lust. A gamut of emotions, but I could sense nothing nefarious. Except someone who was watching me.

Sensing it, I spun around on my seat, searching the growing crowd. Sure enough, Caelum was approaching me. "There you are, old friend," he said. "Bring your ale with you so that we may catch up."

I reached for it, the groups on each side of me not even glancing my way. Leading me from the tavern to the inn, a covered walkway connecting both, before long I found myself in an empty corridor. "We are the only ones on this floor."

With the number of ships at port and size of the crowds, before the Festival of Tides even began, I questioned Caelum on how such a thing was possible.

"Marek somehow arranged it." Caelum gave me a look that said, *"Don't ask how."*

"When—" I started, but my companion shook his head.

"Unsure. I've learned long ago not to ask too many questions where he is concerned." He pointed to a door. "Nerys is in there with Aneri. It's the only room on the floor with a view of the festival below, and neither wished to miss the opening festivities."

I would see her again at any moment. My hands flexed and uncurled, unable to rest. But first: "What is her status?"

"We arrived without incident on a private vessel, though we took extra precaution to escort her and Aneri here separately. She warded the room herself, but it is not as elaborate as Aneri's, though strong enough that we would be alerted. Each of the other rooms are currently occupied with men loyal to her and prepared to defend against an attack."

"They've agreed to remain here at all times? Forgoing the festival?"

"They have, and are stationed belowstairs and at the front and back of the inn as well."

"Good," I said. "I will work the festival, attempt to root out additional threats and stay the tide of any discontent."

"You stand out in a crowd, Rowan."

I already knew what Caelum was saying.

"I won't return after today."

Caelum would not be coming and going but remaining here at the inn, ensuring Nerys was protected. But my skills were best used among the crowds, yet I couldn't risk being followed here.

"We've three days after today before the challenge," he said, his voice barely above a whisper. "Do you think Marek will return in time?"

"With the winds at his back, perhaps. It is a calculated risk."

"One I hope is unnecessary. The mood is unstable, but more accepting than I'd hoped for."

"Agreed," I said. "Though I do not trust her, not since she's shown her hand," I said of the queen.

"Are you certain you will not be recognized? I've heard your name whispered more often than I would like. Her guards continue their search for you."

"Let them look. They'll not find me."

Caelum's eyes darted toward my weapon. "Marek?"

"Aye."

"I attempted to retrieve yours from the palace but was denied. I've sparred with someone much less skilled than you."

"A high compliment indeed," I teased, remembering that first day we met. Little did I realize at the time the reason Caelum was so skilled with a sword. It was a skill valued most by humans, of which he was one. "I will be waiting belowstairs when you are finished. Tongues will continue to loosen as the night wears on."

Watching Caelum leave, I gave silent thanks for his loyalty to Nerys.

Knocking at her door, I was rewarded with her voice.

"Caelum?"

"No," I said. "Rowan."

My tunic suddenly felt tight against my chest as I waited, listening as the door was unlocked. A moment later, it opened.

Nerys was dressed similarly to the day we met, but that's where the similarities ended. I knew her now. Her strength and determination. Her vulnerabilities. I knew the taste of her, and wanted another.

Unfortunately, Aneri watched us closely.

Fuck it, as my modern human friends would say. Shutting the door behind me, I closed the gap between us, grabbed her beautiful face and kissed her. With an audience, I didn't want to create a spectacle, but neither did I want to let her go.

I did anyway, out of respect. But certainly not out of any desire to do so.

With her lips swollen from our kiss, Nerys looked up at me as if she didn't know what to say. Truth was, I didn't either. There was only one way I could tell her of my secret, but that would mean having her accept more than Nerys might be willing.

Accept what is, be where your feet are, and you'll find peace, Sir Rowan of Estmere.

At least, after visiting Seren, I knew my path. Or the one I wished to take. There would be a period of upheaval, but change was never easy.

"Come see," she said as I took her hand.

"Greetings, Rowan," Aneri said with a knowing smile.

I inclined my head. "Greetings, Aneri. I'm pleased to see you both safe and well."

"As well as we can be," she replied, standing by the window. "It is a different experience than most, this Festival of Tides."

Nerys and I stood beside her, hand in hand, watching as the revelries played out in front of us. On the street below, drinking and merriment, smiling faces and mugs of ale clanging in cheers. But the true spectacle was below them, our cliffside perch at a perfect angle to view the bustling docks off to the right and festivities along the beach below.

"So many sculptures," I said, watching as onlookers moved from one to the next.

"The winner is chosen by a council, that person honored during the closing ceremonies as the next festival's chair."

I winced. "Doesn't sound like much of a prize."

Aneri laughed. "The coin that comes with such an honor might sway your thinking."

"What's that?" I asked, pointing to a newly set fire just along the water's edge.

"The Tidefire," Nerys said. "A battle between fire and water as the tide rises. Some years, one is more quickly victorious than the other. At the last festival, the two battled for the entirety of the festivities until the sea reigned supreme."

Aneri brought a teacup to her lips, sipping, and then said, "It is a symbol of the harmony of the elements. A tradition meant to be more of a visual spectacle than anything, if you ask me."

"Is it connected to the legend of a fire clan?"

A "harumph" from Aneri told me what she thought of that possibility. "'Tis merely that. A legend."

"What do you know of it?" Nerys asked. "I've found so little in the Archives, and even Seren admits she's never discovered true evidence of it."

"Just that, before the Aetherians wielded air, Gyorians the land and Thalassarians, the water, Elydor saw a time of chaos. Of fire. And that the fire-wielders' flames burned so bright, it consumed not only the land but themselves with it. And that nature rebelled. The tides rose. Storms raged. The ground trembled. Eventually, the fire was smothered, the fire-wielders destroyed."

"Seren discovered an ancient text once," Nerys said, her hand resting comfortably on my own, "that suggested the flames were not completely extinguished but hidden as embers scattered across Elydor, waiting to reignite."

"Rubbish." Aneri's teacup clattered as she placed it onto its clam-shaped saucer. "A cautionary tale, reminding the clans of the balance the elements must keep."

"Given the legend's warning, the Tidefire's popularity does surprise me."

"Warning?" I asked, having never heard of such a thing.

"Seren showed me once, in the text I mentioned. It said, 'When the fire rises again, the tides alone will not be enough to quell it.' I asked more than one vaelith who had heard the warning before, but it doesn't seem to be common knowledge."

"Interesting," I said, watching as the Tidefire grew.

"Are you attending the opening ceremony?" Nerys asked. "If so, you will want to be down there soon."

What I really wanted was time alone with Nerys, but I was not rude enough to ask for it. Aneri, sans her tea, appeared captivated by the scene below us, despite having seen this festival many times. I could see the appeal. As daylight waned, bright white, blue and teal lights that were strung in seemingly every direction began to glow. All along the shoreline, the water's edge illuminated: some water magic trick, I assumed.

"I am at the future queen's disposal," I said, meaning it. "There is much work to be done, but if I am being honest, there's nothing that I would like more than to watch the festivities here, with you and Aneri."

Nerys's crooked smile told me she knew that last part was not quite true. Her eyes searched mine, and I told her, without speaking how much I meant those words. How difficult being away from her, not knowing if she was safe, had been.

"Caelum says the queen has redoubled her efforts since your escape."

I raised my brows. "Escape. Was I captive then at the palace?"

"For all intents and purposes, you were. Humans have never truly been welcome there. But they will be."

I did not doubt her words.

"How are you feeling?" I asked.

Nerys tore her gaze from mine, glanced at Aneri, whose hopeful smile told me the two had discussed the same.

Stealing her shoulders back, Nerys's chin raised. "Ready," she said with no trace of the hesitation in her voice that had previously been there when talking about the challenge and what came after it. "If she allows me to challenge her."

I wanted to stay. To see for myself that Nerys remained safe. To hold her hand, hold her. But she needed something more than me. Though she did not yet realize it, I had the ability to root out malintent, to help prevent the queen's lies from continuing to spread.

"She will be forced to do so. And to that end." I squeezed her hand. Nerys seemed to understand I was leaving. Aneri did too, judging by her expression. But instead of offering to give us a moment alone, Nerys's guardian looked as if she were about to laugh.

"The tide's retreat only makes its return more cherished, dear boy."

As I suspected. Aneri knew, and had her own reasons for staying.

"Aneri, if you will please—" Nerys began.

"I will not. He will see you in a few days' time. Until then, you need every ally possible to ensure the queen's lies do not take root any more than they have already."

"She's right," I said, reluctant to admit it. Without shame, I leaned forward, kissing her one last time, although I did not linger. "The next time I do that, you will be queen."

"And then?"

Trust me, Nerys. Please.

"Marek is not the only one with a surprise planned. But first, we must get to the challenge."

34

NERYS

"Are you ready?"

Caelum stood at the door's entranceway, waiting. After three days of watching the festivities from my window—from sand-sculpting contests and the daily blessing of the tides to boat-racing and net-casting competitions—the annual festival had gone on without a hitch. Unless you counted the undercurrent that Caelum reported each day, a growing awareness that the queen would, indeed, attempt to refute my right to challenge her.

Somehow, though Caelum could not fully explain it, Rowan had uncovered a plot the day before to manipulate the council into disqualifying me by presenting a forged document alleging my family once allied with a well-known conspiracy against Elydor centuries ago. One of the five council members had been bribed to "discover" the document in the Deep Archives and pressured another to corroborate it under oath. According to Caelum, Rowan was "taking care of it" but didn't elaborate.

The groundwork she had laid to dispute my right to challenge her, along with this claim and my inability to properly train in the days leading up to this day, had done little for my confidence, despite telling Rowan I was ready. In truth, I should have said, *"I am pretending to be ready but am terrified at how the day will play out."*

"If the council does not allow it..."

"There will be riots," Aneri said. "This day will be the beginning, and not the end, of your journey."

"According to law, the last day of the Festival of Tides is the only one the current ruler can be challenged. If she is successful in denying me, at best, we face six months of unrest. Six months until Rowan could even hope to see the Tidal Pearl."

Neither of them disagreed. The stakes were high: for me, for Thalassaria, and for Elydor, the humans especially.

"Put all of that from your mind," Aneri said. "Focus on the challenge, for you may yet be battling a queen today."

"A queen who wields water like none other."

Caelum smiled. "With one exception."

Me.

Whether it was luck or something more that I'd been born with such abilities, it no longer mattered. "I am ready," I said.

It didn't take long, as we left the inn, for the whispers to begin. Surrounded by the same Thalassari who had stayed with me these past days—friends from the palace, two Stormcallers who'd performed the Rite with me, and nobles Caelum had recruited—I was hardly visible. And yet, as we made our way down to the shore, weaving through the bustling seaside market that had popped up for the festival, whispers grew to calls of support. One yelled, "Traitor," which I ignored.

I'd watched her all week, the queen and her retinue sitting on wooden stands constructed for her to view the festivities right from the shore. As we walked down the winding stairs, leaving my cliffside sanctuary behind, my heart pounded so loudly, I could hear it in my ears. Drawing out the calls, I looked for him as my boots hit the sand, but still did not see Rowan.

Nor Marek, who had not yet returned.

Squeezing my hands shut to steady them, I concentrated on the young ones emerging from the sea, laughing as their ceremonial swim marked their coming of age. I could remember doing the same, and though a wave of nostalgia had me momentarily wishing to return to such a carefree time, I refocused on the task at hand.

Be where your feet are.

It was one of Seren's favorite sayings, a reminder that the past could not be re-visited and the future was of no consequence yet.

The queen had spotted me. I'd fooled myself into thinking she was not dangerous. For so long, my mind had rebelled against the idea that someone in her position could want anything but the best for Thalassaria. But as she stood, looking down at me as if I was as insignificant as a piece of sand, her true nature revealed itself.

I prayed to the Goddess Thalassa that, when I became queen, I would never allow power to poison me in such a way.

As the young ones departed and the crowd dispersed to allow me a direct path to the queen, Rowan appeared suddenly by my side. If Queen Lirael disliked me, she openly despised him. The look she gave him may have withered a weaker man. Rowan simply whispered to me, "I believe in you, Nerys. I will return momentarily."

With no indication of where he was going, Rowan disappeared as quickly as he came. Caelum, Aneri... all those surrounding me whispered words of encouragement, dropping back, for this was my moment.

Knowing what must be done and doing it were two very different things.

Wearing the same suit as the day Rowan had openly gaped at me, a memory that would have made me smile if I were not doing all I could to appear calm and confident, I stepped forward. One foot, and then another, until I faced her. The music that accompanied our descent to the beach had stopped. The calls and whistles gave way to only one sound besides my beating heart.

Waves crashing behind me, their relentless rhythm a reminder of the ocean's power... eternal, unyielding, and untamed, like the truth I carried with me. I was more powerful than Queen Lirael, and her time as Thalassaria's ruler had come to an end.

"Queen Lirael," I called. "As Thalassari law and tradition hold, I challenge you on this final day of the Festival of Tides."

Nothing more needed to be said.

Ignoring the murmur of voices behind me, no doubt due to the spectacle I was making, I waited. When Lirael smiled, I knew what would come next.

"You've been a loyal servant, Lady Nerys, which is why it pains me to deny your challenge."

I was prepared for as much. "On what grounds?"

"The threat and instability you and your allies pose to the sanctity of this festival and the safety of Elydor cannot be ignored."

The murmur behind me, and above me all along the cliff as onlookers likely attempted to hear what was being said, grew louder.

"I pose no threat, as well you know. I have been a loyal servant to you and to Thalassaria, as my parents and those before them were."

She stood, the queen's smirk sending shivers down my back. "Interesting that you should mention your parents, and theirs before them. Council member Veylin," she said, her smirk deepening, "perhaps you would like to enlighten Lady Nerys about her family's true legacy?"

To the left of her, all five council members, each of whom I knew well, shifted in their makeshift wooden seats. One, a vaelith who knew better, who knew well he was about to speak a lie, waved a piece of parchment in the air. "A document has come to light that would make Lady Nerys ineligible for the challenge. Your great-grandfather, it seems, was a leader in the conspiracy against Queen Ilyana."

As all those in the stands gasped, I resisted rolling my eyes at their theatrics.

"The document is forged." Rowan appeared, making that claim, as promised. But he wasn't alone.

"Good day, Lady Nerys." Thalon held onto Rowan's arm with one hand, the walking stick always by his side in the other.

"Good day, Thalon," I replied as if we'd just been seated together at the midday meal in the palace and were not surrounded by hundreds of Thalassari standing before the queen.

I could not decide who appeared more surprised by the palace historian's presence: Veylin or the queen, who narrowed her eyes at Thalon.

"That is a serious charge," she said, her voice laced with an unnamed threat.

"As serious as nullifying Lady Nerys's challenge with a fake document. I not only lived through the conspiracy against Queen Ilyana but documented it in my official role as palace historian. Veylin will claim to have discovered that in the Deep Archives, and if the council does not believe me, we will ask its guardian, Seren, to stand witness, since no such document exists."

At Seren's name, Veylin blanched. Had he even visited the Deep Archives, covering his tracks? Likely not. The queen relied on an element of surprise with her false claim, one Rowan countered by bringing Thalon here.

"It is not forged," Veylin called down to us. "But neither is—"

"In holding with Thalassari law, the council will vote," the queen said loudly, for all to hear. She'd likely bribed or threatened each one of them and would move the proceedings along with her forged document stunt having spectacularly failed.

The crowd's impatience grew. Some called for them to vote, others for me to step down, and yet others yelled things I could not decipher. But there was something about the chants that was different than before.

Turning, I was startled to realize those behind me, gathered on the shore, were no longer even watching us. Instead, their gazes were fixed on the same stairs I'd descended earlier. I looked at Rowan.

"Do you think it is possible?"

He shook his head, as if in disbelief. "If it were anyone other than Marek, I'd say nay. But I've seen him sail, so..." He shrugged as an answer.

"I am sorry, Lady Nerys," Thalon whispered beside me, "that she attempts to malign you and your family's good name."

"Thank you for coming, Thalon," I said, watching as the crowd alternately gasped and parted once again. At the first flash of white hair, I breathed a sigh of relief. Would it make a difference? It could not hurt my case to have such an ally, for certain.

Finally, I could see them clearly. Marek and his companions moved through the throng of people toward us. She was even more beautiful than Rowan had described.

Unbelievable. Marek had done it.

He'd brought the lost princess of Aetheria to us, and just in the nick of time.

35

ROWAN

They had the precise effect Marek had hoped for when he first told me of his plan. The arrival of Kael and Mev—a prince of Gyoria and princess of Aetheria, united and standing together as one, was a powerful statement about the future of Elydor. One that would not look like its past, a world on the brink of war.

At least, that was Elydor's potential. We were a long way from such a reality.

"How are you, Rowan of Estmere?" Kael hugged me as if we'd started out as friends when the truth was anything but. He had not trusted me, with good reason. My intentions had been pure, seeking out the lost princess, my alliance with her father long and true. But Kael was perceptive, and like Nerys, could sense there was something more than I'd been able to share.

"You're a long way from Aetheria," I said, the stalwart Gyorian as true to his kind as any. Built like the side of a mountain his kind move, it was Kael's pragmatism that often masked an openness that was buried deep inside. One that allowed him to fall in love with the daughter of his most bitter enemy, now Kael's ally in recovering the artifacts and reopening the Gate.

"This one," Mev said, grinning from ear to ear as if the Queen of Thalassaria was not glaring down on us, "is persistent," she said of Marek. "And I thought Kael was a walking red flag. Holy shit, he has nothing on my husband."

"Mev." I opened my arms, squeezing her tight. "Thank you for coming."

"Red flag?" Nerys asked, staring at Princess Mevlida. She made a striking figure, dressed in traditional Aetherian garb, her flowing silver-and-white robes lifting like ribbons in the breeze. When we first met, her hair had not turned completely white, but now Elydor's magic had taken hold and it was as startling as it was long.

"You look like a princess," I whispered.

Mev laughed. "Because I am." She turned to Nerys, bowing in Thalassari tradition. "You must be Lady Nerys. I am Mevlida Harper."

"Princess Mevlida of Aetheria," Kael reminded her, earning a swat on the arm for it.

"Do not correct me in front of others, husband."

"If you'll remember, we do not use the term 'husband' here."

"No?" she asked. "Funny, 'cause it seems like I just did." Mev gave him a look that said, *We'll discuss this later,* and then said to Nerys, "I'll explain red flag another time. I'm an expert on the subject," to which Kael made a sound of dissatisfaction. "They've not voted yet?" she whispered to Nerys.

"Nay," she replied.

"Which are they?"

"Top left, four men, one woman, all dressed in teal and black."

In the next breath, she raised her gaze to the queen, stepping forward.

"I am Princess Mevlida of Aetheria," she shouted, loud

enough to be heard above the buzz of the crowd. "Together with my husband," Mev continued, "Prince Kael of Gyoria, we have come to witness the challenge which I am told is held in long tradition with Thalassarian law."

That she bowed to Nerys, but not Queen Lirael, was something all would have noticed.

"A challenge," the queen replied, clearly uneasy at this second surprising turn of events, "in question."

"You have two royal representatives, along with a highly respected human who I count as a personal friend, as does my father, before you, standing witness. All three clans of Elydor represented. Perhaps you should think carefully on your answer."

The queen raised her chin. "What is the question?"

"One not addressed to you." She tilted her head slightly, toward the council. "But to you, the council which governs such affairs. I am new to your world but am told the Thalassarian council is a sacred charge, meant to keep the power of your king or queen in check. If I am not mistaken?"

I took a step toward Mev. "Top left. Veylin. He's been bribed by the queen."

"Lord Veylin," she called, not missing a beat. I tried not to smile at how far Mev had come since I'd left Aetheria. And how similar her mannerisms were becoming to her father, though something about Mev had reminded me of King Galfrid from the start, even before the two had met. "You seem to me the sort of man who might be the council's leader?"

"Is he?" I whispered to Nerys.

"Yes. How did she know that?"

"She senses emotion, like me, but more than feelings alone. Mev can detect intention, though I'm unsure how that translates here. Good guess, maybe?"

Either way, it took him by surprise.

Mev's next words were lost in a vision so sudden, so vivid, that I was forced to redirect my attention to it. I'd seen Nerys battling Lirael and was confident this challenge would take place. But this time, instead of being on the periphery, seeing the entire battle, I was on the ship, facing the queen, as if I were Nerys. A subtle movement, the queen's hand moving to her belt and remaining there before whipping out, caught my attention. By now, I was able to focus within my visions, and I did so on the queen's belt. What may have been imperceptible by Nerys in the moment was evident to me, as if the belt were now invisible. A small, black gemstone glowing faintly red.

As quickly as it came, the vision was gone.

I missed what Mev had said to Veylin, but it seemed the council now huddled together as the queen watched them. She was furious, her council members alternately scared, confused, and resolute. But I was less concerned with their emotions than I was with that gem.

"Kael," I whispered.

He spun toward me.

"A small, black gem, glowing red from its inside. What is it?"

Most gemstones that could be found in Elydor were mined in Gyoria. Sure enough, though he seemed confused by my question, I sensed a confidence in him as he spoke. "A shard of the abyss. A forbidden bit of gemstone that, like the Stone of Mor'-Vallis that has the potential to kill its user."

"If it were used by the queen, against Nerys?"

I had no time to decide how to explain my knowledge to Kael. That would have to come later. For now, if the queen planned to cheat, I needed to know how Nerys could combat it.

"It would amplify her power, not unlike the Tidal Pearl but on a smaller scale and in a much different way. But I'm thinking you don't need a history lesson at the moment?"

By now, both Mev and Nerys were listening.

"No, I don't. But I do need to know how Nerys would combat such a thing."

"Why does it matter?" Nerys asked.

I had no choice but to respond, truthfully. "She has a piece of it, beneath her belt. Or will, if not already, before you begin."

To say all three looked at me as if I were mad would be an understatement.

"Have her searched first," Mev supplied.

"How would we explain such a request?" Nerys asked. Realizing she was trying to protect me, despite such secrets holding us apart, made my resolve about the future role of The Keeper even stronger. But that was another problem for another day.

"She won't do it," I said. "And is looking for every reason not to battle Nerys. She could use such a request to invalidate the challenge."

"The only natural counterbalance is aevumite," Kael said. "Which is difficult to find. Impossible outside Gyoria."

Their group went silent at the same time as the council broke apart.

"We have our decision," Veylin said, addressing the queen but with an eye on us as well.

None asked how I knew, but they would. What mattered though was that this council was about to allow the challenge, and the queen had a means to defeat Nerys by cheating.

"It will be allowed."

A roar erupted from the crowd, both on the beach and above us as onlookers all but hung over the railings.

"Nerys, you cannot compete this way. We must call her out if there is no other way."

"I must compete."

"What's happening?"

Caelum and Marek appeared as everything happened at once. The queen consulted with her inner circle as preparations began. Marek had explained that he and the Tidebreaker fleet would assemble and escort Nerys and the queen to the docks where they would board a ship, taking them out to sea so they could harness water from all around.

As Marek approached the queen and council, Nerys explained to Caelum that Lirael planned to use a shard of the abyss during their battle.

"How do you—"

"I saw it."

There was no other way to explain. "You... saw it?"

"There is one other way."

Thalon hobbled up to us from where he stood, close enough, apparently, to have overheard some of our discussion.

"Nerys, you brought an ancient scroll to me once after Seren told you of its presence. One your mother particularly enjoyed studying as it was buried in the deepest part of the Deep Archives."

Nerys's eyes widened. "Purification Rites."

"What are they?" Mev asked.

"Magic so old, it has mostly been forgotten," Nerys said.

"It is time," Veylin announced, his voice now amplified using an Aetherian Echo Stone. A hush fell across the crowd. The queen, now stripped of her robes, stood with Marek and her guards.

"Water rituals are not just about control," Thalan said to Nerys, who leaned closer to him to hear over the cheers of the crowd. "They are about communion with the natural flow of life itself. Use that knowledge to perform the Ritual of the Sacred Waters."

"The only magic strong enough to purify the abyss's corruption," Nerys interrupted to explain to the rest of us. "But it hasn't been used for centuries, Thalan. Even if I could remember it, I—"

"You can remember it, Nerys. Trust yourself. The Sacred Waters are near; use them."

"Are you certain we should not ask the queen to be searched?" Kael's eyes narrowed on the woman in question. "The abyss is a strong, dark magic source. Even the small shard from it will amplify her power."

I was inclined to agree with him. And yet, in my vision, she had the gemstone upon her. It was up to Nerys to decide. I said as much.

"I cannot risk her using my request to invalidate the challenge. I will perform the Ritual and nullify her advantage."

"While battling her?" Mev asked, clearly concerned.

Nerys reached out and took Mev's hand. "Thank you for coming. If not for you, and Prince Kael, this challenge may not have taken place. Thank you all." She released Mev's hand and glanced at Thalon, Caelum and then rested her gaze on me. "For your guidance and support. But now it is my turn to do what must be done."

I would have kissed her if not for the witness of hundreds of Thalassarians all around us. Much too soon, she was called to Marek's side, the spectacle of both women, now surrounded by the Tidebreaker fleet who had been summoned the moment the challenge was issued and who had arrived one by one, a striking one.

It would take some time for them to get to the docks and sail out, close enough for us to witness but far enough from shore that the depths of the sea would be at their disposal.

"Should we watch from there?" Mev asked, pointing to the stand that had been erected for the queen and her inner circle.

"Certainly," Caelum said. "I will get Aneri."

I was less than pleased about this turn of events, though thankful to have had the vision. Unfortunately, Mev must have been thinking along the same thread. Arms crossed, she waited for me to explain.

"Can we discuss this later?"

"Sure," she said. "Maybe we can have a chat about that after we talk about the googly eyes you were giving Nerys."

Though I wasn't familiar with the term, I could discern her meaning easily enough.

"Can't say I blame you," Kael said. "She is quite..." He stopped when Mev cocked her head to him.

"A looker?" she provided.

"A what?"

"Looker."

"What's a looker?"

"This will be quite a shock but... it's a person easy to look at. Get it?"

"Oh, I got it," he said suggestively. "As will you tonight when—"

"Perhaps we should join the others," I cut in.

"Classic dodge," she said. "But you can't avoid me all day. Clearly, there's something going on between the two of you, and I want the scoop."

I looked at Kael, who shrugged.

"Classic dodge, as in... never mind. Two peas in a pod, you guys are."

With that, Mev left us, but Kael and I remained.

"She's different," I said. "In a good way."

He smiled at her retreating backside. "She's becoming her father."

"Most would see that as a good thing."

Kael and Galfrid had a complicated relationship. Once

enemies, they now worked together as family, a fact Kael's father could not have taken gently.

"Have you heard from Adren?"

"Aye. We've much to discuss later. But first, maybe you can answer Mev's question."

"About the shard?"

Kael shook his head slowly. "No. Not the shard."

Nerys. How could I explain it to him when I was just beginning to make sense of it myself?

"As you said, we've much to discuss. Later."

36

NERYS

Perhaps the shard was a good thing.

Rather than concentrating on the queen's glare, one she had perfected over many years of ruling, I searched my mind for the Purification Rite. It was simple; knowledge of the Sacred Waters and pure intent were really all that was necessary. Each town in Thalassari contained these waters, having been built around them. To outsiders, they appeared like any other fountains, but they were anything but.

The largest of the Tidebreaker fleet's ships loomed ahead of us on the docks. It was not one under Marek's command, but he had been given leave to accompany us. He spoke to its Navarch as we halted, the queen not far from me. I could not see her face from here, nor did I wish to.

As far as I could remember, simply invoking the Rite would be sufficient.

You can remember.

Thalon's words were not just a show of support for my memory, which could not be considered superior. Seren believed deeply in ancestral intuition. Whenever Thalon or I were looking for a particular scroll or attempting to pull knowledge together, she would use the words, reminding us that some truths could not be learned or studied; they must be lived.

Channeling the Sacred Waters, something I'd never attempted as it was rarely done—doing so indiscriminately often had the opposite effect than intended—was hopefully one of these instances. I would invoke the Rite with pure intent and knowledge of the waters to fade the corruption of the shard Lirael attempted to use.

"How did he know?"

Marek held out his hand for me as we boarded.

"I am uncertain," I said. "Clearly, he has some form of the Sight, but denied it when we first met," I whispered. "Rowan insists he did not lie to me then, so it makes little sense. He asks for my trust but keeps secrets, admitting as much, so I've no notion what to think, or believe."

Marek guided me to the front of the ship, away from the queen and her companions. We would not be traveling far, and as the ship was readied by its crew, I found it increasingly difficult to steady my nerves. I was about to battle with the most powerful water-wielder on Elydor, one with an advantage tucked away in her belt.

"Look at me."

Serious Marek. A version of him as rare as an unsmiling Rowan.

"I've not traveled anywhere, or met anyone that can wield water as effortlessly as you. Forget everything, and everyone, and show them what you are capable of."

"The shard—"

"Do you know the Rite?"

The ship began to move. "As best I can."

"Nullify the abyss's power as soon as you are able. Do you remember the day we met?"

It was an abrupt change of topic.

"I do."

"I didn't realize it at the time, but that was the day I finally learned what it means to trust someone, completely. Someday, I will learn to deserve that trust. Today is about trust, Nerys, of a different kind. One where you must fully trust yourself. If you do, there is no doubt in my mind we will return to that shore with a different queen than who reigns now."

"What does that mean?" I asked. "Rowan wants me to trust him. You trust no one," I qualified. "Except me," I said, predicting his response. "Trust me. It is such a nebulous idea, trust. Is it not?"

Marek's typical roguish gaze softened, his eyes glazing over in a rare show of vulnerability. "Not when it's earned. Trust is a leap, not knowing where you'll land but knowing that you will, jumping anyway, even when a part of you cautions against it."

Trust is a leap. And I was about to jump.

I tossed my arms around him. "I am lucky to have a friend such as you."

He pulled me tight. "I am the lucky one." He separated us as the ship slowed already. "As is Rowan."

I looked into his eyes, and though Marek said no more, his meaning was clear.

Trust was a leap, and one I would need to take with Rowan too.

"Queen Lirael of Thalassaria. Lady Nerys of Thalassaria," Lord Veylin called to us.

Gathering my courage, with Marek's and Aneri's and Rowan's words of encouragement ringing in my ears, I walked, head held high, to the bow of the ship, where the ceremony would take place.

The twenty or so that were gathered moved aside. If they were smart, they would retreat even further. I'd seen what the queen could do and this was about to get intense.

"The rules are simple. No external aid. No fatal blows. The challenge will last until either participant yields or is incapacitated. The outcome, as you know, is binding."

No external aid.

I could have her searched, but even if the queen allowed it, I'd not win on a technicality. Prepared to perform the Purification Rite immediately, I concentrated on her belt, where Rowan said the shard was hidden.

"Are there any questions?"

The queen's thin lips pursed together, as if answering him was beneath her. I glanced quickly toward the shore where the beach and town above were swarmed with onlookers. Turning my attention back to the queen, I took a deep breath, and said, "Nay."

"You may begin."

She didn't hesitate. Before I could even flick my wrist, Lirael had summoned a wave that cleared the deck and would have seen me swept into the ocean with more than one of the Tidebreaker fleet if I hadn't quickly used the onslaught to shield myself from the blast of water. It was as strong a shield as I'd ever needed to create, no doubt courtesy of the hidden gem's power.

Allowing it to drop, I attempted to summon the Sacred Waters, but they were much further away than the water Lirael brought crashing down upon my head. Its force brought me to my knees. I momentarily abandoned my plan to perform the Rite and constructed a set of water stairs to climb on, a tricky bit of magic which required summoning controlled tide currents to solidify them.

Scurrying to the top, I again attempted to perform the Rite, the fountain's waters just within reach, when our entire ship began to spin. A whirlpool which, left to its own devices, would swallow the ship and its inhabitants whole. Thankfully, every person on board had the ability to survive such an event, and clearly, the queen cared little about preserving the ship, but even if I tried to counter its currents, its precise power and direction would need to be matched.

Instead, I jumped from my stairs to distract the queen and swirled my wrist instead, focusing on the water's flow. By redirecting the energy of the whirlpool into calmer, wider currents, I could spread out its force. It worked, the ship's spinning slowed, but I had no time for anything but the creation of a water shield as Lirael hurled spears made of tendrils of water toward me.

Blood rushing to my ears as I countered one, then two, then three spears, I could hear shouts coming from elsewhere on the deck but blocked them out. I was on the defensive, the queen's advantage taking its toll.

I needed a distraction.

It was nothing but a bit of show, but summoning my water serpents, three massive ones rising from the sea beside us, had the desired effect. The queen glanced at them long enough for me to once again connect with the Sacred Waters well across town. As I did, reaching for them, praying there was not more to the Rite than I remembered, I brought a channel of water from above the crowd, over the shore and hurtled it, flinging my arm toward the queen, at her belt.

A red glow, so small none but me were likely to see it, extinguished.

Using her surprise to my advantage, I summoned an energy

burst from beneath the water's surface that rippled outward in waves, causing the ship to sway. In response, the queen was forced to create a rope of water, preventing herself from being cast overboard. I'd done the same, my rope connected to the ship's mast.

The air crackled with tension as I met the queen's glare. Her surprise quickly morphed into determination as she sent a series of jagged spikes toward me. If I'd not shielded them, one could easily have landed a fatal blow.

So much for the rules that Queen Lirael hadn't followed from the start.

Tightening my grip on the water rope, I reached into the depths of my power, pulled a stream of sea water toward me, and shaped it into a swirling barrier between us. Her remaining spikes struck the barrier, shattering into harmless droplets.

We continued until my fingers ached and my arm felt as if it would drop from my body. At least the Rite had worked. There was a regularity to her attacks that lacked the strength of the queen's first few moves. I tried to imagine, if that shard only intensified a bit of her power, what it might be like to wield the Tidal Pearl.

She would never yield.

All I knew of the queen, both as a part of her court and more recently, when her true nature had been revealed, told me as much. Incapacitating her would be difficult, but as I'd thought about this day, an idea had come to me. One that just might work.

If he'd not shown himself that day with Rowan and me, never in Elydor's realm would I have considered attempting to summon a pelagor. Other water creatures? Aye. But one that would so surprise the queen that it may give me the advantage I needed over her?

He may not come now. They were known to be as independent as Thalassaria itself, serving the whims of none. But as we battled, I tried anyway, reaching far out into the depth of the lifegiving sea surrounding us.

Waiting. Watching. Praying to Thalassa.

I heard the gasps of the crew behind us, the ones that hadn't been already tossed overboard, before I saw its mosaic of blues and purples off the bow. It had the intended effect, and the moment the queen's attention was taken, I twisted my tired fingers, creating three ropes of water. With the first, I bound the queen's ankles together, pulling on them as she slammed to the deck. With the second, I bound her wielding hand to the nearby railing and the third I wrapped around her wrist.

As soon as I did, the pelagor made a deep, booming call, an ancient and haunting echo that carried across the waves. I thanked him as his massive body disappeared beneath the water as quickly as he appeared.

Walking as calmly as I was able, given the circumstances, to Veylin, I handed him my end of the rope. "The queen is, as you can see, incapacitated."

He took it, eyes wide and clearly shaken, without words. The moment he did, Marek was by my side. Like the others, he was soaked from head to toe.

"I've never seen anything like it before," he said, not lowering his voice. "You were brilliant, Nerys."

"Thank you," I murmured, wondering what was to happen next.

37

ROWAN

As we waited for their return, relief flooded through me. If there had been any question before on my path for the future, it had been obliterated when Nerys began to battle the queen. Knowing of the shard, realizing I'd never actually envisioned Nerys as queen, my thoughts ran wild.

What if the shard was enough of an advantage for the queen to win? More importantly, given her behavior leading up to the challenge, what if she "accidentally" killed Nerys, despite being against the rules, using that advantage? Even from this distance, it was evident Nerys struggled at the start.

When the water flew above our heads, and then moments later, Nerys flung it at the queen, everything changed. Murmurs of surprise, questions about why she'd have spent precious time harnessing water from so far away when surrounded by the sea, became gasps and shouts of delight.

"I knew she was powerful," Kael said at one point. "Rumors of her skill reached Gyoria long ago. But I never imagined... this."

Once, when the queen knocked her down, Aneri grabbed my

hand and did not let go. Each time the queen struck, she squeezed it, as if feeling every blow.

But nothing, not even Nerys's spectacular display of water-wielding, had elicited the same response as the pelagor's appearance.

"What is that?" Mev asked, standing for a better look.

"A symbol," Caelum had answered, "that Nerys is the new queen."

He'd been right. Nerys had summoned the creature, using its surprise appearance to her advantage. When moments later, she knocked the queen to the deck, every person on the stands stood and cheered. It seemed everyone in Thalassaria cheered, the celebration beginning almost immediately. Music began to play. From the beach beside us to the town above, I spotted very few unhappy with the result. If the queen had legions of supporters, they'd have been swayed by Nerys's display. She was, without doubt, the most powerful water-wielder in Elydor.

And Thalassaria's new queen.

"They're coming."

Snapping back to the present, we watched a similar procession as when Queen Lirael and Nerys had first headed toward the docks, surrounded by members of the Tidebreaker fleet.

With one notable exception.

"Where's the queen?" Mev asked.

"She comes toward us," Aneri said in response. "If you're speaking of the old queen, though she should be a part of the handing-over ceremony, it appears she and her supporters have gone already to Nymara, a remote and tranquil village to the northwest, where she will live out her days with the other remaining Thalassarian rulers."

"Awkward," Mev said, each of us looking at her, none knowing what she meant.

"It's an expression. Like, 'that's gonna be strange,' or 'ill at ease.'"

"For whom?" Kael asked.

"Nerys. The queen. When she goes there someday. What if the old rulers don't get along? And then all have to live in the same place?"

"Not all. The Balance," Kael said, clearly distracted by the approaching procession.

Aneri didn't wait for them to reach us. She and Caelum headed down the stands, toward Nerys. As much as I wished to do so as well, I didn't trust myself not to make a spectacle of us, to embarrass the new queen, by pulling her into my arms and leaving no doubt about the nature of our relationship. I wanted to hold her and never let go.

"What now?" Mev asked Kael.

"The Balance. I'm sure I mentioned it before."

At this point, Nerys was surrounded by well-wishers. According to Aneri, there would be a ceremony, but by law, she was already the Queen of Thalassari and had been the moment she incapacitated Lirael. The guards that had protected the queen earlier that day now surrounded Nerys, who appeared to be pushing them away so that she might greet all those who approached her. I might have worried for her safety if I didn't know Nerys as well as I did.

"Pretty sure you didn't."

"For some, immortality was never meant to be eternal. The Balance ensures that the lives of immortals remain purposeful, fading once their time has passed. They are immortal only for as long as they serve their role or keep the Balance intact. My guess is that Queen Lirael won't be long for Elydor."

Nerys was looking for me. I smiled as her eyes found mine, telling her our time would come. Our reunion would not be a public display, however. I had things to say, and this moment was for the new queen, not for us.

"Hold the phone." Mev was becoming increasingly agitated. "You're telling me we're not actually immortal?"

"I love it when you have that look."

"Glad to hear it. But I'd love to know what the hell you're talking about. What's the difference between demi-immortal and The Balance?"

Taking my attention from Nerys, I weighed in, helping out poor Kael.

"They are completely different," I offered. "Demi-immortal is a term reserved for the child of an immortal and mortal, or human. As you know, children, like you, may grow up fully mortal, aging as would any human, or they can be demi-immortal, aging so slowly, they have the appearance of immortality. I've known immortals who faded long before some demi-immortals."

The Fade. It was the same word we used when The Keeper finally lost their grip on mortality. I spoke quickly, knowing her next question.

"Elydorians are immortal, but not unceasing. The Balance gives them the ability, willingly, and sometimes not, to step into eternity when their time has come, choosing to fade away. More often, it is a choice, but in some cases, I suspect like the queen's, Elydor will make the choice for them. Which is why every previous Thalassarian ruler will not be found in Nymara. Some have faded. Others were killed. And still others live among the tranquil coral gardens of a place I've heard of but never seen."

"You'd think *someone*." Mev made it clear Kael was that someone "Might have mentioned this to me before? I remember distinctly having this immortality discussion. Seems like it would have been a good time."

"I might have," he countered, "if you hadn't fainted as Lyra told you about being demi-immortal. By the time you woke up, we were on to other matters."

"I remember." She laughed then, clearly taken aback but not truly upset. "Lyra saying you looked like you were going to lose your supper, you were so worried about me."

"Is that how you remember it?" he teased.

"Yep. I do. Are you going to deny it?"

Kael pulled Mev into him, kissing the top of her head. "No, I'm not."

By now, Veylin was attempting to gain the crowd's attention, but even using the Echo Stone, he was unable to do so. With luck, one of Nerys's first orders of business would be to replace the head of the council. His ability to be manipulated by bribery was not a quality she would want in such a position.

"It seems as if the ceremony will have to wait," I said, unable to take my eyes from Nerys. She looked exhausted but happy. Flanked by guards, Marek and Caelum, Nerys and Aneri greeted each and every person that approached them. "Tell me, what news from Aetheria?"

"Mev continues to train," Kael said. "And is quickly growing stronger than any in Aetheria."

I wasn't surprised. Her father was more skilled than any Aetherian that had ever lived, according to some. If his talents had passed to her, I would not be surprised if Mev grew even stronger than King Galfrid, if she remained in Elydor.

"He brags unnecessarily." Mev brushed off Kael's compliment. "I can't imagine anyone growing stronger than my father. Did you know he can whisper to another, if they are skilled enough, from one end of Elydor to another?"

I did know that. Having worked with him for many years, I'd seen him execute that particular skill. "I did. Can you speak with him now?"

Mev shook her head. "Not yet."

"She will. I have no doubt." Kael looked at Mev the way I likely looked at Nerys: with a combination of reverence and respect.

"What of the artifacts?" I asked, lowering my voice.

"Adren reports that my father, as you can imagine, is furious at my defection. He mistrusts Adren, his story of initially coming north with me and then being disgusted by my pledge of support to Mev's father. He and a contingency of my men who Adren's recruited have begun to work alongside your Keepers to locate the Wind Crystal, but thus far have been unsuccessful."

"They will find it," I said, confident in the abilities of those who'd gone to Gyoria to aid Kael's right-hand man in this mission.

"We have no choice but to find it," Mev said, the conviction in her voice having grown even stronger since we'd last been together. Knowing she was worried that her mother would learn of her disappearance, I tried to reassure her.

"Our best estimates, based on those who've passed between Elydor and your realm, suggest a time ratio of 1:3000; that for every day spent in Elydor, only a few minutes would pass in your world."

"We've done the math," Mev said, "and I understand how difficult it will be to gather all three artifacts for my father to reopen the Gate, but..." Her voice trailed. I wanted to offer Mev words of encouragement, but her father had been attempting to locate the Wind Crystal, and to reopen the Gate, for nearly thirty years without success. Even with Kael's inside influence at his father's court, it would not be an easy task.

"And the Tidal Pearl?" Kael asked. "Marek knows of it and said Nerys will allow us its use when the time comes."

"We had no choice," I said, but Kael stopped me.

"Tell who you must. Nothing is more important than gaining use of the artifacts."

It seemed any further discussion would have to wait. Nerys and the others had separated from the crowd and were making their way to the water's edge.

"I think the ceremony is finally about to begin," I said, standing.

We made our way to the back of Nerys's contingency and it became quickly clear something was amiss. I'd watched the palace guards approach, knowing what they carried. The Tidal Pearl was kept locked in the depths of the palace. It was not a crown that would be passed from the queen to Nerys to symbolize her new reign but the artifact that would enhance her abilities, one that would answer to her alone as the strongest Thalassarian.

The guards spoke to the council members as Nerys made her way toward them. Unable to hear them, Mev, Kael, and I inched closer. I opened my senses and felt their panic. Every one of them, from the guards to the council members, were feeling a similar emotion.

"What's going on?" Mev asked, loud enough for all to hear.

It was one of the palace guards who responded. "The Tidal Pearl... is missing."

38

NERYS

It was the final piece.

Before I could lead, I had to surround myself with those who valued the same future for Thalassaria as I did. Amid the chaos of the guard's announcement, one I had known was coming after being briefed on the Pearl's disappearance and recovery, I sought the three men who would help me move Thalassaria toward the shared goals of a united Elydor.

Or rather, those men sought me.

Both Caelum and Marek watched Rowan. He was an essential piece of the puzzle that had been unraveled just before Marek left for Aetheria. He studied the crowd carefully, watching. Listening. Then finally, just as the council looked to me for guidance, he spoke.

"All but one." He nodded to the youngest member of the council, a woman who I knew least of them all.

"The guards?" I asked.

Rowan shook his head.

"I'll admit, I'm surprised," Caelum said. "I thought more would have rejected the queen's treachery."

"That the true nature of man is corrupted and untrustworthy?" Marek made a sound of disgust. "Expect little of people and you won't be disappointed."

Marek's bleak views would have to wait. "Thank you," I said to Rowan, wishing I could say more. We'd been exchanging looks since the competition, but he'd kept his distance. I understood the reason, but he was also the one person I wanted most by my side right now.

That would have to wait as well.

"The Echo Stone, please?" I asked Marek, who was already striding toward Veylin to procure it.

Caelum and Rowan cleared out the path between me and the crowd as I positioned toward them. As the water's edge splashed against my ankles and receded, Marek handed me the Echo Stone.

"People of Thalassaria," I began, the stone carrying my voice all the way up to those at the railings above. I was amazed none had fallen off the cliff yet; the throng of people, some perched atop the railings, pressed forward. "Today, you witnessed my challenge to Queen Lirael."

I was forced to stop as shouts and cheers met my words. If the queen's campaign to sully my name had reached beyond the palace walls, it clearly had not taken root.

"What you did not witness were the lengths Queen Lirael went to prevent it."

The crowd quieted as my confidence in my decision grew. I'd considered preserving Lirael's legacy but would not begin my own rule by shielding a truth as enormous as this one. If not for Rowan's spying before he left the palace, along with Marek's daring and finely tuned smuggling abilities, this would have been a very different speech.

"She attempted to malign me, my name, and my ancestors

once she learned that I planned to challenge her. Lirael nearly successfully bribed a member of the current council to present false documents that would have invalidated my challenge."

I didn't look at Veylin, but did not need to. He would be furious.

"She had a young woman attacked, either believing her to be me, or worse, knowing she merely resembled me, hoping the attack would intimidate me into reconsidering. She also used a shard of the abyss during our challenge, one I was forced to use the Sacred Waters to mitigate."

The crowd's chatter increased, but so did my voice since this last part was the most important.

"Worse, she stole the Tidal Pearl."

I was forced to stop at that, not needing Rowan's abilities to feel the outrage from those all around me. Raising my arm did not get their attention again, but a flick of my fingers and a new sea serpent did. It rose from the sea behind me, but I added a fun bit of magic I'd tested once but never executed. As the crowd watched, the serpent's tongue lashed out, a forked band of water stretching way up to the railings above. Just before it touched the onlookers, I snapped my fingers and the serpent disappeared, the water it was made from splashing to the sand below.

Clapping followed, but I'd not done it for the crowd's pleasure alone.

"As you know," I continued, now having everyone's attention once again. "The Tidal Pearl will validate my reign, and use of it will help protect the people of Thalassaria. Thankfully, those loyal to me discovered it had gone missing and took immediate action to recover it. Captain Marek, Navarch of the Tidebreaker fleet, led a daring mission to intercept Queen Lirael's trusted emissary, who was smuggling it aboard a ship bound for Gyoria. His command of the *Tidechaser* ensured the Tidal Pearl was retrieved before it left Thalassarian waters. Those who knew of her plan will no longer serve at my court. This is not only a day of celebration but one of reckoning. Thalassaria deserves leaders who place its people above personal ambition, and I swear to you that is the ruler I will be."

The crowd erupted in applause, their cheers echoing across the beach. Rowan caught my gaze, his expression steady but proud, and a flicker of warmth settled in my chest. This wasn't just a victory; it was a promise of what was to come.

"To those close to me," I said, "I already know which among you were aware of the queen's plot to steal the Tidal Pearl." Thanks to Rowan and his ability to sense, when the guard first announced the Pearl missing, who was surprised and, more importantly, who was not. "Do not report back to the palace except to recover your belongings this eve. If you do, I will see you arrested."

I looked each and every one of the guilty parties directly in the eyes, landing finally on Veylin. Satisfied at least most would not test the truth of my words, I held my right hand out, palm facing upward, and waited.

Marek reached into a pouch hanging at his side and pulled out the recovered artifact. Though it was no bigger than the size of a regular large pearl, its iridescent color was unmistakable, as would be its power. He handed it to me, winked, and took the Echo Stone as he stepped aside.

Turning toward the sea, I looked out at the horizon, once again silently thanking the ancient pelagor, thanking Thalassa for watching over me, and then dipping my gaze to the ocean's depths where my parents laid for their final rest, thanked them for giving me the strength I needed on this day.

Then, raising my hand to the sky, the Tidal Pearl clutched tight in my grip, I brought it down in one swift motion.

The ocean responded. A thunderous roar erupted as waves surged upward, forming towering walls of water that seemed to defy gravity. The sea shimmered with an ethereal glow as the power of the Tidal Pearl coursed through me. It was an ancient and unstoppable force, binding me to the very heart of Thalassaria.

The crowd gasped as the water began to form the shape of an immense, glowing figure, a sentinel of the sea. I turned to face my people, taking the Echo Stone back from Marek.

"This is Thalassaria's strength. Together, we rise, and together, we endure."

The sentinel bowed its head in acknowledgment before dissolving back into the ocean, the waves cascading gently to the shore. In that moment, the sea was still, but I knew it now carried my promise, to protect and lead my people with all the strength and wisdom of those who came before me.

39

ROWAN

The festivities lasted well into the night.

We danced and drank, the spectacle of the Festival of Tides closing ceremony, with a new queen at its helm, one to behold. By the time we returned to the inn, secured in advance by Nerys's new queen's guard led by Caelum, it was easy to see she was exhausted.

I'd congratulated her, our public embrace short but cherished as I'd wanted to touch her all night. All day, in fact, watching her battle Lirael was one of the most difficult things I'd ever done in my life. She disappeared into the same room she'd shared with Aneri, a testament to the kind of queen she would be. Nerys refused any special treatment, and since Aneri would not be coming to the palace, instead opting to remain in her home.

We'd returned to the palace; Mev and Kael to remain Nerys's guests until returning north, and I'd not seen her since. Locked away all day, she began the process of choosing a new inner circle, putting forth new names for a council. Thankfully, none of those who'd been corrupted by the old queen returned.

Now, as I stepped into my chamber, towel around my waist, I

sat on the bed looking out into the darkening sky and sea below. Knowing its power and seeing that power harnessed were two very different things, and though I respected the magic of Elydor's other clans, it was Thalassaria, and Nerys, that held me most in awe.

The vision came much more easily than the first. I no longer struggled to understand it, or attempted to fight for more than it was willing to reveal. Instead, I simply observed and did not judge.

I stood before the Gate, its intricate runes carved into its surface, their glow pulsing with life as the magic awakened. Most of the etchings shimmered in brilliant blue: the hue of Aetherian power.

Except... not all.

Scattered among the glowing runes were others, faint and dormant, their color untouched by the magic. Instead, they remained the pale, unassuming shade of white marble, almost invisible. I could only make out one of the three, but it appeared to be an old key, its shaft twisted. But the vision faded before I could bring the others into focus.

I had no idea what it meant but understood now why my grandfather kept a leather-bound journal of his visions. I would do the same, in time. For now, they were easy enough to remember, if not to interpret.

My duty to Estmere, and the humans, was clear.

But so was my love for Nerys.

The evening meal was not for some time, but I stood, prepared to dress, when the soft knock stopped me in my tracks. I didn't think she would have been able to get away today, but I knew without using any special abilities that it was Nerys on the other side of the door.

I opened it, Nerys not even pretending to hide her appreciation for my attire, or lack of it. She was dressed in tight, form-fitting breeches and a loose, tunic-style top that fell off one shoulder.

"By Elydor's breath, you are magnificent."

I stepped back. Nerys closed the door behind her.

I was already halfway across the room, afraid to touch her before I said my piece. Once I did, it would be all but impossible to stop.

"How was your day?" I asked, heading toward my leather satchel. With the sun beginning to set, casting a late day glow into the chamber, and the sounds of water's life-giving flow all around us, I'd never felt more connected to this place before. Perhaps it was Nerys, knowing, or hoping, what was to come. Or perhaps it was an echo of my human ancestors' tie to Thalassaria, one I'd never known existed.

"Interesting," she said. "Less contentious than I'd have expected."

Reaching into my bag, I pulled out my Keeper's ring and palmed it, heading to the windows. When Nerys joined me, I turned toward her.

"I don't know if this is the time or place, but there is much I need to speak with you about."

"I'm not due back until the meal." Her gaze dipped, and I steeled myself against a desire so strong that I wondered if it would someday consume me.

I opened my palm, revealing the gold ring, its sole gem representing the runes etched into the Aetherian Gate when it first opened, a reminder that my ancestors were forever tied to it.

"This ring represents my oath," I began, "and promises I've kept, along with ones I have yet to fulfill. It binds me to secrets and traditions that are older than we are. But today, I make a new vow. You asked me once if I thought we could be possible. I did not, believing my duty in Estmere. And though I still owe a debt to the humans that must be repaid, I would do it here, in Thalassaria. If you wish it."

Her eyes searched mine.

Holding my breath, I waited. Would it be enough?

"I wish it, to the depths of my soul. I love you, Rowan, and have vowed to lead Thalassaria on a new path forward. A human king at my side will challenge traditions older than memory itself. Yet I believe in my people, in their strength and wisdom to embrace what is right, not just what has always been. Together, we can show them that unity is our greatest power."

I put the ring in her hand and closed Nerys's fingers around it. "A *human* king. I am, as you will remember, very much mortal."

Nerys would sacrifice as much as me, or me, for us to be together.

"I found a strength within me, one that was always there but buried beneath fear and doubt. When the time comes, I will draw on it and trust that heartbreak will not crush me completely."

Could I live with the knowledge that, someday, I would break her heart?

Aye. More easily than I could walk away from Nerys now.

"Will you marry me, Nerys?" Then remembering she was not human, "Rather, will you partner with me, for my eternity?"

In response, she leaned into me, and I was lost. Kissing her, knowing we were to marry, was a very different sort of kiss. There was no end in sight but a beginning that I never could have imagined coming here.

No longer holding back, I allowed my hands to roam freely. From her shoulders down to her waist, I made quick work of Nerys's top as her hands moved between us.

"I wanted to do that," she said, separating herself long

enough to place my ring on the nearby table and take off her boots, "the second I walked into the chamber."

Standing before her completely nude as Nerys had removed my towel, I marveled at the forces that brought me here. If the Gate had not closed... if Mev had not come through... I could not wish for the suffering my people had been through, being cut off from their families, but at the same time, I could not help but celebrate the wheels that had been put into motion for me to travel here and have met Nerys.

"You best move quickly," I told her, slowing closing the distance between us, "because any piece of clothing remaining on your body when I reach you may or may not remain intact when I do."

Making good on my promise, I did not go gently disrobing my future wife. She gasped as I pulled the form-fitting breeches down, helping her feet from the garment. With nothing but her glorious naked form begging to be touched before me, I lifted and carried Nerys to the bed.

She giggled, a sound I rarely heard from a woman with so many serious burdens to carry, as I tossed her on the bed. When she flicked her wrist, I was surprised to be enveloped by a silencing mist. I was even more surprised when Nerys flipped us around and moved between my legs as I'd intended to do with her.

"What," I croaked out, "are you doing?"

She smiled, taking me in both hands. "Is that not evident? I am pleasing the man that would be my partner."

"Nerys," I started but could not finish. Without warning, she bobbed her head down and took me into her mouth. Gripping the back of her hair, I squeezed its silken strands between my fists. This hadn't been the plan, but reminding myself the woman

I'd just committed to partnering with, I would have to become very comfortable with less predictability very quickly.

And with each flick of her tongue, with every suckle, I understood the reason for the mist. The sounds coming from me were primeval, Nerys's skill something I didn't want to consider. There was little chance I could last much longer. Summoning a will I had no notion I was capable of, I lifted her head and pulled her up to me.

When Nerys licked the corner of her mouth, I nearly came undone.

Sitting up and reaching between us, I smoothed my hand down until my finger was inside her. "So wet already," I said, helping Nerys get into position atop me as she kneeled with each leg on one side of my lap.

"I've been wet for you since the first day we met."

Lying back down, I guided her onto me, the sight of her nearly my undoing. Again.

"I know," I said, remembering.

At her mock indignation, now buried deep inside her, I began to move. Together, we found a rhythm as I blocked out the sight of Nerys between my legs. Thinking of that, of how good she felt now, would not allow me to prolong this lovemaking session, something I very much wanted to do.

But I also wanted to claim her. Possess her in every possible way.

I flipped us, though not gently, and let my need consume us both. Nerys called my name so loudly that I wondered if we'd need the mist every time.

Pinning her wrists beneath my hands, I drove into her, each thrust another promise. It was not the soft beckoning of the tide, rolling gently to and fro along this shore. This was a maelstrom of need and desire and lust. One of love too, and a trust so deep that neither of us were afraid of letting go.

I raised myself up, using my thumb to stroke her, and watched as Nerys became undone. She screamed, thrusting her hips upward as I buried myself deep inside her, flicking and circling her, waiting for that moment.

The one where she forgot everything, and everyone, including me. Where there was nothing but an explosion of pleasure so consuming that nothing existed but her pleasure. When that happened, when Nerys stilled to fully be present in that moment, I drove into her one last time and let myself go.

The vision came as quickly as I did into her. An impossible one, of something so rare in Elydor that I could not possibly give it any credence. One of a babe, not in any particular place or even within the arms of anyone I could decipher. I could simply see its face, rather quickly before the vision faded.

I dared not move.

If this had been my first, or even second or third, vision, I'd have dismissed it. Not trusting myself. Not understanding or even allowing hope to well inside me. But it wasn't. And I knew, as much as I knew Nerys and I had been destined to be together, that the vision was real.

He, or she, was a child who would be born of love.

A rare gift.

And it was ours.

40

NERYS

It was a meal unlike any other.

Four days after Rowan and I agreed to partner, or marry as he called it... four days of upheaval in the palace, from a new staff to changing rules, such as the need to isolate visiting humans... four days of getting to know Mev and Kael as much as possible amid the chaos... four days planning this night with Rowan. And now, it was done.

After having fetched Aneri, and with very little ceremony, we were partnered. Rowan and I wished to do it before Mev and Kael returned north, and with the excitement of the challenge behind us, a big celebration could wait. Instead, we posted the banns, allowed all of Thalassari to learn of our plans, and said the vows that bound us together for life.

Or more accurately, his life.

For his part, Rowan was even more anxious than I to see it done. There were things, he said, that we could discuss after we were wed. But those would have to wait until after the meal. Aneri insisted, if a large partnering celebration was not going to happen, that she could at least plan and decorate for this meal.

Everyone, old and new, who worked at the palace had been invited. The Tidebreaker fleet, my fellow Stormcallers... The dining hall was filled to capacity with the glow of lanterns crafted from sea glass, casting shimmering reflections on the walls like waves in motion. Long tables were adorned with coral centerpieces and pearl-lined runners, evoking the beauty of the ocean depths brought to life above.

With Rowan beside me and the raised dais empty, we sat with those who had helped make this day possible.

"A toast." Kael raised his silver goblet high. "To the new Queen of Thalassaria and her mate, a man I am proud to call friend."

We toasted, not our first, as the final course was finished.

"Not always," Mev said beside him. "Remember your first meeting?"

Kael gave her a look and explained to Aneri, who was sat beside him. "He came upon us on the road as we traveled to Aetheria."

"Back to Aetheria," Mev cut in, earning her a look from her partner. "Sorry. I'm sure I'll stop busting your ass about our meet-cute one of these days."

Mev said the strangest things at times, though I was fairly certain of her meaning since I'd heard this story before.

"Anyway," he continued to Aneri with Marek and Caelum listening, "Mev took to him immediately, being human and all. I may have needed a bit more convincing."

"A bit?" Rowan said.

Kael shrugged. "I believe we're missing the point which is that I'm glad for you both."

"As we all are," Marek said. "Another round of drinks to celebrate?"

"I would like to speak to you alone," Rowan said in my ear. I nodded.

"Please continue the celebration without us," I said as Rowan, now standing, pulled my seat for me. Forgetting I was no longer simply Nerys but the queen, when the entire table stood as I did, the remainder of the meal's guests doing the same, I vowed to eliminate that silly tradition. "Sit," I called to the crowd. "And stay. I leave but that does not mean the meal is ended. I wish, this night and every night, for you to come and go as you please."

"Is it wise," Aneri asked, "to dispense with too many traditions at once?"

"A good question, although that one seems innocuous enough to alter. But I will think on it after I speak privately with Rowan."

"You wish to *speak* to your new partner? Is that so?" Marek laughed, earning a stern glare from Aneri.

"You are incorrigible," she chastised him.

"You adore me for it."

Caelum grinned.

"I can assure you that is not the case," Aneri shot back.

As the two of them continued their disagreement, I bid a good eve to our guests.

"You've moved your belongings to our new bedchamber?" I asked as we left the hall.

"I have, but wondered... before we retire," he said the words with a smile, knowing full well we would be doing anything but, "I thought perhaps we could speak in the Garden of Luminous Tides?"

"Of course," I said as we walked through the corridor as Aelois followed. As Captain of the Guard, he was never far behind me. "You will need to choose a captain too," I reminded him, "after the ceremony."

"Are you surprised at the public sentiment thus far?" Rowan asked.

We had anticipated a mixed reaction to the announcement and had received it, but more Thalassarians had accepted that they would have a human king, once I was officially crowned, than we'd expected.

I thought about the question. "No," I said finally. "You have been our neighbor for hundreds of years. If it is not time to fully accept Estmere as one of the four clans of Elydor, then when will it be? In five hundred more years? A thousand? Even those among us who value water-wielding above all other skills can recognize the contributions humans have made."

We reached the cascading vines; I twisted my hand, parting them.

"I should have realized that day," I said, as Rowan took me into his arms the moment the vines closed behind us, "you were special. To be admitted here. The pelagor. Seren's ready acceptance of you. This was meant to be, Rowan. You were meant for Thalassaria."

"I was meant for you," he said, kissing me, his lips covering mine as we fell into a blissful embrace that I'd have been glad to last forever. Unfortunately, we were here to talk and Rowan seemed intent on doing just that. He broke away, guiding me to the same bench by the water's edge where we sat the other time.

"But I was also meant for another purpose."

Rowan took my hand. The change in his demeanor had me angling my body toward him, intent on not missing even a word. This was important, obviously, and Rowan's countenance said as much.

"I took a vow not to utter these words aloud to anyone without the blood of my ancestors running through them. The only exception being my wife. It is the same vow my parents, and grandparents, and theirs before them took. The vow of The Keepers."

"The Keepers? What is that?"

"Have you heard of Richard Harrow?"

"The first human to come through the Aetherian Gate?"

Rowan nodded. "As did all humans who entered after him, Richard passed through with his own brand of magic already. He was a seer in his time. A psychic in the modern realm of humans. We call it having the Sight."

"Richard could see the future."

"Aye. Pieces of it. Ones that sometimes made little sense, in his realm. As you know, when humans come to Elydor, their innate abilities are enhanced, and it was more so with Richard than any other. He could not simply see fragments of the future, but clear visions. And not just of himself but of all those in Elydor."

As I understood it, the Sight was more akin to the fragments Rowan mentioned. "How clearly?"

"Enough to identify people and places. To predict events in the future. It was a powerful gift that he quickly realized needed to be kept secret lest his life be endangered. When he died, the ability was passed on to another as it has been every generation since. The Keepers are his ancestors, by blood or marriage, who know of this power. Eventually, this network grew, their secrets encompassing not just The Keeper's identity but another purpose: to protect the Gate. To advance the humans' cause. And these past years, to find a way to help King Galfrid open the Gate."

"And you are one of them? Richard Harrow was your ancestor?"

"Not only one of them," he said. "I am *The* Keeper."

I thought quickly. Not just a human spy with a lineage dating back to the first human who came through the Gate but... one chosen to receive a special ability for a new generation. The Sight, but stronger. "You can see the future?"

Rowan sighed. "Before I came here, on my way from Aetheria, I visited my home in Estmere and learned my grandfather, the former Keeper, was ill. When I told you of my sole ability, to sense emotion, it was the truth. But days after I arrived"—he looked to the pool of water before us, lost in thought—"my grandfather died. I knew only because of the visions I began to receive, my training having prepared me for the possibility, though I will admit I never actually thought it possible to have been chosen."

When he turned back to me, Rowan's eyes were glazed. He'd lost his grandfather, a man Rowan thought highly of, one he loved, and he had grieved alone. With a lump forming in my throat, I reached for him. Holding on tight, stroking his hair, I offered my condolences. My sorrow was his.

"What a terrible way to learn of his death," I murmured into his chest.

When he didn't respond, I pulled back, wiped the wetness below his eyes with my thumbs and held his face in my hands, as he once did to me.

"I am sorry for your loss. Sorry you were forced to bear it alone. And sorry to have accused you of lying to me."

"Nerys—"

"We will find a way to honor your grandfather," I said, holding his gaze.

He swallowed, taking in a deep breath. "I wish I could have told you before."

Letting go of his face, I took both Rowan's hands in mine. "Your honor, the vow you took, is one of the things I love most about you. I will never doubt your loyalty to me, not that I had before."

I wanted to know about his visions. What they were like. What Rowan had seen. But now was not the time. He was a grieving grandson first.

"When you asked if we were possible, I could not see a way. My place, I believed, was in Estmere, furthering the human cause."

"Is it not still?" Though I did not want to ask the question, afraid of the answer, it seemed to me nothing had changed if he was still The Keeper.

"I met two Keepers in Thalassaria, much to my surprise. First, in The Moonlit Current—"

"Nerithia."

He nodded. "I was as surprised as she was. There is a phrase, known only to Keepers. 'The winds remember the first crossing, and the stone keeps their weight.' When she said it, I was confused at first as my grandfather had said nothing of her. I learned later he did not know of her, and neither do I know how Nerithia guessed my identity. But she was able to get a message to Estmere, telling them of my status. Later, she received a message back from them which is what guided me to the Deep Archives."

"Why Seren?"

The corner of Rowan's lips turned up as if he wished for me to guess.

Seren knew more of Thalassaria's history than anyone. "Did she know one of your ancestors? Perhaps she had a connection to..."

He continued to smile.

"No. She cannot be."

"I said the same, at first. It seemed impossible, given her age. Her father was Caius Harrow, one of Richard's sons and the second Keeper. Apparently, being guardian of the Deep Archives gives her a brand of immortality tied to it."

"Which is why she never leaves."

"Precisely. She told me of her father and more of my ancient ancestors than I'd ever known before. They did not always live in Estmere but were more akin to diplomats, seeing their purpose not only as keeping our family's secrets but of furthering the humans' cause by living among the people of Elydor, helping to make them see our commonalities. Over time, that purpose was lost. We have been isolated, as your people have, for too long."

"You can be The Keeper from here?"

"I'd not have thought so, but so often we are stuck thinking the way things are done is the only way forward. I may need to leave, at times, but aye, I aim to both serve as The Keeper, and your husband too."

"And as the King of Thalassaria."

"You are the true ruler here. I am but your servant, Nerys."

His gaze dipped to the deep cut of my gown.

"Is that so?"

"It is."

I knew where this conversation was heading. But first, I had to be certain Rowan understood how deeply I appreciated his sacrifice. It would have been easier to carry out his duties from Estmere, and it was as likely he would receive resistance from his fellow Keepers, as I had in taking him as a partner.

"Thank you, Rowan."

He reached up between us, tracing my bottom lip with his finger.

"Thank you for trusting me." The mischief in his eyes told me what was coming next. "A stranger, come to beg a favor of the queen."

His hand moved from my lip, Rowan's deft fingers gentle as he tucked loose strands of hair behind my ear.

"What, pray tell, is the favor you ask of me?"

Rowan moved closer to me. "My queen," he said, his voice thick with promise. "I ask for use of the Tidal Pearl so that we may reopen the Aetherian Gate once again."

I pretended to consider his request. "What do you propose to offer me in exchange?"

His smile left no room for interpretation on precisely what my partner was offering.

"I accept."

Rowan tossed his head back, the sound of his laughter settling on my soul.

"That," he said, leaning forward with a kiss, "was unexpectedly easy."

EPILOGUE
ROWAN

I never expected it to be this difficult.

When I decided to travel with Marek, Mev, and Kael north, Marek to deposit me in Estmere en route, Nerys and I knew it was necessary. Neither of us wished to be separated so soon, but I needed to speak with my family. There were big changes afoot, ones they needed to learn about from me directly.

But now, standing on the docks, having said goodbye many times already, I wanted to take her into my arms again and, this time, never let go.

"This is the most miserable I've seen you look since we met," Mev said as the others prepared to board.

"It will be difficult, being separated," I admitted.

"But maybe good for her too. Caelum said there was a pocket of dissent in Maristhera to the idea of a human king?"

"Some of the queen's supporters. But thankfully, it seems to be the exception and not the rule."

"Any word from Nymara?"

"None," I said, having received a report just the day before.

The queen appeared to have peacefully transitioned into a new life, for as long as she would live. Neither Nerys nor I trusted the transition would continue to go so easily, and Caelum had placed men in Nymara to keep watch.

Mev was about to respond when a shout could be heard at the end of the docks. With Nerys in attendance, there were guards everywhere, but she insisted all remain otherwise normal. The activity worried Caelum, and with whatever was currently happening, I was inclined to agree. I was at her side before she could be surrounded, the shouts growing louder.

"You need to listen to him," I said of Caelum, who had run toward the source of the ruckus.

"I will consider it," she teased, clearly unconcerned. "Look, he's speaking to the man in question, who doesn't appear to be a threat."

When the man, a Gyorian or human by the look of him, handed Caelum a missive, he did not move off. Instead, he watched as the missive was delivered to... Kael?

"How strange," Nerys said, echoing my thoughts.

Even stranger was the expression on Kael's face when he read the missive. He ran to Mev who, in turn, called for Nerys and me. All I knew, as we boarded Marek's ship, was that a private discussion had been called for, his ship serving its purpose.

With all eyes on us, Nerys, Marek, Mev, Kael, and I huddled on the deck of the ship as it swayed from side to side, the sea rougher than usual this day.

"A message from Adren." Kael tucked the missive into a leather pouch at his side. "It is a miracle he reached us in time, though was ordered to deliver it to you," he said to Nerys, "if we'd left Thalassaria already."

"We need to embed a Whisperer here," Mev said to Nerys. "So that we might get messages to you more quickly."

"A good idea." Kael peered over to the dock, where all eyes were on us. It seemed all activity had come to a stop, the spectacle we made one I was certain would be a topic of conversation for days to come.

"What's the message?" Mev asked.

"I don't know how he did it. Or how Adren knows for certain, but..." He paused, his nostrils flaring. I couldn't discern if the news was good or bad. "He found the Wind Crystal."

Stares of shock followed his announcement.

"He said that? In a missive?" Mev asked.

"It was coded."

"Obviously."

Kael tried not to smile but he was unsuccessful. Looking at Mev like he was unsure what to do with her, a common expression of his but one that amused me, Kael cleared his throat and continued.

"By found, I mean he has discovered its whereabouts but does not have it in his possession."

I assumed as much but dared to hope.

And that was where the hope ended. As if reminded of the precise contents of a missive that had been moments away from missing him, Kael looked as he had the day he'd been forced to send Mev to Aetheria while he stayed to stop his brother from following her. I understood now, and was grateful for the brief respite to my own separation from Nerys.

"Where is it?" Marek asked, apparently sensing Kael's dread.

"Interesting you should ask."

"Why?" Nerys squeezed my hand, clearly worried.

"Have you heard of the Maelstrom Depths?"

Marek winced. "Of course. I've avoided them on more than one journey." He seemed to remember something. "There are rumors of a cavern deep within the Depths."

Before he even finished, Kael was nodding. "Somehow, though I have no notion how he managed it, my father apparently hid the Wind Crystal in those caverns."

"What now?" Mev asked. "Start from scratch." Marek's puzzled gaze had her amending, "From the beginning."

"The Maelstrom Depths," Marek said, "are located off the coast of Gyoria, hidden within its rugged coastline of cliffs and rocky shores. It's a massive underground network of sea caves extending deep into the earth and only accessible by navigating through treacherous, storm-swept waters. The rumored entrance is hidden in a sea-bound cove. Rumored because no one would be foolish enough to attempt to reach it."

"Then how did he manage it?" I asked, already knowing Kael didn't have the answer.

Shaking his head, he looked up to the sky, saying nothing. Then turning to Mev, his expression bleak, he said finally, "I simply don't know. A few have attempted it. All have perished."

"Perhaps with a bit of magic..." Mev's voice trailed off as she likely realized what we all already knew. There was no magic that could calm a maelstrom. Unless?

I looked at Nerys, who shook her head.

"It has been attempted by Thalassarians too," Nerys said. "Powerful ones lured by the promise of gemstones more powerful than could be found anywhere in Gyoria. But the water is too deep, the maelstrom too powerful. Even with the use of the Tidal Pearl, I cannot drain the sea. Push it back? Aye. But the force of it returning to its natural state would decimate anyone in its path."

The group was silent.

"There has to be a way." Mev appeared ill and I understood her anguish. Without that crystal, the Gate would remain closed.

Forever.

No one spoke.

"Sometimes," Marek said finally, "magic isn't enough."

I knew that tone. It wasn't one of defeat but resignation. All heads turned toward him.

"Thankfully, you've enlisted the aid of the most skilled seafarer in all of Thalassaria."

"And humble too," I murmured, Marek ignoring me.

"No," Nerys said, her voice unwavering. "Marek, no. You are immortal, not invincible. Those waters are treacherous. None have survived attempting to navigate them. No one."

Marek turned serious. "Is that a friend's suggestion or an order from the queen?"

Mev paled. Kael and I remained silent as we watched Nerys's expression change from surprise to... sadness. I knew before she responded what her answer would be. It would devastate her to lose Marek. And from what the others said, the chance of that happening if he attempted to reach the caverns of the Maelstrom Depths were high.

"It is a friend's suggestion. One who loves you and does not wish to see you perish."

"I don't intend to perish. But if the Wind Crystal is needed to reopen the Aetherian Gate..." He looked at me. "To reunite humans who never intended Elydor to be their permanent home." And then toward Mev. "And your parents, who were so rudely torn apart."

Marek had such a way with words.

"I will navigate the Maelstrom Depths." He grinned from ear to ear as if he was not facing imminent death. "And retrieve the crystal."

★★★
MORE FROM C. L. MECCA

Another book from C. L. Mecca, *Whisper of War and Storms*, is available to order now here:
www.mybook.to/WhisperofBackAD

ABOUT THE AUTHOR

C.L. Mecca is the author of romantic fantasy and also writes contemporary small town romance as Cissy Mecca.

Discover your Elydorian clan by taking our exclusive bonus quiz in Whisper of War and Storms. Sign up here to become a Mecca Romance Insider!

Sign up to C.L. Mecca's mailing list for news, competitions and updates on future books.

Follow C.L. Mecca on social media here:

- facebook.com/MeccaRomance
- instagram.com/meccaromance
- tiktok.com/@clmeccaauthor

ALSO BY C. L. MECCA

Heirs of Elydor Series
Whisper of War and Storms
Tide of Waves and Secrets

Boldwood EVER AFTER

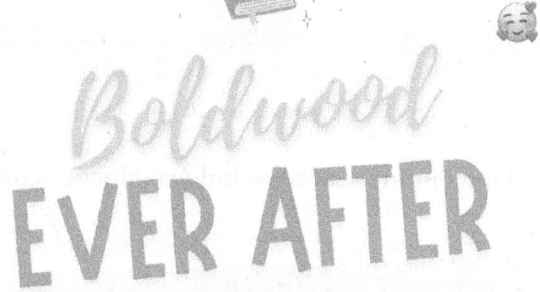

xoxo

JOIN BOLDWOOD'S **ROMANCE COMMUNITY** FOR SWEET AND SPICY BOOK RECS WITH ALL YOUR FAVOURITE TROPES!

SIGN UP TO OUR NEWSLETTER

HTTPS://BIT.LY/BOLDWOODEVERAFTER

Boldwood

Boldwood Books is an award-winning fiction publishing company seeking out the best stories from around the world.

Find out more at www.boldwoodbooks.com

Join our reader community for brilliant books, competitions and offers!

Follow us
@BoldwoodBooks
@TheBoldBookClub

Sign up to our weekly deals newsletter

https://bit.ly/BoldwoodBNewsletter